"Kira, you should have been standing here beside your brothers," he said.

She started in surprise. "Me? You wanted to promote me?"

"Yes, I believed you deserved a title and to be given your own command."

Taejo grinned broadly and nudged Kira. "She would make an excellent officer, Your Majesty!"

Eojin smiled. "I know." He glanced over at the impassive face of General Kim. "But it is not to be. I've argued for many hours with my advisers on this issue and I could not get them to agree."

Eojin sighed. "Our world is not ready for a female leader."

"I'm not surprised," Kira said. "But it doesn't matter. I don't need a title."

"I know that," he replied. "It wasn't for you. It was for others to recognize you and your value. But I fear that they are still intimidated by the Demon Slayer."

WARRIOR

· A PROPHECY NOVEL ·

ELLEN OH

An Imprint of HarperCollinsPublishers

To my wonderful Mom and Dad, who used to always call me Xena, the
Warrior Princess. This warrior wouldn't be here without you both!

Love, Xena

HarperTeen is an imprint of HarperCollins Publishers.

Warrior
Text copyright © 2014 by Ellen Oh
All rights reserved. Printed in the United States of America.
No part of this book may be used or reproduced in any manner whatsoever
without written permission except in the case of brief quotations embodied
in critical articles and reviews. For information address
HarperCollins Children's Books, a division of HarperCollins Publishers,
195 Broadway, New York, NY 10007.
www.epicreads.com

ISBN 978-0-06-209113-0

Typography by Carla Weise
15 16 17 18 19   PC/RRDH   10 9 8 7 6 5 4 3 2 1
❖
First paperback edition, 2015

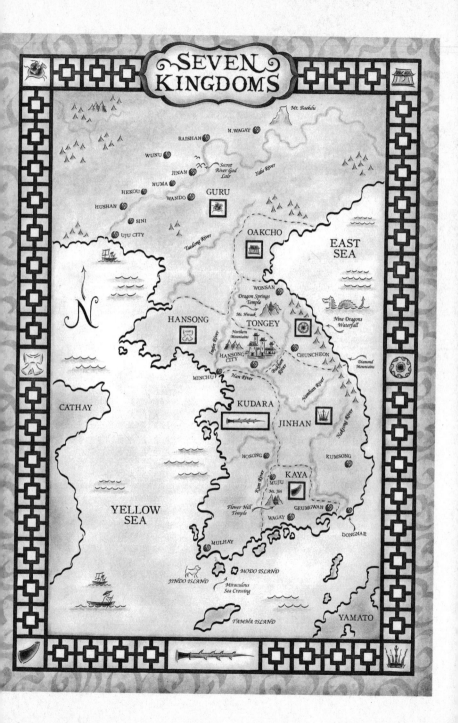

Kira was on the hunt. Her boots crunched softly on snow-covered ground. Icicles hung like shimmering crystal blades from the bare tree branches above her. Yet the delight Kira initially had for the wild, breathtaking landscape and the beauty of the ancient forest was short-lived. She had no idea where she was and she no longer felt the deep isolation of the eerie woods. There was a trail of human footprints before her.

She was not alone.

Welcome to the Sea of Trees, a voice whispered in her head. Stay here with us forever. Stay. Stay.

Suppressing a shiver, she studied the tracks. One person. Heavy gaited, large in size, and most likely male. The footprints led her to the entrance of a cavern that gaped open in the forest floor—a fierce black maw, as if a gigantic imoogi, a cursed half-dragon, half-snake–like creature, had tunneled its large serpent body and erupted from the ground. Unrelenting darkness layered with cool fog met Kira's gaze.

She blinked and her yellow tiger's eyes adjusted to give her night vision, but it was still difficult to see.

She descended with caution down the rough stone staircase, slick and treacherous from the snow. The interior walls of the cavern were made from ancient lava flows and were draped with sheets of ice. The long narrow corridor twisted and turned before entering a large cave. Huge ice formations hung from the black ceiling and lava shelves decorated the walls. Toward the end of the cave was a narrower passage that led down into a chamber filled with red light and pulsing heat. As Kira approached the beckoning light, the floor became wet with melting ice. Although she'd hardly felt the winter cold outside, down here in the caves, she could feel the heat emanating from underground.

Bending low, she entered the narrow passage and walked through. It opened into a wide cave dominated by a pool of molten lava that boiled in the center, shooting up large flames. The lava began to churn and bubble over explosively. From the depths of the fire rose a dark gray column that erupted into the blazing figure of a demonic visage. Once again Kira was faced with the Demon Lord.

"You have failed me!" The voice sounded like the grumbling of earthquakes.

A figure lay prostrate before the Demon Lord. He wore a

heavy silk brocaded coat, and his hair was oiled and slicked into a fan-shaped queue topknot that was folded forward. When he raised his head, Kira focused on the long jagged scar etched into his cheek and jaw. Even with his bearded face contorted with fear, he was a cruel-looking man. He displayed a large, jewel-crusted gold medallion on his chest, and the richness of his clothing established his high ranking.

Small winged imps flew out of the Demon Lord's gaping mouth, launching themselves at the nobleman's face with sharp talons that scratched, pierced, and pinched his exposed flesh.

"No, my lord!" The nobleman tried to protect his eyes, fighting off the imps that were attacking him. "I have done all that you've asked. Please! Spare me! Let me prove myself to you!"

The imps subsided with one last painful gouge. They hovered in the air above him, their claws outstretched in readiness. The nobleman lowered his trembling hands from his bloodied face and prostrated himself again before the Demon Lord, begging for mercy.

"Why should I bother? You will only fail me again."

At his words, a larger group of imps assaulted the man, shredding his fine robes and ripping chunks of hair. His once immaculate appearance was now a tattered mess. They left him shaking violently on the ground.

"Please, master, please give me another chance," he cried.

Kira felt a sick kind of pity for the nobleman. He was nothing more than a puppet for the Demon Lord, and yet she felt sorry for him.

The nobleman pulled himself slowly to his feet, keeping

himself in a bowing position before his master. "The Guru king and the Hansong prince will die soon. I promise this my lord. I shall not fail you again."

Kira gasped. This was Daimyo Tomodoshi, the human medium of the Demon Lord. He was the reason for the Yamato invasion of the Seven Kingdoms. He was the reason for the loss of her parents. Her pity disappeared as fury ignited within her.

Now she knew the face of her enemy.

Now she knew who she had to kill.

Another flock of imps flew at the daimyo. They ripped the clothes off his body and slashed his naked flesh with their razor-sharp claws, until he was a bleeding mass from head to toe.

The great demon head laughed. "No, you will not fail me again. I have something for you." Another imp flew from the gaping mouth holding a long rectangular box in its claws. The daimyo cringed as the imp screeched and flung the heavy metal box at his feet before returning to the flames.

The daimyo opened the box with shaking hands. Inside were seven daggers with long, thin, sharp black blades that came to a wicked tip. Each blade was inscribed with unreadable characters etched along the middle. Smoke seemed to rise from the lethal weapons as they glistened. They whispered of a dark death.

"Don't touch them with your bare hands if you value your life," the Demon Lord said. "They carry something very special on them—a part of my essence. Choose your assassins wisely!"

Tomodoshi snatched his hand away and snapped the box shut. "It will be as you command."

"And what of the girl?" The flames shot higher.

"She will not see another birthday," Tomodoshi said with an ingratiating bow.

"No," breathed the voice as the figure in the fire began to fade. "Bring her to me alive. I have other plans for her." The imps raced into the fire as the demon face disappeared with one last mocking laugh that sent shivers down Kira's spine.

One imp spun around and came flying at her face, its claws extended. Kira ducked and ran, feeling the claws snatching at her hair as she fled from the overpowering heat.

Hansong Palace

Ten days had passed since Kira had defeated the evil shaman and his imoogi. Ten days since the Iron Army had beaten the Yamato army and freed Hansong. She was finally home. And yet in those ten days, Kira had not returned to her family house. She'd been avoiding it. Her brothers had asked her to look for her mother's treasure box, which was hidden in her mother's rooms. They'd refused to let the servants into the area, wanting Kira to have her private moments alone with her memories. But Kira hadn't been ready.

She'd been present when her father was killed. It was his heroic sacrifice that had allowed her to save her cousin, Prince Taejo, from Lord Shin Mulchin and the Yamato army. But she'd been forced to leave Hansong without seeing her mother, only to hear that Shaman Ito had murdered her mother and trapped her spirit in the shadow world with his dark shaman magic. When Kira had killed Ito, she'd freed her mother's spirit so she could alight to heaven. But Kira had never forgiven herself for leaving her behind, even knowing she had no choice. Every day, she was filled with a desperate longing for her parents. She missed their love and wisdom. Being in Hansong again, Kira ached for them with a fierceness that was almost crippling at times. But her guilt had kept her from her family home. Until now.

After a few days of finally feeling safe, the frightening visions had started again. Shaken, Kira sought out the one place that she'd always felt the safest—her mother's rooms.

Kira stood in the women's quarters of her family home. Here her mother had sat on the cushioned warmth of the heated floor, embroidering on luxurious folds of colored silk. Now the large lacquered chests that held the silks and threads were destroyed, their delicate contents befouled by the muck of enemy boots.

Kira walked through the doorway that separated her mother's inner sanctum from the outer chambers. She shivered as the cold winter winds swept through the broken walls.

Entering the room, she was catapulted back into the

past, remembering the comfort of a childhood spent hiding in her mother's sanctuary. Instead of the broken pieces of furniture and slashed embroidery, she saw it the way it once was. At the far wall stood an eight-paneled folding screen of a plum tree painted through the four seasons. Several small and large chests inlaid with mother-of-pearl designs of peacocks and flowering branches framed the room. She could see her mother, sitting beside a low table covered with threads, bits of fabrics, and small embroidery scissors. Her blue *hanbok* billowed around her as her long slender fingers worked the needle through the delicate silk. Smoothing down the dark, shiny fabric on her lap, she smiled and beckoned to Kira.

Kira stepped forward and the vision faded, leaving her standing in the dusty ruins. The loss of her mother was like a knife through her heart, causing her wrenching pain when she thought of her. Kira wondered if she would ever be able to think of her mother without agonizing grief.

She picked through the debris, hoping to find unbroken mementos to treasure. The Yamato had done a thorough job, but they didn't know about the secret panels hidden beneath the floorboards and behind the walls.

Kira pushed away the memories and pawed through the torn cushions, damaged hanboks, and wrecked furniture. She paused as she collected fragments of her mother's belongings. Beads from a broken headpiece, the tooth of a jade comb, a small pair of jeweled embroidery scissors—Kira's fingers caressed all of them. Each item was a distinct memory of a time shared with her mother. Lessons learned, laughter shared, meals eaten together in private, hidden from prying eyes. She could no longer keep the tears from falling as she sorted through her mother's things. Wiping her eyes with her sleeve, Kira continued to pick through the remains. Anything salvageable went into a large bag slung over her shoulder, but there was very little left unbroken.

She pulled aside the woven carpet in the far left corner of the room. Underneath, the floor was layered with sheets of thick, oiled paper over large flat stones that covered the network of flues carrying the heat. But this corner contained no flues.

She'd always complained about how cold this one spot had been. It wasn't until she was thirteen that she'd discovered the reason why, for this was where her mother kept hidden the Kang family treasures. When Kira had asked her mother why she kept them in the floor and not in a locked chest, she'd been told that some things needed to be hidden. She respected her mother's decision. The locked chest, which had held some coins and valuable silk hanboks, had been completely destroyed, but the floor had been untouched.

Kira ripped the yellowed, oiled paper and lifted up the farthest corner stone. Within the deep cavity lay a large bundled box. Grabbing it by the knot, she lifted it up from its hiding place, coughing as clouds of dust flew all around her. She waved the worst of it off and untied the wrapping cloth, revealing a large rectangular box covered with an ornate design of two dancing dragons.

Opening the lid, she was dazzled by the treasures within the box: jewelry she'd never seen her mother wear, gold coins, and other items worth a small fortune. In the corner, there was a small silk-wrapped parcel with her name written on the cloth. She was glad the Yamatos had not gotten their hands on her family treasure, but she would have traded it all to see her parents one last time.

She leaned against a wooden beam and opened the little parcel. Inside it, there was a small scroll and a black embroidered bag. She unrolled the scroll and found her father's bold calligraphy of the flowing pictorial characters of *hanja*. A bolt of emotion shot through her at the sight. Her father's presence shone through his words, reminding Kira of all she'd lost.

Unlike other noble fathers, who barely spent any time with their daughters, her father had trained her to be a fighter since she was a little girl. He'd always said, "Kira, if you'd been born a boy, you could become the greatest general in all the Seven Kingdoms." She'd laughed and said, "Just like you, Father!"

Even when the king would make his dislike and contempt of her clear to all, her father had always stood by her side. When the entire court and citizenry had followed the king's lead and shunned Kira, her father had always protected her.

As a young child, she'd once asked him why everyone hated her.

"*They don't see the real you,*" her father had said. "*They see only the outside and are frightened by your differences, and in their blindness they can't see how truly wonderful you are.*"

"*And my uncle? Why does he hate me?*" she'd asked him.

"*He doesn't hate you, he is afraid of you—a small child who can see demon possessions and who was able to save the prince's life. Instead of recognizing your worth, he fears your strength because they are powers he doesn't have and can't understand. But I will help you fulfill your destiny and train you to be the greatest warrior of the Seven Kingdoms, and one day you will be respected and loved by all.*"

Her father trained her to be the best soldier and the prince's bodyguard, which saved her from the king's enmity. In her heart, she knew that if she had not become useful to her uncle, he would have found a reason to be rid of her long ago. Even the love of her aunt, the queen, wouldn't have been enough to protect her.

She missed her aunt. Bright and beautiful, she was a larger-than-life figure. The queen had always kept Kira's mother by her side. They were sisters, but more important, they were the best of friends. Even though Kira had been more likely to clash with the queen, she'd loved her very much. The queen had supported General Kang's decision to train Kira as a *saulabi*, a member of the king's elite army. She was the one who insisted Kira would be the prince's bodyguard.

For the queen's sake, Kira had agreed to dedicate her life to protecting her cousin, Prince Taejo. She was seven years old the first time she saved him from a demon who tried to sacrifice him to an imoogi. Despite her uncle, Kira and Taejo had always been close. To Taejo, Kira was not only his bodyguard but also his big sister. And now he was the one, the future king of the prophecy, destined to unite the Seven Kingdoms. Protecting him was the most important priority for Kira. As the Dragon Musado, it was her destiny. It was her father who had first said she could be the Dragon Musado, the one to fulfill the Dragon King's prophecy—the warrior who would unite the kingdoms and save their world from the Demon Lord. Even when the Dragon Springs Temple monks, who'd studied the prophecy for centuries, had proclaimed that her cousin, Prince Taejo, was the one, her father had believed in her. She didn't know how he'd known, but he'd been right. Unfortunately, he hadn't lived to see Kira fulfill her destiny.

"I believe that one person can change the world. Whether he is the Musado or a girl with a tiger spirit. The monks teach that we mere mortals cannot question fate. But I say that we control destiny by our every action. Our power lies in the choices we make."

If the loss of her mother was a knife through her heart, the loss of her father was the hammer that pounded on it. She missed them fiercely.

In the upper corner of the scroll was an ink brush

painting of a tiger. Underneath it, a caption read "Golden Tiger." Quickly scanning the writing, she realized the scroll was the court shaman's prediction of her fortune, written at her birth. The characters for death and betrayal leaped from the paper before she rolled up the scroll, unwilling to read any more. She didn't need to know what was in store. It was bad enough that she was plagued with prophetic visions that nearly always came true. There was a danger in knowing too much of what the future held.

Setting it aside, she opened the little bag and removed a thick gold chain with a small tiger medallion. She'd never seen it before, but it was clearly a gift for her. No one else in the family had been born in the year of the tiger. She wondered why her mother had never given it to her. What had she been waiting for? What would she have said when presenting it to her? Kira's heart hurt to think of another missed opportunity.

She remembered a long-ago conversation with her mother when she'd been only five years old. They'd been sitting in this very room, her mother embroidering a tiger on a pillow for Kira. It was the first time that her mother had told her about the tiger dream.

"See this tiger?" her mother asked. "It is your animal symbol, your protector."

"Like me. I am the year of the tiger," Kira said.

Her mother nodded. "But it is also something more. It represents you as I first saw you, before you were ever born."

"How is that possible?" Kira asked.

Lady Yuwa caressed the silk before passing it over to her daughter.

"It was in my dream. I was in a meadow bordered by a thick bamboo grove, sitting on a large rock before a beautiful persimmon tree filled with ripe fruit. Chills ran down my spine when I sensed something behind me, stalking me. From within the bamboo grove, I spied two golden-amber eyes ringed thickly with deepest black. Only then did I realize that it was a large tiger, sleek and sinewy, its immense head held low to the ground while its golden eyes stared fixedly at me. Suddenly, it leaped toward me. I was so frightened I fell off the rock and landed on my back. The tiger was right on top of me and I flung my arms over my head, thinking I would be devoured. When nothing happened, I opened my eyes and found the large beast lying on its stomach before me. It yawned and shook its massive head as if it was nothing more than a house cat, batting a paw at a passing insect.

"Slowly I sat up, and the tiger rose onto its front legs. It raised its right paw and placed it gently upon my thigh. Within its razor-sharp claws was a perfect pink peony. It uttered a low purring growl and nudged me with its head, knocking me over and out of my dream."

Lady Yuwa had a faraway expression on her face, as if she was reliving the vision in her head. Kira waited for her mother to continue.

"It was definitely a good omen, but of what? I called the local village shaman who entered into a trance to commune with the spirits. When she revived, she told me I would bear a child in the year of the golden tiger, who would be the greatest warrior of all the seven kingdoms."

"That was me?" Kira asked.

Yuwa nodded. "After you were born, your father laughed to hear that the great warrior was an infant girl. But I knew my dream was an omen, for when you opened your eyes at me, they were the same golden amber as my tiger's eyes."

Kira was quiet, surprised by the story. Was this an explanation of why she was so different?

"Is that why Father makes me do my taekkyon training?" she asked. "So I can be a warrior?"

She'd been so proud to think she was special.

"Never doubt that you were born to do great things, my child," her mother said.

Her parents had been right: she did have a tiger spirit. Ever since she was a little girl, whenever she'd been sick or injured, she'd dreamed of a tiger that would comfort her. Now she knew it wasn't a dream but the spirit of a large gentle tiger that would curl up beside her and emit a golden light surrounding them both. Its *ki*, pure tiger energy, would transfer into her body and heal and rejuvenate her. Kira and her tiger spirit were deeply connected. Without it, she would have died a long time ago.

The bright golden medallion gleamed in the dim light. Kira heaved a deep sigh. She still grieved for her parents, missing them terribly.

She replaced the medallion in its small bag and closed the box, her hands trembling as she retied the wrapping cloth around it. With a heavy heart, she hoisted the treasure box onto her shoulder, leaving behind the ghosts of her past.

3

"*Noona*, you're late! Where've you been?" Taejo, prince of Hansong, nephew to King Eojin, and heir to the Guru throne, called to her as she entered the elaborate dining hall. This was the first of many dinners to be held for the various political groups coming to honor the Guru king.

Heading toward her cousin, Kira was surprised to note that he wasn't sitting on the royal dais with their uncle. Instead of sitting in a place of honor, Taejo sat at a lowly table a far distance from all the other nobles. The prince, along with his tutor, Brother Woojin, and Kira's brother Kwan, sat next to their friends Jaewon and Seung. While Jaewon's lineage was noble, Seung was a commoner. A rush of affection and relief warmed her to see her cousin's loyalty and his lack of pretentiousness. Besides, she was always happier sitting with her friends.

She eyed the beautiful court ladies who were being presented to their new king. They reminded her of the old court ladies of Hansong, none of who had ever been nice to her. Although she'd had no interaction with any of their female guests, she was grateful that King Eojin had not placed her in the women's quarters with them. Already she was aware of the glances and could hear the whispers of the visiting women.

Within the hall, the nobles vied for the attention of their new king. They'd come with the Tongey and Oak-cho delegations, and each noble family seemed to have a marriageable daughter in tow that they were eager to introduce to the widower. The king had made clear to Kira and Taejo that he would not remarry. He'd lost his entire family to influenza many years ago and still grieved for them. But looking around the room at the coquettish maidens, Kira wondered if he could stand against their determined onslaught.

Kira knelt by Taejo's side, noticing that round-faced Seung looked uncomfortable sitting in a royal banquet hall. She exchanged a glance with Jaewon, who smiled at her. Kira averted her face, reminded of her disfigurement.

She touched her eye, feeling the puckered grooves of the scar that ran across her eyebrow and eye and down her cheek, compliments of the traitorous Lord Shin and his whip. It was completely healed now, thanks to her tiger spirit, but her face would be marked forever. Most people flinched when they saw her. Yet she found it a marked improvement from the fear that she used to inspire. She was self-conscious about the ugly scar, but in some ways she thought it suited her. It was a constant reminder of who she was—a demon slayer and the prince's body-guard. The only time it bothered her was when she was near Jaewon. And that fact irked her even more.

"Noona." Taejo sighed. "You're not answering me—where were you?"

A servant placed a small table setting before her with a bowl of rice, several side dishes, a plate filled with deli-cacies from the main service table, and a bowl of white oxtail soup garnished with minced scallions. She snagged a pair of silver chopsticks and shoveled a large glob of rice into her mouth before answering.

"Just canvassing," she said. Hungry, she placed deli-cate pieces of marinated meat, bean sprouts, soy sauce potatoes, and pickled cabbage into her bowl.

"Is everything safe?" Taejo asked.

Kira hesitated. *Safe* was a relative term. "We must always stay on our guard."

He nodded with a serious look on his young face. "Everything must be extra safe for the coming celebra-tion."

"Don't worry," her brother Kwan said. "It will be great."

He turned his attention to Jaewon. "What's this I

hear about you gambling on *baduk* again? There have been a lot of unhappy rumblings from the officers."

Jaewon waved his hand in annoyance. "Hey, I can't help it that they all stink. You would think trained military officers would be better at a game of strategy."

Kira hid a smirk. Baduk was a simple game of strategy involving black and white stones on a board. The object of the game was to control as much of the board as possible by capturing or surrounding the opponent's stones. The rules were deceptively easy—baduk was an extremely difficult game to master. The first time she'd ever seen Jaewon, he'd been raking in a huge win off of a merchant. He was one of the best baduk players she'd ever met.

From across the table, Seung gave her a shy smile and pushed over a small teacup, which smelled of ginseng and honey. Kira sighed but took it with a nod of thanks. Every day Seung had been pushing his herbal remedies on her, insisting on treating her as a patient still. It was a very sweet gesture on his part, and Kira appreciated it. She grimaced as she prepared to drink the tea.

"I put a lot of honey in it," Seung said earnestly. "It will taste much better."

She held her breath and gulped it down. Shuddering, she forced herself to smile at him. All the honey did was add a cloying sweetness to what was a strong, bitter, and nasty brew.

"Thank you, I feel better already," she said. "I don't think I need any more."

Seung shook his head. "Oh no, you must drink it every day for at least a month to get its full efficacy."

Kira blanched as her brother snickered, and even Taejo gazed at her in amused sympathy.

"I don't think Kang Kira likes the taste of ginseng, Seung," Jaewon said. "In fact, I'm pretty sure she hates it."

"No, really?" Seung asked with a shocked expression. "But ginseng is so delicious! It's earthy and aromatic and so good for you. I can't imagine anyone disliking it."

"That's because you have strange taste," Jaewon said. "You're the only one I know who actually likes to eat those nasty Cathay century eggs."

"They are a real delicacy," Seung retorted. "Only a person with true gourmet sensibilities can appreciate the depth of flavor that a century egg contains."

"Sorry, I'm not eating anything that smells of horse urine," Jaewon said.

As Taejo giggled and gagged with exaggerated disgust, the two friends continued to bicker about food. Kira took the opportunity to share her findings with her brother.

"I found Mother's treasure box," she whispered to Kwan.

Kwan's face brightened. "That's wonderful! At least we have something left of our family."

"Were you able to recover anything of Father's?" Kira asked.

"No, the Yamato burned down Father's quarters and his office. There was nothing left." He sighed. "Were

Mother's things hard to find?"

Kira shook her head, swallowing over the lump in her throat. "Although I wonder if we would be better off leaving them hidden. I'm not sure where we could keep them safe."

"Why wouldn't you just keep them here?" Taejo asked, his face curious as he pointedly eavesdropped on their conversation.

The siblings looked at each other. Kira knew neither of them would speak about their deepest fear: that Hansong would be taken again.

"Send your family treasures to Dragon Springs Temple," Brother Woojin cut in. "Master Roshi can keep them safe for you there. There are several of my fellow monks here at Hansong who will be making the pilgrimage to the temple. They will be leaving a few days from now. I'm sure they would be able to deliver them for you."

Kwan nodded in agreement and thanked the monk, but Kira was hesitant. She sensed that she might never see her mother's treasures again.

All of a sudden, shouts rose over the drone of conversation. Everyone turned to face the doorway, where a new group of arrivals appeared. Kira recognized the supercilious Lord Yu of the Tongey delegates. She clenched her jaw in anger. He'd once tried to throw her out of a military meeting with the heads of state. When King Eojin had refused his demand and let Kira stay, Lord Yu had never forgiven either of them. The mutual dislike between Kira and Lord Yu was both intense and public.

One particularly brash Tongey nobleman jumped forward and shouted into the crowd, "Your Majesty, the Tongey are celebrating today! After the murder of our beloved King Asin, we believed his bloodline was finished. But we have discovered that we were wrong. We are proud to introduce to you to the late King Asin's nephew, the lost heir of Tongey, Prince Namhoe!"

There was a loud gasp of surprise and disapproval from the gathered nobles. Glancing toward her uncle, Kira was not surprised to see the king's impassive countenance, but behind him, she could see the anger in his advisers' faces.

"The Tongey are rejoicing in our good fortune," proclaimed Lord Yu. "Perhaps you were premature in naming your heir, Your Majesty."

Kira gritted her teeth to bite back her temper. The Tongey had made clear their displeasure with King Eojin's announcement of Taejo as his heir. They'd never been happy pledging their fealty to a Guru king. This was their response.

The antagonism in the room was strong. Guru soldiers, who usually stood unobtrusively in the background, had stepped forward with their hands poised over their swords. Nobles quieted and froze, staring avidly at the tableau before them. The whole chamber radiated discord.

Before emotions could escalate, her oldest brother, Kyoung, intervened, standing before the Tongey prince with an elegant bow. Tall and handsome in his uniform of black and silver, he was a commanding presence. Kyoung efficiently diffused the situation, calming down the rowdy Tongeys and bringing them to a table of honor near the king's station.

"Your brother is not only a gifted leader but a natural diplomat," Brother Woojin said with a pleased smile.

Kira nodded, absently flexing her hands, which had been tightly fisted during the confrontation. She noted the worried frown on Taejo's face.

"Don't worry about it," she said with a gentle nudge. "Uncle would not replace you." Under her breath she muttered to herself, "I'd never let him."

She felt a tug at her sleeve. Turning her head she glimpsed Kwan's grim expression. "I don't like the look on Lord Yu's face. He looks like trouble. We need to keep an eye on him," he said.

Kira agreed. Lord Yu had never been happy with Eojin's forced merger of Tongey and Guru. And he was not alone. Kira could already see what was going to happen next. Tongey would urge Eojin to renounce Taejo and take the new Tongey prince as his heir instead.

Whether or not he was a true prince and heir of Tongey was irrelevant. For this, she vowed, would never happen.

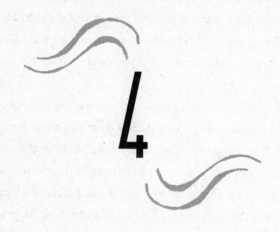

4

She could smell the demon somewhere in the palace. The foul odor assaulted her senses, making her eyes burn and tear. But no matter how hard she looked she couldn't find it.

The corridors began to change. She was no longer in the palace grounds.

She was in a cave, lost in a warren of tunnels. The scent was stronger than ever. It was all around her. She held up her sword, ready for the attack, but the tunnels were empty.

The sound of chanting came from behind her. She followed it down a narrow tunnel that was strangely familiar to her. When it opened into a cave, Kira recognized it immediately. This was the cave where she had first seen Daimyo Tomodoshi speaking with the Demon Lord. In front of the glow of a gaping maw filled with lava stood a man wearing a grotesque mask and dressed in black silk robes, muttering before the remains of an animal sacrifice. Jewels glittered on his hands and around his neck. Kira knew that she was in the presence of a powerful shaman, but was it the daimyo?

Several guards stood to the sides, overseeing a group of prisoners chained to the walls. All the prisoners were young men, ranging in age from sixteen to no more than twenty years old. They looked healthy and strong but terribly frightened.

"Bring the first prisoner!" the shaman shouted. He spoke in the Yamato tongue, and yet Kira could understand every word. It was as if something in her head was translating the words for her.

A guard unchained a young man, who fought hard to escape, punching and kicking until he broke free and ran wildly for the exit.

"Keep him alive!" the shaman commanded. The guard shot an arrow through the prisoner's leg and dragged him to the center of the cavern.

"Please, just kill me!" The wounded man wept.

The shaman ignored his words, focusing instead on the arrow protruding from the man's leg. He snatched it out with a twist, causing the prisoner to scream in pain. Blood flowed heavily from the wound. The shaman captured the blood in a brass bowl and then tossed the entire bowl into the fiery pit. A large demon shot up from the lava, its grayish-black leathery skin immune to the flames that licked at its feet. As soon as the demon sighted the bleeding man, it tried to lunge at him but came up short. It roared and raged within the confines of the pit but could not leave.

Two of the shaman's guards approached cautiously and picked up the prisoner, holding him directly before the demon. The demon licked its lips and tried to leap once again at the offering placed so close, and then it froze in place, bound by the hypnotic chanting that the shaman had begun.

Kira did not understand the words of the chant. It was a language such as she'd never heard before. It sounded harsh and ugly, a tongue made for speaking only the foulest of things. The shaman paced along the perimeter of the lava pit, continuing his binding magic. Only the demon's black lidless eyes moved as it watched the shaman. The prisoner, who had been whimpering in fear, began to scream in terror as his body floated in the air toward the frozen demon. The shaman's chants had grown steadily louder as he guided the prisoner's writhing body toward the demon's immobile one. At the moment of impact, the shaman slammed his hands together and Kira watched in horror as the two bodies began to meld into one. It was as if the demon body was consuming the human one, absorbing it whole until the screams were silenced forever.

The grayish-black skin of the demon began to bubble and explode, cracking and peeling off to reveal human-looking skin. The binding spell was broken as the demon began to writhe in agony, its body morphing. Curved spine and limbs began to straighten as its head shrank. This was the darkest type of magic. Kira could not look away, riveted by the mutation occurring before her. It was only when the demon stopped writhing that she realized what it had become.

A half-breed.

With a flick of his hand, the shaman moved the half-breed from the lava pit to stand before him. The creature got down on one knee and bowed his head.

The shaman began to laugh. "I will build a new army of half-breeds made from demon fire and human blood. And then we will rule the world!"

At his words, Kira knew who it was. She didn't need to see under the mask to recognize him.

It was Daimyo Tomodoshi.

And Kira knew that he must be stopped, no matter what. She would bring about his end, or she would die trying.

5

Three days later, Kira walked by Taejo's side as they entered Hansong palace's magnificent throne hall. In all her seventeen years, Kira had never been allowed inside the elaborate building. It was two stories tall and built upon a multi-tiered stone base. Its red double doors opened into a large room with a vaulted ceiling painted with two golden dragons. Toward the rear of the room stood the king's and queen's thrones on a dais. A painting of the sun, moon, and five mountain peaks, the symbols of the king, dominated the wall behind the throne. Kira had peeked into the throne hall many times, but only now could she appreciate the details of the architecture and paintings.

King Eojin stood on the edge of the dais before Kyoung, Kwan, and Captain Pak. The king's right-hand man, General Kim, stood behind him. As Eojin announced their promotions, each soldier stepped forward to accept a gift of a newly forged sword. Kyoung was raised from lieutenant colonel to general, Captain Pak was raised to major, and Kwan was now a captain.

Kira and Taejo, the only two spectators in the room, clapped their hands loudly as the two Kang brothers grinned and congratulated each other on their promotions. They turned to pound Major Pak on his shoulders with good-humored affection. He stared at the king's gift, mesmerized by the craftsmanship of the gleaming sword, before replacing it in its ebony sheath.

Then, King Eojin called for Kira and Taejo to come forward.

"Kira, you should have been standing here beside your brothers," he said.

She started in surprise. "Me? You wanted to promote me?"

"Yes, I believed you deserved a title and to be given your own command."

Taejo grinned broadly and nudged Kira. "She would make an excellent officer, Your Majesty!"

Eojin smiled. "I know." He glanced over at the impassive face of General Kim. "But it is not to be. I've argued for many hours with my advisers on this issue and I could not get them to agree."

Eojin sighed. "Our world is not ready for a female leader."

"I'm not surprised," Kira said. "But it doesn't matter. I don't need a title."

"I know that," he replied. "It wasn't for you. It was for others to recognize you and your value. But I fear that they are still intimidated by the Demon Slayer."

The king gave General Kim a pointed look. "There are those who will never accept a woman in a man's world. You shake up their beliefs and they don't like that. They aren't ready."

"As long as you believe in me, that's all that matters." Kira smiled at her uncle.

He looked down at her with worried eyes. "But what troubles me is that I won't always be here."

Taejo gasped and spoke in a hushed voice. "Don't say that, Uncle. You must not say that."

The king smiled. "Death is inevitable, young prince. Don't fear it. My concern is more for those I leave behind."

"Nothing shall happen to you while I'm by your side, Your Majesty!" General Kim said with a sharp bow.

Eojin eyed his right-hand man with a concerned expression. Kira perceived a certain wariness in his gaze. It surprised her. She was not fond of the general and he made no effort to hide his dislike of her. But she knew how much her uncle relied on him. There was no doubt that the general would die for the king. His obsessive loyalty was unquestionable and unwavering.

"It is as heaven wills it," Eojin said.

"Even the heavens will see your destiny and dare not take you from us!" the general responded.

Eojin sighed. "Do not taunt the gods, General Kim. They do not like mere mortals such as us to question their powers."

"I do not fear the gods," the general retorted.

"Such hubris is dangerous," Kira said in a quiet voice.

The general whirled around to glare at Kira, his eyes narrowing into slits. She could hear the angry grumbling of her brothers as they moved closer. The general also took note of their reactions, as he seemed to catch himself before answering.

"You must learn to keep your opinions to yourself, young mistress Kang."

Kira was unfazed. "Why? Because I'm female or because I'm a Demon Slayer?"

"Because you are not important," he said. "Didn't you know that?"

Kira flinched at his words.

With a final contemptuous flicker of his eyes, he excused himself and left the room. Kyoung had to keep a furious Kwan from going after the general, and even Pak looked perturbed.

Eojin nodded to the three men. "You may leave us now," he said.

Taejo stood by Kira's side as the others left. He placed a comforting hand on her arm. "I don't like him," he said in an outraged voice. "He doesn't know what he's talking about."

"He is wrong. You are very important," Eojin said. "Never doubt that."

Kira swallowed her anger and tried to smile. "His words don't matter to me."

"Unfortunately, he is not alone in his beliefs and that is why I worry," he said.

A certain sense of bitter resignation had filled Kira since the general's abrupt departure. Some things would never change.

Kira shrugged. "I can take care of myself."

The king shook his head. "I have no doubt of your strengths and your capabilities. But you must also know your limitations. Know when you need help and do not be shy about asking for it."

"Your Majesty, it is not always easy to know whom I can ask for help," she answered.

Eojin put his hands on her shoulders and looked her deep in her eyes.

"You can always ask me," he said. "I promise, I will always help you."

As heartening as his words were meant to be, Kira was beset by a powerful unease that she couldn't explain.

6

The palace was filled with the bustling of visitors, servants, and performers. Tonight's celebration would be the first royal banquet for the new king on the night of Seollal, the lunar new year, which was also the second day of the second month of the solar calendar.

All Hansong's nobility, as well as those from neighboring kingdoms, would attend the gala event in the palace. Outside, on the streets, a large festival was in progress for the common folk, who would also enjoy the new fortunes associated with being part of the great Guru kingdom. Merchants had flocked to Hansong once again, eager to take part in the celebrations. Although it was a very cold night with frigid winds, no one was willing to miss the fun.

A thunder roll of drums signaled the arrival of the entertainment, as brightly dressed acrobats rolled and flipped into the center of the palace courtyard. From the elaborate garden pavilion, Kira stood surveying the festivities under the midnight blue sky. The acrobats sailed in complicated maneuvers in the courtyard below her but she couldn't care less.

The entire palace grounds were swarming with shamans protecting the area, but still Kira was uneasy. Her gut churned with a sense of impending danger. After she'd shared her nightmarish visions with her brothers, they'd doubled the number of guards surrounding the king, but nothing could contain her worry.

She reached for the little bag that hung from her neck, which she always wore close to her chest. It contained the little jade *haetae* statue her father had given her and the tidal stone, the first of the Dragon King's treasures. The large ruby gave the Dragon Musado the power to control water. Its magic had helped Kira save Hansong from Shaman Ito and his evil imoogi, a monstrous half-dragon, half-snake creature. She usually found it comforting to hold her treasures, but not tonight.

She hadn't stopped moving all evening, as if chasing some elusive spirit she was only vaguely aware of. All night her senses had stayed on high alert.

She moved down toward the banquet hall again,

following the servants carrying trays of elaborate food for the dinner that night. Inside the hall, she breathed in the delicious aroma of the finest delicacies Hansong had to offer. Long tables were set with steamed whole sea bream in a ginger-soy sauce marinade; stewed chickens stuffed with ginseng, sweet rice, and chestnuts; clear noodle dishes stir-fried with vegetables; oyster and scallion pancakes; meat dumplings; soups and stews; and a variety of side dishes. Another wide table was set solely with desserts—sweet rice balls, pastries filled with red bean paste, layered rice cakes, and assorted drinks made of rice or persimmons. It was a royal feast befitting a conquering monarch.

She prepared to take another circuit around the hall when a whiff of a foul stench twirled her about, away from the laughter of the guests.

The odor was fleeting, but enough to send her tearing after it. Somewhere in the palace was a demon presence. Catching her brother Kwan's eye, she waved him over. With him came Jaewon.

"I smell something," she said, still walking, following her nose. "Stay close to Taejo for me."

Kwan nodded and joined the tail end of the royal procession, which was now entering the banquet hall. Her cousin, Prince Taejo, was following their uncle to the dais set in the back of the brightly illuminated chamber.

Jaewon stayed by her side.

"What is it?" he asked.

Kira breathed deeply, just barely catching the trail

again. "Demon," she said, and started running, taking a huge lungful of air as she ran. The source of the odor continued to elude her. It led her up toward the southern walls of the fortress, then past the sentries standing guard and up into the darkness of the cliffs. There it abruptly disappeared. Kira scanned the murky depths of the Han River. Had she chased the demon into the water?

"What happened?" Jaewon asked, breathing hard by her side.

Kira looked wildly about her. Was it really gone? She couldn't tell. "I don't know," she whispered as she began to pace.

Jaewon gripped her by the arms. "Calm down," he said. "It's all right. Just breathe and think."

Kira closed her eyes and cleared her mind as she opened her senses once again.

Her gut began to twist and the tidal stone at her chest burned red-hot as she realized her mistake.

"Oh, Heavenly Father, I've been tricked!"

Cursing, she ran for the banquet hall. She just hoped it wasn't too late.

Precious seconds ticked off as she raced through the corridors of the palace. How could she have been so stupid? She should never have left Taejo's side. They'd lured her away.

Unsheathing her sword, Kira ran for the stairs.

"We've got to return immediately!" she shouted at Jaewon.

Their leather boots pounded the pavement as they reached the exterior of the palace hall. Guards seeing their approach came to immediate attention.

"The king is in danger!" she yelled. "Follow us!"

Something terrible was about to happen, but she didn't know where the danger was. She shoved past gawking servants and burst through a side door of the banquet hall. Nearby observers glared in disdain as her gaze swept over them. Kira scanned the entire room. Where was the assassin? Who could it be? The guards came up right behind her, causing a commotion among the guests closest to the door. She ignored the complaints and slowly paced around the entire room, moving ever closer to the royal dais.

In the middle of the hall, a troupe of red-gowned dancers stood in two circles, one within the other, their large feathered fans overlapped in perfect symmetry. They began to dance. A group of musicians sat in the far corner playing a variety of delicate stringed instruments.

Kira scanned the guests, looking for the assassin. She motioned for the guards to surround the room. Jaewon stayed close by her. From across the room, Kira signaled to her brother Kwan where he stood not far from Taejo's side. He nodded and unsheathed his sword. More guests stirred anxiously, noticing her and the guards' drawn swords.

The acrid stench of demon magic hit her nose. She whipped her head around to face the dancers. And then the odor disappeared. Kira ground her teeth in frustration. Where could it have gone? In confusion, she scrutinized the dancers. Red robes swung in unison, fans flipped open and closed in harmony.

There was the odor again. But which of the women was a demon? She focused on the dancers, studying each dancer's face and posture. Pretty faces, wide smiles, and glittering eyes—all except one. Kira concentrated on one dancer, whose sharp smile and narrowed, intense eyes caused Kira's flesh to tingle in alarm. The woman was clearly not a demon, but all Kira's senses were at high alert.

She began to walk toward the dancers, her uneasiness drawing her forward like an irresistible force. As Kira approached, the intense-eyed dancer flipped open her fan, causing the ripple of demon magic to shimmer slightly around the spokes.

"Assassin!" Kira shouted as she launched herself at the dancers.

The woman flung her arm at the king and prince, and several blades instantly shot out. Kira leaped forward, and twirling her sword in a furious circle, she sliced the blades out of the air. She landed in front of the assassin and thrust her sword through the woman's chest. The woman peered down at the blade and then up at Kira. Her heavily painted face pulled into a macabre smile as she choked on a laugh, her fan still extended over Kira's shoulder.

"You missed one," she said, before slumping down dead.

Only then did Kira hear the screams behind her. Pushing the assassin off her sword, Kira ran for the dais, her eyes seeking Taejo. Her heart didn't calm down until she saw his pale face staring at her.

She looked to see the king next to him and saw that the assassin was right. One black blade protruded from the king's abdomen. His skin was turning a grayish black and the poison was spreading rapidly. There was nothing they could do to save him.

"It's a cursed blade!" she shouted. "Don't touch it!"

But it was too late, Kyoung had already reached over, trying to remove the blade. He recoiled in pain, staring in shock as his fingers turned the same grayish black and the poison spread quickly down his arm.

Kira raced to her brother, her left hand reaching for the tidal stone, commanding it to help. Her right hand turned to ice and she grasped him by the wrist, fighting the cursed plague with the purity of the tidal stone. She didn't question the logic of the stone, only relieved to see that it worked. The dark gray stopped spreading and began to recede, slowly moving past the wrist and up the palm of his hand until only his middle and ring fingers remained dark and hard as stone. Though she questioned the stone, no answer was forthcoming. There was nothing else she could do to heal Kyoung's fingers and return them to normal.

Someone seized her by the nape, yanking her away from her brother and toward the paralyzed figure of the king.

"Help the king!" General Kim shouted. "Your duty is to the king!"

His brutal grip dug deep into the tender flesh of her throat before he finally released her with a furious shove.

Kira forgot the throbbing pain as she caught sight of her uncle's ashen face. An unnatural pallor emphasized the blue capillaries under his skin and his breath came in short painful rasps. The king was dying.

She shook her head at the general. "I'm sorry, it's already too late."

Enraged, the general whipped out his sword and held it to her neck. "You will try or I'll kill you myself!"

She heard her brothers' outraged responses as they came to her defense. With a fierce glare at the general, she shoved his sword aside and turned to the king. Kira tried to place her icy hand on the black blade, but the force of the curse repelled her hand. She asked the tidal stone for all of its help. There was an immediate surge of ice that coursed through her arms.

Struggling hard against the evil, Kira put all her concentration to push against the power of the blade. She circled the gray flesh with her arms and poured the clean energy of the tidal stone into the king's body. Eojin wheezed and choked, but she didn't stop. Sweat streaked down her face as she fought with the cursed blade.

A deep, malicious voice rang in her ears, speaking to her.

Why fight me? Let go. Let go.

She recognized the voice from her dreams. The blade was cursed by the Demon Lord himself.

Kira gritted her teeth as the curse attacked her with thousands of needle pricks across her skin, trying to burrow into her flesh. Only her determination kept it in check, but she could feel herself wavering. She moaned as pain stabbed at her and something popped in her nose. Fluid coursed down her mouth and chin. She tasted blood. Pressure filled her ears, causing excruciating pain.

She heard her brothers calling her name. She tried to respond, but her mouth had dried up, leaving her tongue swollen and useless. Her eyes rolled back as her lids began to flutter wildly. The power of the tidal stone ebbed against the demonic onslaught. The Demon Lord's deep, mocking voice rang in her head.

Soon you will be mine also.

Tears burned in her eyes as her body began to tremble. She was trapped by the curse. No longer was she trying to save the king—now she was fighting for her own life.

Release came swiftly. Her body was wrenched away by Kwan. With a moan she collapsed to the floor and was gently lifted to a sitting position by Jaewon and Taejo. Before her, Kyoung stood nose to nose with the livid General Kim, Kwan seething in anger by his side. If her brothers had not been there, Kira knew that the general would have gladly killed her.

Jaewon pressed a cloth to her bleeding nose while her young cousin hovered over them.

"I'm all right," she said. "Help me up."

On her feet again, Kira despaired to see the dark stain spreading across Eojin's torso, up to his neck and his extremities. Within minutes, his face was a mottled gray and black. Eojin let out one last raspy breath before stilling forever, his face frozen in an expression of agony.

General Kim turned on Kira. "You!" He spat at her feet. "You failed the king! How convenient that you stopped the assassin's blades from hitting the prince! And instead of turning your immediate attention to the king, you save your brother first! You are a traitor!"

He raised his sword.

Taejo was the first to defend her, bravely standing up to the general's wrath.

"Stop! I command you to drop your weapon!" he shouted.

The general froze, but his sword remained drawn.

"Your Highness, she is a traitor to the throne. Stand aside. You must not protect her!"

Kira was still too weak to defend herself, but it was her brothers' swords that met General Kim's in a clash of screeching metal that drew screams from the spectators.

"You are out of line," Kyoung said in a low, fierce voice. "My sister did everything she could to save the king. And

I will kill you right now before I let you speak ill of her again!"

Two other advisers pulled General Kim aside, forcing him to lower his weapon.

"It's true. We all saw her try to save the king. You were wrong to accuse her," Lord Hwang, the Guru minister of foreign affairs, said. "There was nothing she could do."

"General Kim is overwhelmed," another adviser spoke up. "But how can we blame him? This is a disaster for us all. Without the king, who will lead the Iron Army? Who will fight the Yamato?"

"The army will continue its current leadership. We will lead it under Taejo's rule," Kyoung said.

"He's just a boy! He cannot be king!" General Kim's voice was filled with anger and despair.

Kira gripped Taejo's hand hard. His body was shaking from the ordeal. Putting an arm around her cousin, Kira studied the faces of the king's advisers. Shock and grief were second to anger. Overwhelming anger.

"The Tongey will revolt! They only joined due to King Eojin's leadership," General Nam, Guru vice minister of military affairs, said.

The advisers congregated around General Kim trying to lead him from the king's body.

"There's no way we can continue the war! We are doomed!" cried General Kim.

"Quiet!" Kyoung roared. "We must move on. We must continue the fight. The Yamato will not stop because

Eojin is dead. We fight on."

He turned to Kwan and Jaewon. "Take Kira and the prince to their quarters and keep them safe."

Kwan bowed and steered Kira and Taejo toward the exit. Jaewon put a bracing arm around her waist, supporting her. Kira didn't complain. She was feeling sick and still in terrible shock.

The banquet hall was now empty of all guests; only grief-stricken soldiers remained. Kwan quickly led them out and to the west side building, where the Kang family and the prince were now housed.

They stopped for no one until they reached the safety of the prince's quarters. Jindo, the prince's devoted white dog, bounded over. Taejo knelt and buried his face in Jindo's soft, thick fur.

"What happened? What was that blade?" Jaewon asked.

"It was cursed by the Demon Lord," Kira said. She rubbed her eyes and patted her nose, relieved to find it had stopped bleeding. "I don't think I could have saved the king even if I had tried immediately."

Kira was worried and defensive about the action she'd taken. She knew her first allegiance should have been to the king, but when she had seen the threat to her brother's life, her instinct had been to save him first. Despite the split-second decision, she had known in her heart that while she couldn't save the king, she could save her brother.

"You did the right thing, Kira," Kwan said. "You had no choice. The blade was cursed. We saw what it did to you and Kyoung. Given the type of injury the king sustained, it would have been impossible to save him even if it wasn't cursed."

Taejo nodded. "Noona, I will speak for you. No one will be allowed to accuse you of wrongdoing!" He sat curled up amid a tower of cushions, hugging Jindo tightly.

Kira thanked him and sank heavily down onto the floor, then held her head in her hands. Her arms and legs ached as if she'd fallen down a mountain cliff and smashed her body against the rocks. Her stomach heaved and her head pounded. Everything hurt.

She felt someone wrap a blanket around her and looked up into Jaewon's concerned face.

"Do you need anything?" he asked.

Shaking her head, she leaned against the wall. "Just tired."

Everyone sat quietly, until broken sobs filled the room. It was all too much for Taejo. Kira was close to tears herself, but fear overcame her sorrow. Without Eojin, who would protect Taejo's right to the throne of Hansong? She'd been so grateful that the Demon Lord's cursed blades had not touched Taejo. And yet he was in more danger than ever before.

"What's going to happen now?" Jaewon asked.

She had no answer, for she feared the worst.

7

Her brothers arrived early the next morning, their faces tight with worry.

Kira leaped up to grab Kyoung's left hand and survey the damage.

"It's all right, little sister," Kyoung said, trying to ease her fears. "I was a fool. I should have known better than to touch that blade."

Ignoring him, she carefully examined his hand. Both the middle finger and the ring finger were still grayish black. They were smooth yet cold and hard to the touch, like stone.

"I can't feel anything there, but I'd rather have them

than not," Kyoung said. "I've no doubt you saved my life, little sister. Thank you."

Kira held her brother's hand between both of her own, trying to contain the emotions that threatened to spill over in a surge of hot tears.

"But I didn't save the king," she whispered. All night long her mind had kept replaying the moments of the assassination in an endless cycle. If she'd moved faster, if she'd killed the assassin sooner, if she'd seen the blade that had slipped past her. How could she have failed the king so completely? Her last remaining uncle was dead. Her brothers and Taejo were the only family left.

Kyoung placed a comforting hand on her head and leaned his forehead to hers. "No one could have saved him. It wasn't your fault. I won't have you blaming your-self. Do you hear me?"

She nodded and took in a shaky breath. In her mind she knew he was right, but her heart refused to relin-quish the guilt that had sunk deep into her soul.

She was also in pain from the ordeal with the Demon Lord's dagger. Her tiger spirit had not come to heal her in the night as usual. She didn't know if it was because of her inability to sleep or her guilty mind, but she missed it sorely. She could still feel the effects of the curse, still hear the Demon Lord's voice in her head.

A scuffle and sharp protests could be heard from the courtyard. Major Pak's soldiers had been ordered to let no one into their building.

"That sounds like Kim Jaewon," Kwan said.

"It *is* him," Taejo said. He leaped to his feet and raced for the door. Kwan stopped him and pushed him aside with a firm but gentle grip. He then opened the door and stepped into the hallway. A moment later, he reentered, bringing Jaewon, Brother Woojin, and Seung with him. Seung stood by the door, looking uncomfortable, as always. Catching Kira's eye, he frowned in concern. With a bow, he quickly exited the room again.

"The kingdom is in pandemonium. Even with Oakcho and Hansong honoring the Guru agreement, Tongey is going to be problematic. They've already openly refused to accept Prince Taejo as King Eojin's heir. And General Kim is calling for your arrest," Jaewon said. "What are we going to do?"

Everyone turned to Kyoung. Kira was not surprised by this. Her eldest brother was one of the most respected men in all Hansong. His mere presence was heartening— tall, broad, and muscular, with a weathered face both young and old. Looking at him now, she could see how much like their father he'd become.

"The Tongey diplomats didn't waste any time at all," he said with a deep sigh. "They've declared Prince Nam-hoe the new king of Tongey and are now pushing for him to take over the Guru throne."

Angry shouts filled the room and Kira clamped her hands over her ears, her head still hurting from her encounter with the cursed blade.

"Those traitorous dogs! They swore an oath of fealty to Guru!" Kwan said.

"They swore fealty to Eojin and now that he's dead, they claim they are released," Kyoung said. "They don't accept Prince Taejo as the rightful heir and seek to take over the Guru empire, including Hansong, in one fell swoop."

"Has their army attacked?"

"No, it is all diplomacy right now. They aren't stupid enough to think they could win against the Iron Army. So they are using persuasion to speak to Oakcho and all the military leaders. They're after Kira, claiming she's in league with the Demon Lord and allowed the king to die."

Kira snorted. "That's no surprise."

Kwan let loose a long series of creative and inventive curses that caused Taejo to gawk at him. Even Kira had to smile at that.

"We should gather the army and crush them," Kwan said.

Kyoung shook his head. "No, this is not a fight of strength. This is fight of words. A show of force would only exacerbate the situation. We must find a way to prove to them that they are wrong."

"But how?" Kira asked.

At that moment, Brother Woojin stepped forward, shaking his head.

"There is only one thing we can do," Brother Woojin said. "We must find the other two sacred treasures of the Dragon King. Only then will the people believe that Prince Taejo is our rightful king."

The Dragon King's treasures and the prophecy were the monk's greatest concerns. Kira could still remember sitting in the temple with Brother Woojin and Master Roshi and listening to legends that were now becoming true.

Seven will become three. Three will become one. One will save us all. But only in the hands of the Dragon Musado will the Dragon King's treasures destroy the Demon Lord, wreaking the vengeance of the heavens on earth.

"So we are to leave this mess behind and head to who-knows-where again?" Kira asked.

"What other choice do we have?" the monk replied.

"Stand and fight!" Kwan interjected.

"That's not an option!" Kyoung said sharply.

Her brothers began to argue. Kira closed her eyes and shook her head. It was starting all over again. Just when she'd thought they'd found security and stability, the peace was destroyed. Someone knelt by her side and she knew it was Jaewon. She breathed in the clean essence of his sweat and the woodsy smell of his clothes. There was always a certain sense of warmth that Kira felt around him. He was a comforting blanket that cocooned her.

"Come with us north—it isn't safe for you and the prince here," he said.

Kira looked up at him in surprise. "You're heading north again? Why?"

A shadow of pain passed over Jaewon's face. "When the Yamato invaded, my clan headed north, toward Mount Baekdu. Seung needs to be with his family, and it's time I faced my parents for my crime," he whispered.

"How do you know where they are?" Kira asked.

"They are at our ancestral lands of what was once the Puyo kingdom near Mount Baekdu. Many centuries ago, long before Guru conquered it, my ancestors lived there. My father has always spoken of returning to Puyo and the village shaman believes that the source of shaman magic lay within the heart of Mount Baekdu. He would persuade my father to take the clan as close as possible because that is where his power would be strongest."

"Are you ready for that?" she asked in sympathy.

Before he could answer, Brother Woojin approached with a serious demeanor.

"Young mistress, you promised me that we would continue our quest. Therefore none of these political issues matter right now. All that matters is that we find the treasures," he said. "Besides, your duty is to keep the prince safe. Hansong has now become the most unsafe place in the world for him."

This was absolutely true. Kira knew this the way she always knew when danger was present. They must leave Hansong soon, before it became impossible to do so. She heaved a great sigh. Given her restlessness and the constant nightmares she'd been having, it wasn't a difficult decision for her, but she knew it would be hard on Taejo.

"He's right, *Oppa*," she said looking up at her oldest brother. "We don't have a choice."

"I'm not sure that's a good idea," he replied.

Kira shook her head. "No, Oppa, this is something I must do," she said.

He was quiet, his expression worried as he gazed at Kira. She kept her eyes steady on his, trying to assure him that this was the right path for her to take.

"What is it you seek now?" he asked.

"The jeweled dagger," Brother Woojin said. "The Dragon King carefully hid his three most prized possessions so that they would be found only in a time of our greatest need. They are the tidal stone that controls the seas, the jeweled dagger that controls the earth, and the jade dragon belt. Your sister already has the tidal stone. She must find the next two treasures. The dagger can cause earthquakes, and the belt controls the fourteen dragons of the heavens but only when reunited with the dagger and the stone."

"And you know where this second treasure is?" Kyoung asked.

"In theory, we know where it *should* be," the monk said.

"Where is it?"

"The land of shadows, which can only be accessed from Mount Baekdu," Brother Woojin replied.

"Sunim, when you say shadows, you mean the dead, right? Which means the shadow world is actually in the underworld," Kira said.

"Correct, although it is separate from where the Demon Lord resides," he said.

"And how are we to access the shadow world?" she asked.

"The door to the land of shadows will open for the Dragon Musado," Brother Woojin assured them.

"And you are sure of this?" Kyoung cut in.

Brother Woojin hesitated for a moment. "It is what my brothers have learned from the ancient text."

Kyoung nodded and bowed to the monk. "Then we will all leave on your quest as soon as we possible."

Kira started at his words. "But aren't you needed here?"

Her brother's tanned face grew darker. "I'll not see my family hurt again. We'll stay together."

With a relieved whistle, Kwan clasped arms with his elder brother. Looking at her two brothers together, Kira breathed a sigh of relief. Having them both would be a great comfort to her on the trip that was to come.

"One word of caution," Brother Woojin said, his kind old face looking unhappy. "The jeweled dagger is guarded by a dangerous dragon called Fulang. Not much is known about it other than that it emerges from the underworld every hundred years, hunting for treasures from all over the world."

There was a long pause as the Kang siblings considered his words.

"Well, then it is a good thing that I'm coming along," Kyoung said with a grim smile.

The door slid open and Seung reentered, carrying a tray with a steaming cup of tea. He crossed to Kira's side, setting down the hot beverage on a small table that he placed before her.

"This will help you feel better," Seung said with a gentle smile. "There's no ginseng in it."

She took a deep breath and was grateful to take in the sharp aroma of ginger mellowed with the sweetness of honey. Kira thanked him gratefully and sipped the healing draught, her senses stimulated by its soothing fragrance.

Brother Woojin clasped his hands together. "I will start the preparations." Patting Seung on the back, he said, "You will not be rid of us so easily."

Seung smiled in happy confusion. "Where are we going?"

Jaewon gave Kira a satisfied smile. "North," he said. "Again."

Four days had passed since Eojin's assassination, and Hansong was once again in chaos. Fierce debate raged over who would now control the Guru state of affairs.

Kira could see how difficult and stressful the situation was for Kyoung. Constantly sought by Guru ministers and military chiefs for his advice and leadership, Kira's oldest brother had become a voice of calm and a stable force in uncertain times. But he was adamant about leaving Hansong.

"The northern passes are no longer safe," Kyoung said, his face grim and tense. "General Kim has lost his mind and blames everything on Kira. He knows the only safe route for us is to head north away from the Yamato. He has men and mercenaries everywhere."

"Maybe I can lure them from here, so you can get the prince to safety," Kira said.

"Absolutely not!" Kwan was adamant.

"No, young mistress," Brother Woojin said, raising a hand to keep the others quiet. "You are the Dragon Musado. Prince Taejo is safest with you."

Kyoung nodded. "You must stay with the prince. General Kim would capture him to get to you."

"But then where do we go?" Kira was frustrated and upset.

"We should head west to the Yellow Sea," Brother Woojin said.

Jaewon cleared his throat. "*Sunim*, we need to head north. Isn't that where the next treasure is?"

"We can't head north over land, it's too dangerous," Kyoung said. "But General Kim won't expect us to go west. It would make no sense to him. He's a Guru soldier: he never thinks of the sea as an option. But once we are at Minchu port, we can take a ship to Uju. It's the largest port city of Guru, right on the Yellow Sea. We can trade for horses there and head inland, toward Mount Baekdu."

Taejo smiled for the first time since the king's death. "The Yellow Sea! I've never been to the sea. I've always wanted to go."

Jaewon looked unhappy. "Is this the only way? I don't enjoy boat rides."

"It's true. He gets terribly seasick, even on the calmest ferries. He always throws up." Seung gave Jaewon a worried look. "Always."

"Well, they're not looking for the two of you, so you can still head north to your clan," Kyoung said.

Jaewon shook his head, his eyebrows drawing tight. "No, we have to stick together."

"So then it's settled," Taejo said. "How soon can we leave?"

Kyoung paused, his eyes looking uneasy. "I just don't know of a safe way to get you off of the palace grounds. The general's men patrol the entire perimeter of the palace and city gates."

"What about the tunnels?" Taejo asked.

Kira shook her head. "General Kim had me show him the tunnels all over the city for security reasons. And then he sealed all but one. There's no way we can use any of them."

There was a knock at the door and a voice called for General Kang.

Kira felt a sharp pang to hear the title that was once her father's. Her eldest brother rose to his feet and slid open the door. Lord Hwang, Guru minister of foreign affairs, and General Nam, Guru vice minister of military affairs, entered the room.

"General Kang, you must not leave us now. The Iron Army needs you," Lord Hwang said.

"Soldiers loyal to General Kim have broken off and

are now supporting his claim to the throne. The Tongey are pushing for their new king, and everyone else is confused and scared. You are our only hope!" General Nam said.

"This is not my problem. My sister and Prince Taejo are in grave danger as you well know," Kyoung retorted. "I need to protect them or there will be no hope for any of us!"

"This *is* your problem!" General Nam shouted. "The soldiers are looking to you for leadership. They trust you! You can't turn your back on those who would still support you and the prince."

Kira could see her brother's anguish at General Nam's words. Kyoung had been trained by their father to be a leader to his men at all times. The idea of leaving them behind would go against his very nature. She understood the reason for his turmoil; he was caught between family and duty.

Lord Hwang faced Kira. "Your brother is right. You are both in great danger. You aren't safe here in the palace and your chances of leaving the city aren't good. I understand your brother's concerns. But without his leadership, keeping you both safe will become moot. There will be nothing left."

Kira rubbed a tired hand over her eyes. As much as she had hoped both her brothers could accompany her, it was not to be.

"Oppa, you must stay here," she said. "Your job is

to keep the army together for Taejo until we finish our quest. We will keep him safe."

"But who will protect you?"

Kira scoffed. "I can take care of myself and the prince! Now stop worrying about us!"

Kyoung slammed his hand down on the low table. "I don't even know how to get you off the palace grounds—how can I not worry?"

"General Kang, if you stay, I can get the prince and your sister out of Hansong."

They all turned in surprise to the Guru minister of foreign affairs.

"But only if you stay," he repeated.

9

The morning of their escape was cold and overcast, in keeping with Kira's mood. She couldn't shake off the feeling that it would be her last time in Hansong. There was nothing to hold her there anymore, only painful memories. And yet it was depressing to think of leaving forever.

For the last seven days, Kira had been confined to the western building of the palace. Too many spies were watching her every move, eager to cash in on the huge reward General Kim was offering to bring her to him, dead or alive.

For his safety, Taejo was never left with anyone but Kira or her brothers.

She chafed at her imprisonment, anxious to depart from Hansong. The impending sense of doom was suffocating her. Her tiger spirit had not visited her since the king's death. Kira was tired and short-tempered, still not completely healed from her ordeal with the cursed dagger.

However, Kira had something far worse to contend with. She could not speak of it to anyone, and no amount of Seung's herbal tea remedies would heal her. Ever since King Eojin's death, an insidious voice whispered in her ear at odd moments in the day and woke her up from sleep. It was loudest when she was all alone and depressed, missing her parents. It would speak to her of death and destruction and the utter hopelessness of resistance. Taunting her and belittling her, it was the voice of an entity more frightening than a thousand imoogis. The voice she'd heard as she'd tried to save Eojin's life.

The Demon Lord.

At first, she thought it was a figment of her imagination, for the voice delighted in blaming her for Eojin's death. Perhaps her own guilt and stress were causing her to hallucinate. She wanted to believe this. The thought that the Demon Lord might actually be speaking to her was frightening. But as time passed, it became impossible for her to tell what was real anymore. All she knew was that she had to fight it.

Trying to keep herself calm, Kira concentrated on sewing. She sewed socks, satchels, undergarments, hats—anything to keep the voice at bay. She packed and repacked her traveling bag, trying to keep it light as possible but knowing she could never return to Hansong. It wasn't too hard. Anything of true value had been sent on with the monks who'd left for Dragon Springs Temple before her uncle's assassination.

The door slid open and Kwan entered the room. Taejo jumped up at his appearance, bombarding him with questions.

"The city's turned into a madhouse," Kwan said. "People are leaving Hansong because they don't feel safe anymore. And to make matters worse, more Guru soldiers are deserting and wreaking havoc."

"This is terrible news," Taejo said.

"Not necessarily," Kwan replied. "It may be the best thing that has happened to us."

Kira nodded in agreement. He was right. All the commotion would help them slip unnoticed from the city.

"Major Pak and Brother Woojin left the city today. They headed north and then plan to backtrack to Minchu port. They'll find us a boat and crew. We've been sending small groups of our most trusted soldiers into the eastern mountains with horses and supplies," Kwan said. "No one pays any attention to them because they just look like another group of deserters. The trick will be to get you and the prince out safely. I hope Lord Hwang's plan works."

Kira sighed. So much was riding on the minister. It

galled her to be dependent on another. She felt useless, and she didn't like it at all.

"One thing," Kwan said. He paused as he eyed Taejo. "Jindo left with the major and Sunim."

"What? Who ordered that? You shouldn't have done that. He needs to be with me!"

It wasn't only anger in Taejo's voice but fear. Kira tried to calm him down.

"There's no way we could have brought Jindo with us," she said. "You know that. And if we left him at Hansong, he'd try to follow you. You know how he is."

Taejo's small face reflected his hurt and betrayal. "You should have told me first."

"I'm sorry about that. We felt it was better this way. But don't worry, he'll be safe," Kwan said. "And you'll see him soon."

They saw him wipe away a tear as he ducked his head down into his arms.

That afternoon, Minister Hwang appeared with a group of beautiful *gisaeng*, female entertainers, and servants bringing an elaborate luncheon. Kira and Taejo stayed hidden in a small inner chamber during the meal. Hearing the gisaeng giggle irked her as much as listening to them eat and smelling the food while having none of the delicacies themselves. It made Kira cranky.

An hour later, Kyoung ushered in two of the gisaeng. The women bowed and then escorted Kira into an adjoining chamber and closed the door.

"Quickly," the older gisaeng said. "We don't have much time."

The younger one began to disrobe. Underneath her beautiful hanbok she wore a white servant's uniform. She took off her elaborate hairpiece while the other gisaeng tried to help Kira into the discarded hanbok.

"It would be easier, young mistress, if you took off your uniform," she said.

Kira refused with a sharp shake of her head.

"Mija is the tallest of all of us and still you are taller," the gisaeng complained. "You will have to slouch when you leave with us. Especially since you are still wearing your boots."

The gisaeng named Mija then plaited Kira's hair into a low bun and covered it all with the elaborate wig. Kira winced in pain as the hairpins were stabbed into her head.

With all the layers of the hanbok tied into place, the older gisaeng began to apply makeup to Kira's face.

Kira turned her head in agitation. "Must you put that goop on me?" she asked.

"It's the only way you'll blend in," she replied. "But please keep your eyes down. We can cover your scar but not your eyes."

Kira held her complaints and aggravation and let the gisaeng powder her face and rouge her cheeks and lips. When they were done, they began to apply charcoal to her eyebrows and eyes. It was hard sitting still under their determined onslaught. Without the benefit of a mirror, she could only imagine how ridiculous she looked.

Kyoung reentered the room.

"Nami, you must hurry," he said addressing the older gisaeng.

"Patience, General, beauty takes time," Nami answered.

Kira saw her brother gaze at her in surprise. She scowled, causing him to laugh.

"Didn't recognize you for a moment," he said. "That's a good thing."

Still chuckling, he sauntered out.

"Please, young mistress, try not to frown. You are creasing your makeup," Nami said. "If you don't stop, you'll look like one of those masks the shamans use to ward off evil spirits."

Mija giggled. "Then you'll look more like an scary ghost than a pretty gisaeng."

Putting down her hands, Nami gave Kira a careful once-over. "No, not pretty," she announced, and continued putting on the makeup. "Never pretty. She's too different to be pretty."

"You are being too hard on her. While her scar is unfortunate, with her looks and figure, she would have made a famous gisaeng."

"I didn't say she wouldn't have been a great gisaeng," Nami retorted. "I said she's not pretty. She's striking, which is much more interesting than mere prettiness. Especially with those eyes."

Mija gave Kira a shy smile. "I had heard that they were an ugly yellow, but it's not true. Your eyes are like a golden honey. I think they are beautiful."

"Um, thank you," Kira said, blushing. She was not used to receiving compliments.

The older gisaeng finally put down her jars of makeup. "There, you are all done."

"But her scar still shows," Mija said.

"Don't worry," Nami said. She opened up another small bundle and retrieved several colorful silk scarves, which she proceeded to pin into the wig, letting one purple scarf drape elegantly over Kira's scarred eye.

Both gisaeng pulled Kira up to her feet and circled around her, looking her over. Mija clapped her hands together.

"You look wonderful!"

Kira swallowed her exasperation, not wanting to offend the two women. All she could think about was how itchy the face paint was and how ridiculous she felt. It would be a long day.

Nami nodded before telling Mija to wash her face off quickly. "You must look and act like a servant until we return to our quarters."

Ignoring the other two women, Kira gathered up her weapons and pondered how to hide them under the voluminous skirts.

"No weapons," Nami said, snatching them from her hands.

"I need them," Kira said. "Give them to me."

The other woman shook her head and handed them to Mija. "There are other ways to defend yourself." Reaching up into her hair, she pulled at the end of an elaborate hairpin and removed a long sharp dagger.

Kira had to smile. "That's very nice, but only effective close-up. What do we do if we need to fight?"

"Run," Nami said. She sighed before speaking to Kira with cool proficiency. "Listen to me, it is imperative that you follow my lead. This is not a military mission. We won't be fighting our way through this. If we run into any trouble—" Nami slashed her dagger through the air. "Quick and quiet. That's how we will proceed. If you are suspected, you endanger us all. Is that understood?"

Kira scowled again.

"Stop frowning!" Nami's voice was sharp.

Adjusting her facial expression, Kira nodded.

"I can't leave my weapons behind," she said.

"Don't worry, they will be taken care of with your travel bag," Nami said. She waved Mija over, who wrapped the weapons in a heavy cloth and tied them down. Kira bit her lip hard to keep from protesting.

"You will stay close to me," Nami continued. "If anyone addresses you, do not answer. I will speak for you. You will keep your eyes lowered at all times. Is that understood?"

Kira nodded again.

"Good," Nami said. "Then we have a chance of actually surviving this day."

"I do appreciate all that you have done for me today," Kira said, "but may I ask why you are helping me?"

Nami looked at her in surprise. "Because Minister Hwang asked me to, of course," she replied. "Why else would we do it?"

Kira was puzzled by her response when Mija tapped her arm and began to attach ornaments to her hanbok. Kira was surprised at the change in the other girl. Without her makeup and her gisaeng silks, Mija faded into obscurity with her pale face and white servant's clothes. But then she smiled, and her face was a younger, prettier version of the exotic gisaeng Kira had met at first.

"You look so different," Kira said.

"You too," Mija said. She attached a large, three-part *norigae* decoration to Kira's hanbok.

"This is what you will use should the need arise," Mija said. The norigae had three decorative components. Two of the decorations were intricate enamel pendants with hanging knotted tassels. The third was a jeweled *eunjangdo*, a woman's knife. Most women wore them on their hanboks not only as decorative pieces but to help protect their virtue. Kira had never thought they were anything but toy knives. Eyeing Kira's expression, Mija seized the sharp dagger hidden within the mother-of-pearl design. Kira was surprised to see it was bigger than she expected.

"It may look like a toy," Mija said, "but, believe me, it's sharp enough to carve out a man's eye with one move."

Kira nodded in approval. "Nice," she said. "But do you know how to use it?"

The young gisaeng twirled the dagger in her hand before throwing it in one fluid move. The jeweled handle protruded from a narrow beam on the far wall.

Grinning, Kira looked in admiration at the other girl.

"I'm impressed," she said.

Mija inclined her head as she retrieved the knife and replaced it in its ornate sheath.

"Even pretty things can be deadly," Mija said.

They entered the next interior room, where Kyoung waited impatiently. He nodded in approval when he saw his sister's transformation. Standing behind him was a small servant boy who grinned at Kira.

"Is that the prince?" Kira started in amazement. Taejo was now an ordinary-looking boy dressed in clean commoner clothes. A beige vest made of hemp over his white jacket indicated his status as a palace slave. His hair had been thickened with a hairpiece and made into a coarse braid. A wide beige headband was wrapped low over his eyebrows. In his hands, he held a small tea tray.

"It's going to work, Noona!" he said. "No one will recognize us."

Before she could respond, Mija went over and reminded Taejo to keep his eyes lowered.

"Let's start the show," Kyoung said.

Slinging an arm around Kira and Nami, he pushed them toward the outer chambers. Mija slid open the doors and bowed as they exited, Taejo hidden behind her. Kira saw the younger gisaeng's smile as she followed her brother's lead.

"Minister Hwang, while I appreciate your gifts to me, I must return them to you, for I fear I am too drunk and too tired to enjoy their services," Kyoung said.

Kira kept her eyes down, as Nami disengaged herself from Kyoung and linked arms with her.

"Hold up your hand to your mouth and giggle," she whispered.

Controlling her urge to gag, Kira did as she was told. From the corners of her eyes, she noticed several gisaeng were entertaining high-ranking officials in the large chamber. She saw Mija and Taejo shuffling toward the other end of the room, blending in with the other quiet servants.

"It is time for the men to speak and the pretty ladies to leave," Kyoung said. He gave a coarse laugh and slapped Kira on her back. Suppressing her natural instinct to punch him, Kira giggled again and followed Nami out of the room.

In the hallway, the other gisaeng crowded close together, keeping Kira in the center. Kira peeked behind her and was assured to see six servants surrounding

Taejo and Mija. She was relieved to see that Mija carried the long parcel that contained her weapons as well as her travel bag.

They left the west side of the palace grounds and headed to the northeast side, where the lotus pavilion was located. Kira had never been in this side of the palace grounds as it was an area reserved for the gisaeng.

It was a beautiful place filled with elaborate gardens and ornamental ponds hidden behind high brick walls. Here in the far northern end of the compound, the mountains made a majestic backdrop and gave the illusion of another world. It was the perfect place for entertaining and romantic intrigue.

They stepped through the gate that opened into the inner courtyard and came to a sudden stop. A group of soldiers stood waiting for them in the shadows.

Their leader stepped forward, his sword raised menacingly.

"Look at the pretty flower girls coming to service us," he said with a greedy leer. He seized the nearest gisaeng, pulling her against him and feeling up her body. Kira drew a hissing breath, wishing she had her sword with her. Before she could do anything, she felt Nami give her a hard pinch on her arm.

"Don't do anything or you will kill us all," she whispered, before stepping forward.

10

Nami stepped to the front, pushing Kira subtly behind her. "Are you truly that stupid that you would risk the wrath of Minister Hwang?"

"Minister Hwang? Who's he?" The guard laughed. "We take our orders only from General Kim."

The other five soldiers surrounded the women, reaching over to finger their dresses or caress their skin. Kira stood in the middle, watching the danger through narrowed eyes.

"So, we heard that you ladies were over at General Kang's quarters, entertaining the Kang brothers. Is that correct?"

The women stayed silent. The guard released the gisaeng he'd been fondling and choked Nami by her neck.

"I asked you a question!"

Nami whimpered in pain, her hands fluttering to her throat. "Oh please, sir, we were just called to entertain them! We didn't listen to their conversation and don't know anything about the war plans!"

"Stupid wench," he said. "I don't care about that. I just want to know if you set eyes on the Demon Slayer."

"No, she never came out of her rooms," Nami said. "We never saw her!"

"Did you hear her? Did you have any reason to believe she was not in her rooms?"

"I don't know! General Kang would walk into the inner rooms, a few times during the night. I think he was taking food and drink with him," she said. "We assumed it was for the prince and his bodyguard."

"Bodyguard!" The soldier spat on the ground. "She doesn't deserve that title!"

He released Nami so abruptly she fell against the other gisaeng. She pushed forward and faced the guard again.

"You've gotten your answer, now leave at once!" she said.

"Watch your mouth, bitch!" The soldier backhanded Nami, causing her to stumble, her mouth bleeding from the hard blow. "We don't take orders from whores!"

Kira's hands closed into tight fists, but she stayed

still. She noted the casual demeanor of the soldiers, the way they stood at ease, certain that there was no danger here. Kira watched as Nami straightened, holding her head high. She dabbed a handkerchief against her lip, wiping away the blood with a curious smile.

"You may not want to listen to us, but if Minister Hwang finds you here, he will kill you all," she said.

The soldiers began to laugh.

"And who's going to turn us in?" the guard asked with a sneer.

The gisaeng smiled as she stepped closer. "No one," she said. Pulling her dagger from her hair, she slashed the man across his throat. Only then did Kira realize that all the other gisaeng had positioned themselves before a soldier. At Nami's action, they moved as one, whipping out their daggers and killing them in the space of a breath.

Only one man was alert enough to avoid the knife that had been aimed for his throat. He shoved the gisaeng down, kicking her hard before running for the courtyard gate.

Kira snatched her eunjangdo, slid the blade from its decorative cover, and threw it with deadly accuracy. He dropped to the ground, skewered through his neck.

She made to retrieve her weapon when Nami stopped her.

"Leave it," Nami said. "I don't want you staining your robes."

Nami wiped off her own dagger, replaced it with a pat to her hair, and ordered the servants to stash the bodies in a nearby storage room. Within minutes, the courtyard was pristine and beautiful again. Kira couldn't even see any blood on the cobblestones.

"We must move quickly, girls," Nami said.

Kira's eyes searched for Taejo. He was watching everything with keen interest and admiration.

They hurried into the main room of the women's quarters, where the women picked up silk-wrapped parcels and put on long heavy coats for the journey. Mija came forward and pulled a quilted coat over Kira's shoulders.

Thanking Mija, Kira made her way over to Taejo.

"How are you doing?" she asked.

Taejo smiled. "These gisaeng are quite handy with their knives."

"And you're happy about it?" she asked in mock surprise.

"No, I was shocked," he said. "And so were those soldiers. That's why they're all dead."

Kira agreed. "Even I underestimated the gisaeng."

"They're pretty amazing." Taejo leaned against a beam, watching the others rush around the room. "You know, I always thought that you and my mother were the strongest women I knew. But any woman can be powerful and dangerous, if she chooses to be."

"Yes, I think you're right," Kira said.

Taejo grinned. "General Kim is an idiot."

"I agree with you," she said. "Mostly because he can't see what a great king you will be."

He looked alarmed at her words. "Not yet," he said. "I'm far from ready. But one day, with your help, I will try to be the best king I can."

Kira gave him a deep, respectful bow from her waist. She was so proud of him.

Not long after, their group departed from lotus pavilion and headed for the east gate.

Guards were everywhere, and Kira was surprised that no one stopped them. None of the women looked around as they walked, but they chatted to each other in a light tone, laughing and giggling as if they hadn't just brutally killed six men. Kira stayed quiet within their group, very aware of Taejo walking silently behind her. Her senses were on full alert as she sniffed the air for any demon presence.

By the time they reached the outer palace gate, Kira's nerves were strained to the breaking point and even the ever calm Nami looked tense.

"The beautiful Nami and her flower girls are leaving us today," a guard called to them at their approach. "We will be brokenhearted without the sight of your loveliness."

Nami inclined her head. "Our master is too concerned for our welfare to risk losing us in this upheaval. Have our soldiers arrived?" she asked.

"Yes, along with your carriages," he replied. His eyes swept across all of them, stopping on Kira's face.

She immediately dipped down and lowered her head as another gisaeng stepped in front of her with a tinkling laugh.

"Tell the truth, Officer Cho, it's me you'll miss the most!" She leaned over and patted his cheek with a saucy grin.

"Oh yes, my precious lily, the sun will no longer shine on us without your presence." The guard flirted with the gisaeng as Nami hurried the rest of them through the gate.

On the dirt road outside the palace walls, twenty soldiers guarded a caravan of horse-drawn carriages.

The carriages were designed like small rooms with tightly curtained windows. Servants lowered the rear wall of the carriage, allowing Nami, Kira, and one other gisaeng to climb in. The interior was well padded with floor cushions and backrests. It was clearly a nobleman's carriage.

"The minister must care very much for you," Kira remarked.

Nami smiled. "We are not safe yet," she replied.

"Where is the prince?" Kira asked as the carriage began to move.

"He will be in the last carriage," Nami replied. "But do not fear, the rear guard is made up of your brother and friends."

Kira was relieved to hear that Kwan, Jaewon, and Seung would be near Taejo. Since Jindo was with Major

Pak and Brother Woojin at the seaside port, the only person she trusted to protect the prince was her brother.

"Quickly, you must change and hide," Nami said as the conveyance began to move.

Kira was confused. "What do you mean?"

The women pushed aside the large cushions in the middle of the carriage floor and pulled up the woven rug. Underneath was a trapdoor.

"You must stay hidden until we reach our rendezvous point," she said. "The prince will be in a similar hiding spot."

The two women removed the scarves and hairpiece and helped Kira undress. Nami opened a small oval container that held a grainy white paste, which had a light floral scent with hints of an earthy undertone.

"This is a rice bran and camellia oil paste that we use to remove our makeup," she said. "Knowing how much you enjoyed your first experience, I'm sure you're eager to take it all off."

Kira nodded gratefully. Her skin felt greasy, itchy, and suffocated. Nami slathered the paste all over Kira's face. She then filled a basin with water from a large gourd and removed all the paste and makeup with a wet cloth. Afterward, she slid open a small hatch on the bottom of the carriage and poured the water out. When it was empty, she threw the soiled cloth into the basin and put it aside.

Relieved and happy, Kira let down her hair from

its topknot and quickly braided it. With a final nod of appreciation at the other women, she crawled into the narrow space beneath the carriage floor. Nami threw in a heavy rug to ward off the cold and closed the trap-door. The weak afternoon light filtered in through the cracks of the wood at Kira's feet. She wrapped herself tight within the rug and pressed herself to one side of her box. The slow pace of the plodding horse lulled her to sleep.

She wasn't sure how long she'd slept when she heard a sharp voice ordering them to stop.

"We seek the Demon Slayer. If you allow us to search your carriage, we will not harm you," the voice said.

"Very well," a guard answered.

Kira heard the door of their carriage pulled open.

"Captain, there are only two gisaeng in here," a soldier reported.

"Search the other carriages!"

After several long minutes, the voice ordered them to continue. But still, Kira was nervous. Without seeing Taejo before her, she was unnerved and worried. When the carriage began to move again, Nami opened the trap-door and offered Kira water and some food.

"You will have to stay there until we reach our meeting place," she said.

"How much longer will it take?" Kira asked.

"We hope to get there before night falls," Nami

answered. With one last reassuring smile, she pulled the trapdoor closed, leaving Kira in darkness once more.

Kira woke up to the glow of a lantern as she was pulled from her hiding space.

"Your brother has signaled for us to stop," Nami said. "This is where you leave us."

Nodding, Kira tried to stretch her body before exiting the carriage.

"Thank you for all your help," she said. "I will never forget you."

Nami smiled. "I think it would be more truthful to say that *we* will never forget *you*, young mistress." With a bow, the gisaeng sank against the cushions and let the servants close up the carriage and continue on.

Kira felt Taejo wrap his arms around her waist.

"I was so scared when we were stopped and you weren't there with me," he said.

She hugged him and then greeted the others, grateful to see that they brought with them her travel bag, heavy coat, and weapons. Kira hurriedly put on her coat and strapped on her weapons. It was a relief to feel the weight of her bow, arrows, and sword on her back. She no longer felt as vulnerable as she had in her gisaeng outfit.

"Let's go," Kwan said.

They walked straight into the mist-covered forest and up into the mountains, vanishing into the darkness.

Kwan led them to a soldiers' encampment near an abandoned shrine, where fifteen men waited for their command with more than twenty horses. They would ride at night until they reached the coast.

Kira took the lead. The light of the moon filtered through the clouds above them, allowing limited visibility. They galloped when the roads were straight and clear and walked their horses when the roads were harder to see. Several hours later, they arrived at the port city of Minchu on the Yellow Sea.

They broke for camp in the forests outside the city

limits, waiting for the sun to rise and the town to wake up.

In the morning, Kwan entered town alone, and returned with Major Pak and Brother Woojin. The joyous reunion between Taejo and Jindo was heartwarming to see. Despite his initial reaction, Taejo had been brave and positive throughout their planning and their escape. But seeing him with Jindo showed just how hard it had been to be parted from his faithful companion. Kira realized how much her cousin had matured.

"Good news!" Kwan said. "Major Pak bought us a ship to Uju."

"Bought? Did we really need an entire ship, Major?" Kira asked.

The major bowed and gave a small smile. "That's not quite correct," he said. "When I arrived, I came across a merchant who had fallen upon hard times. His ship was about to be auctioned for failure to pay his debts. His last cargo had been stolen by pirates. I struck a deal with him. I repaid his debts and in return he would arrange safe and completely discreet passage to Uju on his cargo ship."

"Very nice, Major!" Kira said. "But what made you believe he was worth helping?"

"Simple—instead of abandoning him, his captain and most of his crew were trying to help raise money to save his ship," the major said. "It speaks to the honor and integrity of the merchant that his crew would stand by him even during a crisis."

"I must agree with the Major's assessment," Brother Woojin said. "Master Hong is a very good man. I believe you would like him very much, young mistress."

Kira was impressed. "When do we sail?"

Major Pak looked at Kwan and nodded. "We'll set off tomorrow at dawn. I'll go tell the captain to prepare for the voyage."

For the first time in over two weeks, Kira had felt the presence of her tiger spirit revitalize her as she slept in the frigid outdoors. It kept her warm and healed all her pains from the curse. Unfortunately, the voice of the Demon Lord still haunted her. It whispered in her ear in the morning as she washed her face and cleaned her teeth.

Come to me. I am waiting for you.

She cringed, clapping her hands over her ears and shouting the evil down with her inner voice. Kira couldn't help feeling afraid. Was she going mad or could the Demon Lord really communicate with her? Or was it the cursed dagger? She just didn't know for sure. She quickly finished her morning routine and prepared to leave. The streets into town were dark and empty when they headed toward port the next morning. Kira pulled the collar of her heavy quilted coat up around her face, her trusty *nambawi*, her winter hat, pulled down low over her eyes. She felt inconspicuous, just one of an early group of traders coming to town.

At the harbor, they met Master Hong, the merchant whose business Major Pak had saved. He was a short, thin man with a kind face who appeared with several servants laden with straw baskets covered with cloths.

"The major tells me that it is at your behalf that my family and I are saved," he said with a bow to Kira. "Thank you, kind sir. Please accept these baskets of food as a token of our appreciation."

The light was dim, but Kira pulled the brim of her nambawi even lower and accepted a basket with a nod and a low thank-you.

The major appeared and intercepted the merchant with a warm smile.

"Master Hong, thank you for all you have done for us," he said.

"No, no, the honor is all mine." Master Hong kept bowing.

Major Pak grabbed the merchant by his arms to keep him from bobbing up and down.

"Take good care of our horses for us," he said. "If we do not return for them by the season's end, they are yours to do with as you wish."

"But of course we will!" Master Hong replied. "And they will always be yours, no matter when you come. We are forever indebted to you."

He peered around the major to smile at Kira who inclined her head. She found herself liking him; his genuine kindness showed on his pleasant face. She was glad Major Pak had helped him.

They left Master Hong behind and headed to the harbor, where tightly planked, narrow wooden piers extended into the shallows in varying lengths. They approached a merchant ship that was bustling with activity. The ship was large and well made, with two tall masts and rectangular sails. They climbed a rope ladder to get on board, while a large basket was lowered for Jindo. They were met by a stern-faced man with keen, narrow eyes and an air of command.

"Welcome aboard. I am Captain Lee," he said, giving them all a precise bow.

"Thank you, Captain," Major Pak responded. "This is Master Yoon and his brother."

He introduced Kira and Taejo under false names. The captain seemed preoccupied. He hardly glanced at her and she was certain he hadn't recognized her as the Demon Slayer. But to be safe, Kira stayed behind the others and kept her nambawi low over her eyes.

"I am very pleased to meet you both. By saving Master Hong, you have done us all a great service and we are happy to provide you with safe passage to Uju City."

The captain then introduced them to his second in command, a scrawny-looking man named Chong with a scruffy beard who wore his hair long and loose.

Chong led the soldiers, Jaewon, Seung, and Brother Woojin to the cargo hold. Jaewon was already pale and looking sick just from stepping onto the ship. Kira couldn't help but wonder if being cooped up in the hold would be worse for him.

When the captain mentioned sending Jindo belowdeck, Taejo shook his head and wrapped his arms around Jindo.

"I'll take care of him. He won't bother anyone, I promise," Taejo said. "I've done it before. Don't worry about him. He's my family and I'll take care of him."

"And I'll come up and assist him every day," Kwan said.

Kira faced her brother in surprise.

"Aren't you staying up here with us?"

"We'll be with the men," Kwan answered. "It's better that way. But we will check on you often."

The captain showed them to a cabin situated aft of the main deck. The cabin was small but comfortable, with two small berths for sleeping and a desk with several chairs set up in the middle of the room. Kira appreciated the privacy that she and Taejo were given. She knew that Major Pak and her brother wanted to keep them as far away from the crew as possible.

"We have a strong wind," Captain Lee said. "The sooner we leave, the better time we'll make.

"While you are expected to stay in your cabin for most of the voyage, you will be allowed on the main deck twice a day to enjoy the air. One of our crew members will come get you. Please stay inside your cabin for most of the journey. It is for your own safety." With a short bow, he departed.

Taejo tugged on Major Pak's sleeve. "Is it all right if we watch our departure?"

"I'll ask the captain," Major Pak said.

Within the hour, the ship was pulling out of port. Kira and Taejo walked onto the main deck and stood breathing in the cold sea air. The sun peeked over the mountains, sending shimmering light across the blue seas. Major Pak and Kwan were on deck, speaking intensely with the captain.

Jindo barked as the cold ocean spray hit them. A chilly wind blew across the deck, sending the ship's flags fluttering. Kira breathed in the clean, salty air and found it refreshing.

Now that the sun had risen, Kira noticed that the crew members were eyeing her with growing alarm. She had been recognized.

Kwan came rushing over. "I think you should return to your quarters right now," he said.

Before she could leave, the captain arrived, Major Pak in tow.

"It appears that we have the Demon Slayer on board with us," he said in a neutral tone. "Which must mean, then, that we also have the great fortune of having the crown prince of Hansong sail with us."

He bowed to Taejo, who nodded in return, thanking him gravely.

"A word of caution, Your Highness," the captain said. "It would be best for all our sakes if your bodyguard were to stay unseen as much as possible. While my men are a good and loyal crew, they are very superstitious and the Demon Slayer is alarming them. They've already begun speaking of her presence as a bad omen."

Kira was irritated that Captain Lee avoided speaking directly to her.

"I will do my best to avoid upsetting your crew, Captain," she replied.

"I would appreciate it," he said grimly.

He waited before her until finally she returned to her cabin, sighing in frustration.

While Kwan and Major Pak kept Taejo company above and below deck, Kira remained secluded for two days. None of the crew would come near the cabin. She had to rely on her brother and Taejo to bring food to her.

The constant whispering voice of the Demon Lord grew louder the longer she was alone. Frightened, Kira decided to go belowdecks and check on the others.

Jaewon sat huddled under a blanket, leaning against the bulkhead, his face an unhealthy shade of pale. His faithful friend Seung sat nearby, trying to get him to drink some water.

When she came to sit by his side, Kira grew alarmed. Jaewon was so sick, he didn't notice her presence.

"Hey." She brushed her hand across his loose hair. It was soaked through with sweat. "You'd better not die on me or I will hunt your spirit down and beat you senseless."

A slight smile quivered around the corners of Jaewon's

parched lips. "Only if you can catch me," he whispered.

"Oh I'll catch you all right," she replied. "A one-legged grandmother could catch you, you limp noodle."

He moaned and then cracked open one eye to peer feverishly at her. "Please don't mention food, evil one, or I fear my revenge will ruin our friendship."

Kira caressed his pale cheek. "Don't be silly, nothing could do that."

But Jaewon didn't hear her, having fallen into a feverish sleep.

The wind was strong but steady and was pushing them through relatively calm seas. To Kira, the motion was a slight and pleasant rocking. If they were to hit rough waters, how would Jaewon survive? He already looked deathly ill. Concerned, Kira turned to Seung.

"Is there anything we can do?" Kira asked Seung.

Seung shook his head. "The most I can do is give him a few pieces of dried ginger to help his nausea, but there is no cure for him but getting off this ship."

"I will pray for smooth sailing so that we can arrive at Uju as soon as possible," she said.

By the third day, the weather took a sharp turn as the winds picked up and the waves began to buffet the ship. Kira could hear Captain Lee shouting at his men.

"I've never seen a storm as big and as fast as this before. The waves are as tall as mountains. It's as if the heavens themselves are seeking to crush us!"

The sailors began to pray to the gods. From the window

of her cabin, Kira saw the angry glances they sent in her direction. She didn't need to hear the mutterings to know that the sailors were blaming her for their misfortunes. She wasn't surprised, but she was beginning to worry. The storm was getting worse. Kira took out her tidal stone. Could it help them in this situation? Brother Woojin had pulled her aside before the voyage and warned her to never reveal the stone to anyone. That in no case was she to use the stone during their voyage or it would let the Demon Lord know where they were. Closing her fist, she let it drop into its pouch with a heavy heart.

Peering through the window again, Kira marked the frequency of the glares and desperation on the faces of the sailors. Her gut churned and the sense of danger grew strong.

"Quick, let's go belowdecks to check on the others," she said.

Taejo and Jindo hurried after her as she headed belowdecks. She ran to the hatch, hearing the sailors cursing at her.

Belowdecks, Kwan and Major Pak were making the rounds with their men, trying to ease their minds. Most of the men looked queasy, but it was Jaewon who Kira worried about the most.

Jaewon's face was clammy and leached of all its normal color. His eyes were sunken into his sockets and his teeth were clenched so hard, Kira could see his neck muscles straining. He had rolled himself into a ball, shivering under a heavy blanket.

"Is he going to be all right?" Taejo asked Seung.

Seung looked really worried. "He hasn't been able to eat any food and has only drunk a little water. He can't keep anything down. We've got to get him onto land."

Jaewon retched. Kira felt helpless watching her friend suffer. She reached over to touch his face and found him burning hot with fever.

Grabbing the water gourd, she motioned for Seung to lift Jaewon up as she pried his lips apart and poured a little water in his mouth. He moaned and tried to fight them off.

"You've got to drink or you're going to die," she said. "And I told you that I was not going to let that happen! Now drink!"

Jaewon stopped fighting and dutifully opened his mouth. Feeling relieved, she gave him some more water. When he was done, she patted his cheek lightly and whispered, "Good job, now you can sleep."

With a faint sigh, he settled down in his pallet, only to rear up retching again.

Disheartened and scared, Kira could do nothing but watch as he threw up the pitiful amount of water he had ingested. She knew he had to get off the ship, but what could she do?

The ship pitched and rolled. It felt like it would be bludgeoned to pieces by the waves or capsized.

Nearby, Brother Woojin was chanting in prayer and

several soldiers huddled together in fear.

Kwan came over to their side, and shook his head at her. "You shouldn't be down here! This isn't a good place for either of you."

Jindo was whining, his big head buried into Taejo's side.

"To be honest, I was getting a bad feeling being in our cabin," she said.

"What do you mean?"

Before she could answer, the hatch door crashed open and a large group of crew members came running down the stairs.

"There she is! There's the evil one!"

Kira exchanged a look with her brother just as he jumped to his feet, his sword drawn. Major Pak stepped in front of him, his hand resting on the hilt of his sword.

"What is the meaning of this?" Major Pak asked in a furious voice.

"This thunderstorm is unnatural! We have angered the gods by having that creature on our ship!"

"It's because of her that our ship is going to be destroyed!" A crew member pointed at Kira. "Throw the Demon Slayer overboard before we all die!"

The crewmen came forward, only to be met by the steel of Kwan, Major Pak, and those of their soldiers who were not seasick.

"If you even think of touching my sister, you will die a slow and agonizing death," Kwan said fiercely. "Now get the hell out of here before I kill you anyway!"

The crewmen were forced to leave at the point of Kwan's sword.

Kira got up abruptly and faced Brother Woojin.

"Sunim, I know we agreed to keep the tidal stone secret for fear of the Demon Lord finding us. But this storm is his doing," she said. "I think he already knows where we are. And I don't think we have a choice anymore."

Not waiting to hear his response, she followed Kwan up onto the main deck, Major Pak and several of their soldiers keeping close guard.

The upper deck was a nightmarish scene. The captain was yelling at his crew to return to their stations as waves washed across the ship. Even as Kira tried to balance herself on deck, a wave swept one of their soldiers off the ship and into the sea.

Horrified, Kira proceeded to the bow as fast as she could, holding on tight to the rigging and the rails. A crewman came charging at her, intent on pushing her overboard. She twisted her hands into the netting hanging above her head and kicked the man hard in the chest with both her feet. He went sliding across the deck and narrowly escaped going overboard. Several others tried to attack her and were met by Kwan's sword. Ignoring the crew, she climbed up onto the bow.

"What are you doing?" Captain Lee shouted. "Get back inside! I don't need to be worrying about you on top of everything else!"

Kira pushed past him and stood at the prow. The skies were a surging force of dark gray to black clouds that were barreling toward them. She knew that when the storm hit them, the ship would be destroyed. There was no time to lose. The large red ruby glowed warm and vibrant in her hands, throwing a bright light in the dark of the storm.

"What is she doing?" she heard the captain ask behind her.

"Leave her alone," Kwan said. "She's going to save us."

Kira's connection with the tidal stone was immediate and strong. She held the stone before her and the water calmed in front of them. The captain swore in shock as the hurricane continued to rage just beyond the ship. It was as if they were in a tunnel, protected from the elements.

Why fight me? What is the use? Your efforts are pitiful. Soon you will be mine.

Kira shook her head hard, trying to rid the Demon Lord's voice from her head.

Don't fight me.

The tunnel began to collapse as a wave washed over the ship, causing it to list sideways. The men screamed as Kira struggled against the mocking voice of the Demon Lord. She could hear the wind tearing through the rigging, threatening to break apart the masts.

"No! I will never let you win!" Kira yelled into the storm. She let her mind meld with the tidal stone. Instantly the evil voice was quieted as the tidal stone took over and filled her with calm. The ship straightened and the waves receded, leaving them safe in their tunnel again. Kira thought only of the tidal stone and let it work to bring them to safety. The winds blew them quickly through the seas, but still the storm raged all around them. It was well over an hour before the ship found itself clear of danger.

Kira staggered, exhausted by her struggle against the Demon Lord. Jumping forward, Captain Lee steadied her as she stepped down from the bow of the ship. "Young mistress, I do not know what magic you wield," he said. "But I do know that you have saved us all."

Kwan met his sister with an anxious look. Noting her weariness, he wrapped his arm around her waist and helped her across the deck. The entire crew cheered, yelling "Demon Slayer" over and over again.

Kira kept her eyes closed, letting her brother steer her past the others. Worry gnawed at her. She'd been right. The storm had been supernatural. Even wielding the tidal stone, it had been difficult to ward off the tumultuous winds and waves. She knew the Demon Lord was behind the storm, which meant he knew where they were going.

Kira was truly frightened, for she knew this was just a taste of what was to come. Their journey was only going to get much worse.

12

They sailed into Uju City on the last day of the second month. The storm had sent them way off course and what should have been at most a five-day trip took them over a week. By the time they reached port, Kira felt normal again. The use of the tidal stone in such a major way had drained her so greatly that it took two nights with her tiger spirit to be completely healed.

Uju was a large port city that had developed around the mouth of the Yalu River, which divided the city in half. They entered port on the south side, at the captain's insistence. The north side was dangerous, overrun with bandits and mercenaries. The captain was unwilling to risk the ship and crew.

When they reached shore, Jaewon was desperate to get off the ship. He was too weak to walk on his own, so Seung and Kwan helped carry him off the ship and onto shore.

Dropping to his knees on the sand, Jaewon sighed in relief. "May I never take another boat ride for a thousand years!"

As Kira prepared to disembark, she was surprised to find the sailors lining up on the main deck, waiting to present her with tokens of appreciation: a parcel of nuts, a handful of sweet dried dates, a carved wooden statue of a dragon, a satchel made from what looked like sailcloth. They were all small but thoughtfully given. Kira was overwhelmed and moved by their gifts.

The last person to see her off was the captain.

"We are truly fortunate to have had the great Demon Slayer on our vessel," he said. "It will be a story to tell our grandchildren."

Kira looked at the satchel, which was now full of their gifts, not knowing what to say.

"There have been so many stories told about you. Some say you are a *kumiho* who seduces men or a soul-sucking demon. Others claim you slew an imoogi that would have destroyed Hansong. That you are our savior, the Musado.

"But I see a young girl with extraordinary talents who would do anything to protect our future king. I see a strong young girl who will grow into a formidable woman and I am grateful that the prince has such a powerful protector."

The captain pressed into her hand a beautiful red ribbon with a decorative gold design.

She gaped at the gift. Unmarried girls wore these ribbons tied to their braids to signify their status. But Kira had never worn one. Had never wanted to wear one. She didn't quite know what to say.

"Although you are a Demon Slayer, you are still a girl," he said with a smile. "Wear it when you want to remember that fact."

It was lovely and part of her wanted to tie it into her hair, while the other part scoffed at such a silly impulse. A ribbon? For a soldier? She had to smile at the thought. Even though she'd probably never wear it, she would treasure it.

"Thank you, Captain," she said. "I will not forget."

Uju City was home to an interesting blend of Guru and other nationalities. As Kira and her group departed from the harbor, they found themselves in the midst of an open marketplace. Many of the trade stores were run by the Cathay. There were tea stands, silk merchants, and even a jewelry shop that displayed the huge ivory tusks of some poor elephant. In a side alley, tribal folk displayed their wares of baskets, pottery, blankets, and rugs. The mix of various languages filled the air and made for a unique experience.

Taejo walked close by her side as they passed food stalls selling a variety of items from the mundane to the exotic. A street vendor hawking hot fish cakes on skewers was located right next to another who sold fried scorpions, centipedes, and seahorses. Taejo paused in front of a food stall that held baskets of roasted grasshoppers.

"What does that taste like?" he asked.

The vendor gave him a grasshopper and smiled toothlessly.

Taejo recoiled and shook his head, causing the vendor to cackle.

After over a week at sea, Kira was eager for a hot meal. The city was not as cold as the ship, but the wind still blew hard through their coats.

They headed for a local inn, where Jaewon sat with relief on a square stool at a small table with Taejo and Brother Woojin.

"Kira, you'll stay here," Kwan said. "Major Pak, Seung, and I will seek horses and supplies. The soldiers will take orders from you."

While Brother Woojin ordered food, Kira organized the soldiers for guard duty and meals by shifts. At first she had been concerned that they would rebel against her lead, but her actions on the ship had cemented their respect for her. They saluted her with deep respect and followed her orders with great alacrity.

Sitting down next to Taejo, she was delighted to find her food was ready and waiting for her. She breathed in the delicious aroma of a hot bowl of noodle soup piled with chicken, scallions, dried seaweed, boiled eggs, and pickled radish. The next few minutes were filled with the sound of slurping noodles. Jaewon, who was drinking only chicken broth, looked on enviously.

"It's very cruel of all of you to give me broth while you guys are eating delicious noodles," he groused.

"Just following young Seung's prescription," Brother Woojin said. "I promised him that I would not let you eat anything solid while he was gone."

"Seung is evil and no longer a friend of mine," Jaewon complained.

He nudged Taejo and made a pleading gesture for one of his noodles. Taejo covered his bowl with his arm and pulled it closer to him. Jaewon frowned and then reached stealthily over to Kira's bowl, trying to snag a piece of chicken. Kira hit his thieving fingers with her chopsticks and shook her head.

"You are all mean and I don't like any of you anymore," Jaewon said, subsiding with a huff. Taejo giggled.

While she ate, Kira kept her eyes roving around the room, taking note of every person coming into the inn. She was particularly interested in the commotion that was happening in the far corner, where a dirty, disheveled-looking man with badly shaking hands sat drinking from a bowl.

Finished with her meal, she rose to her feet, motioning for Jaewon to stay with Taejo and Brother Woojin. Keeping her nambawi low over her eyes, she wandered the room until she stood but a few steps from the frightened man and a small group of spectators.

"You've been drinking again, Lee Shin," a nearby man said. "Who would believe such a story?"

"I'm telling you the truth!" Lee Shin sputtered, his drink spilling all over his coat. "The whole village was possessed. They attacked my caravan and ate the merchants and my crew! They ripped them apart with their bare hands and *ate* them! I was lucky to get out of there alive."

"That merchant group from Cathay who hired you last week to take them to Wando?" someone asked. "With these weather conditions, you never should have taken them in the first place! In fact, the truth is, you probably got your group killed in an avalanche or they froze to death."

Lee Shin just kept shaking his head. "They were real. Their eyes were big and all black. No white at all—like a frog's." He shuddered.

"So they're all dead? What about their wares? Did you bring 'em with you? That's a mighty big windfall."

Lee Shin glared at the other man in disbelief. "Are

you crazy? Did you not hear a word of what I've been saying? I nearly died! I had to leave the caravan behind!"

He then started to laugh, but it was completely mirthless. "I know what you are thinking, but don't do it. It's just silks and ivory! It ain't worth your life."

The two men smiled at each other over Lee Shin's head. One of them ordered a new bottle of soju, distilled rice liquor, and poured more into Lee Shin's bowl.

"Well, we'd better warn everyone of the danger. Where did you say this happened?"

"Over at Hekou. It's like they're lying in wait for people, and then they attack." He whimpered and took a deep drink. The two men who'd been so attentive got to their feet and quickly left the establishment.

Kira had heard enough. She retraced her steps and returned to the others, quickly filling them in on the details.

"Demons for sure," she said.

Jaewon agreed. "We just need to chart a route around that village."

Kira couldn't help but worry if that was enough. The closer they got to Mount Baekdu, the harder it was to keep the voice of the Demon Lord quiet. It questioned her, seeking her weaknesses, looking for a way to erode her confidence.

You cannot defeat me. My servant raises an army of half-breeds that will destroy your world. Stop running from me, Musado. Join me and I shall reward you with greatness. You will be the most powerful human in the world.

It was taking more and more effort to ignore the voice. Sometimes she had to scream inside her own head to shut it up. But it was ever present, and so was her fear. Fear that the Demon Lord was somehow connected to her. Fear that she was losing her mind.

They waited uneasily for the others to return. Kwan and Seung arrived first, sitting down and ordering three bowls of noodles.

"We've obtained horses and supplies," Kwan said. "There's even a squirrelly-looking guide who's offered to take us for an outrageous fee."

"We're going to need that guide," Kira said with a grim look. "How are we situated for money?"

He waved his hand. "Not an issue. Our brother made sure we were well funded."

Major Pak arrived and sat down just as the server brought over bowls of noodle soup for him, Kwan, and Seung.

"We're almost ready to leave," Major Pak said. "But I hear we may be in for some rough weather. It'll be slow going to Mount Baekdu."

"That's not all we have to worry about," Kira said. As they ate, Kira filled them in on the news of the demon-infested village. The three men ate quickly, wolfing down their noodles in giant gulps. When they were done, Major Pak sent Seung out again.

"Go and fetch that guide we met with earlier."

Seung bowed and pulled on his coat to brave the cold once again. As the major spoke with Brother Woojin and Kwan, Kira turned her attention to Jaewon, who was holding a conversation with Taejo.

"How do you feel?" Taejo asked.

Jaewon smiled. "I think I'll live."

"You seemed like you were getting better once we passed the storms," Taejo said.

"Only because I had nothing left to vomit," Jaewon replied.

"So now we have to find your clan. Do you know exactly where they are?" Taejo asked.

Jaewon looked pensive. "I do. They'll be on the western side of the mountain, across the Yalu River."

"How do you know?"

"Ever since I was small, my father would show me the old maps of our heritage. He didn't want me to forget where we came from."

"I can't believe it! You were so close to your family when we were at Wando City," Kira interrupted. "Why didn't you tell us?"

Jaewon's face changed as intense grief overcame him. "I was too afraid to see them. I ran away again."

"Are you ready to face your family now?" Kira asked.

"I don't know." His eyes were so bleak that she struggled against her urge to comfort him. "I'm so scared. The nightmares are getting worse. Every night I relive that day on the temple steps, watching Jaeho fall. He lies there, bleeding on the ground, my bow still in his hands, and he asks me, 'Why? Why did you hit me?'"

"It was an accident," Kira said. "It was just a terrible accident."

"He was a little boy! I should have let him have my bow. I shouldn't have gotten mad at him. I shouldn't have—"

He stopped to compose himself, his lips trembling.

"Sometimes it is hard to breathe at the thought of seeing my parents again. I don't know if I will ever be ready. But I must, for Seung's sake. He has been without his family because of me."

It was the right thing to do, but it pained her to see her friend suffer.

"I'll stand by your side, no matter what happens," she said.

"Me too!" Taejo piped in.

"Thank you," Jaewon said. "You don't know how much that means to me."

His eyes were warm and tender, making Kira squirm in discomfort. They were quiet as Taejo stood up and wandered over to sit with Brother Woojin.

"You know you saved my life," Jaewon said in a low voice.

Kira raised an eyebrow in surprise. "I think you are confused. It was Seung who saved your life."

He shook his head. "It was you. Your constantly yelling at me not to die was what did it." He leaned closer. "To tell you the truth, I was scared of you."

Smirking, Kira reached over and tapped him on his nose. "You should be."

Before she could pull her hand away, Jaewon caught it and pressed it to his cheek.

"Thank you," he whispered. In the next moment, he released her, avoiding Kwan's fierce glance. Kwan stood glaring at both Jaewon and Kira before finally being called by Major Pak.

Only then did Jaewon let out a relieved sigh. "Tell you the truth, your brother is starting to scare me too!"

Kira laughed. "We have that effect on most people."

Seung soon returned in the company of a small, dark man with a slick smile and keen eyes.

"Major Pak, here is Jeong Chul Soo as you requested."

The guide took off his thick fur hat and bowed before taking a proffered seat. He unrolled a map of Guru.

"So you're going to Baekdu Mountain." He snickered as he showed them the route. "That's seven hundred sixty li if we were going straight. But with the mountains and the bad weather conditions, it would be more like eleven hundred li. I used to stop at Wando but not anymore. There've been demons spotted south of the river heading east. No guide will take you that way. We cross the river at Sini and stay north."

Kwan whispered to Kira, "We want to avoid Wando at all costs." He gave her a pointed look.

She understood. There was no telling what rumors had reached Wando. It would be dangerous for her and the prince.

The guide scratched his head. "We'll stop at Jinan instead. That's right on the river. It isn't a walled city, but it should be fairly safe."

Kira stood up and gazed down at the map. "Show me where Hekou village is."

Jeong pointed at a spot midway between Uju and Jinan. As she had feared, the village was directly on their route.

"We must go around that village," she said.

"That will add an extra fifty li to our trip!" he exclaimed.

"Can you take us or not?" Kira asked.

Jeong surveyed the group, his sharp eyes resting the longest on Kira's face.

"I can take you as far as Baishan. It's farther north than I like to go at this time of year. But it's as close to Baekdu as I'll go," he said. "What you do after that is not my concern."

"Fair enough. We'll leave tomorrow," she said.

Jaewon's anxious face reminded her of the turmoil he must be enduring. Part of her wished he hadn't come. She feared what would happen to him if his reunion with his family did not go well. She could once again hear Brother

Woojin's words when they'd first learned of the tragedy in Jaewon's life.

"He carries a heavy burden. I hope one day he will be able to forgive himself or else . . . it will destroy him."

That night, Kira was grateful for the opportunity to sleep in a warm room. It would probably be the last time in a long while.

A little after dawn, Kira roused Taejo and prepared for the cold day before them.

"Bundle up tight," she told him. "Remember how cold the north is."

The prince nodded as he layered up under his heavy coat. "How long will it take to reach Mount Baekdu?"

"Two or three weeks if we're lucky," she said.

He groaned. "At least I have Jindo with me."

"Yes, lucky you have your own personal heat source," she teased.

He smiled. "I'll share him with you, Noona."

She tousled his hair, something she could only do in private. But she worried for him. Would she be able to keep him safe? She prayed to the heavens and her parents to help her.

"How are your lessons with Sunim?" she asked.

He sighed. "I'm so tired of Confucius! Is it really important for me to know all the classics?"

"'Ignorance is the night of the mind, but a night without moon and star,'" Kira quoted.

He glared at her. "You sound like Sunim," he griped.

"'He who learns but does not think is lost. He who thinks but does not learn is in great danger,'" Kira continued with a sly grin.

"Stop quoting the *Analects* to me!" Taejo covered his ears.

"'When anger rises, think of the consequences.'"

"Argh!" Taejo threw a pillow at Kira as she laughed.

He flopped down on his futon and heaved a long sigh.

"You know, it's not fair that you can't ever be a government adviser just because you are a girl," he said. "You're so much smarter than any of the nobles who sit for the civil service exams."

Kira grinned at him. "It's a boring job anyway. And I'm not the most diplomatic person in the world."

Taejo laughed. "I want you to know that when I'm king, I'm going to change that law so girls can receive an education and sit for the civil service exam if they want a chance at a government position," he promised.

"I really appreciate the sentiment, but you will make a lot of enemies if you do that," Kira warned.

He sat up indignantly. "Good! I would rather know who my enemies are! When I'm king, there's no one else in the world I would rather have as my primary adviser than you."

Tears pricked at Kira's eyes, pride filling her heart. Taejo would be a great king. She bowed and gave him a big smile. "On my honor, I will serve you faithfully, in whatever capacity you will ask of me, until the day I die."

They left town with a packhorse loaded with supplies to help them survive the brutal winter weather. The snow was light and intermittent, but the wind was cold and biting. Kira worried that the wind would pose a problem for her in sensing any demon presence. To stay vigilant, she kept herself circling their group at all times.

During the first camp break, their guide squatted in front of Kira and examined her closely as he chewed on a long piece of dried squid.

"So you're the legendary Demon Slayer of Hansong, huh," Jeong said, with his mouth wide open, half of a long tentacle hanging from his lip. "You don't look that scary to me."

Kira let her eyes narrow as she took in his insolence.

He cackled, pieces of dried squid spraying from his mouth.

"Your eyes don't frighten me, Demon Slayer! I've seen the ghost of a murdered maiden who's been said to kill all who laid eyes on her. But she didn't get *me*." He pointed to himself with a smug smile. "I've seen monsters that live in deep water and suck you down into the depths, but not *me*. Cause I'm too smart. And I see right through you. You're nothing but a girlie and you're no scarier than any other girlie girl. Except my dead wife—now, she was a frightening woman."

With that, Jeong stuffed the last of the dried squid in his mouth, stood up, stretched, scratched his behind, and sauntered off.

"What an idiot," Jaewon said.

"Oh, I don't know. I kind of like him," she said.

"What?" Jaewon sputtered on the hot barley tea he'd been drinking.

"He thinks I'm a girlie girl," she said with a grin.

Jaewon laughed and sat down on the log next to her.

She nudged him with her shoulder. "It's good to see you normal again."

He shuddered. "Are you joking? I will never be the same again. I'm half the man I was before getting on that boat. That experience has ruined my life."

"Well, I guess you won't be going with me to fetch the third treasure."

"Of course I'm going with you. Why would you say that?" he asked.

"Sunim informs me that it is located on Jindo Island."

Jaewon froze.

Kira tried not to laugh at his horrified expression. She realized how grateful she was to have him as a friend. "Don't worry, I won't make you get on another boat, I promise."

Consternation still covered his face as he swallowed down his hot tea. "Perhaps Sunim is mistaken and the last treasure is actually somewhere on the mainland," he said.

"Oh no, there's no mistake," Brother Woojin piped in from nearby. "We've studied the scrolls for centuries and it is clear that the last treasure was placed into the keeping of the monks of Tiger's Nest Temple, which is on Jindo Island."

"Sunim, it seems too easy. Do you think the monks will just hand over the last treasure to me?" Kira asked.

He shook his head. "I said it was placed in their keeping. They then hid it deep in the caves of the temple that is built on the highest cliff of the tallest mountain of Jindo. Even if they wanted to give it to you, they couldn't. It is the most guarded treasure in our world. But the bigger problem is that they won't want you to take it from them," Brother Woojin said.

"They don't believe in the prophecy?" she asked.

"They don't believe in the Dragon Musado," he replied. "But they do believe that the last treasure is the most dangerous one of all and should never be released into the world. For, you see, the jade dragon belt will allow the

Musado to control the fourteen dragons of the heavens and the powers of wind, rain, lightning, and all the other physical elements. It is a truly destructive power you will have."

Jaewon whistled.

"Well, that would explain why they don't want it getting into the wrong hands. But you are the Musado," Jaewon said to Kira, "and battling monks won't be too hard for you. They don't take lives."

Brother Woojin shook his head. "No, my son. These monks are savages and have never taken such a vow. They will gladly kill any who trespass on their mountain."

"Of course! And why should it be easy? That was just foolish thinking on my part," Jaewon said with an exaggerated sigh.

Seung, who had been listening closely from his station near the campfire, cleared his throat.

"Young master, I hesitate to remind you of this, but once we are reunited with our clan, you must think about your duties as the chief's successor," he said.

Jaewon's face contorted with despair before it closed up.

"That will never happen, Seung," Jaewon said, his voice as cold as the wind that buffeted them.

He walked away, not responding even as Seung called to him in remorse. Kira thought to chase him down, but she didn't know what to say. How could anyone help alleviate his torment? Jaewon's guilt over the death of his younger brother was a heavy burden on his soul. Her heart was tight as she wished there was something she could do to ease his pain.

What he sought was atonement, but Kira feared it was impossible.

14

Seven days later, they found themselves in the middle of a heavy snowstorm. The horses were struggling, and they had to stop frequently to clear the snow and ice out of their hooves. They had to find shelter before the blizzard conditions worsened.

Villages had been few and far between. Ever since crossing the Yalu River, they'd found nothing but deserted farms and abandoned houses, with no signs of people.

Jeong was leading them to Hushan village where they would find a reputable inn to stay for the night. Yet when they reached the village, it was completely empty. Snow-covered streets remained unmarked by any human or animal passage. Kira's gut told her something bad had happened here, but she could detect no signs of any demon activity.

Major Pak had his men search all the buildings. As much as Kira wanted to get Taejo and Brother Woojin into a shelter, she was worried about the mystery behind the abandoned village. Kira rode slowly, checking each passing building for demons. She could detect nothing, but for some reason, that didn't relieve her.

She knew they needed shelter soon. Both Taejo and Brother Woojin were shivering nonstop, heavy snow covering every inch of them.

Kira circled the town center before leading them to a large building that was clearly the village inn. She entered the building first. It took only a few minutes for Kira to determine that it was safe, at least from demons. Only then did she bring the others inside. Seung hurried over to the central fireplace and started a fire.

"I'm going to look around, see if there are any clues," Kwan said. He went upstairs to search all the rooms.

"What happened to everyone?" Taejo asked.

Kira surveyed the room and took in the signs of hurried abandonment. Bowls of food sat on tables with overturned cups that had spilled onto the floor. She stepped outside and entered the adjacent structure that housed the kitchen. Several pots of food still hung over cold hearths. Opening up a trapdoor, Kira found an underground storeroom that was half-filled with vegetables, rice, eggs, and even some meat. Everything was frozen. She found a large brass kettle that was filled with ice and carried it into the main building.

Going inside, she placed the kettle on the now-roaring fire and told Seung about the food situation. His gentle, round face lit up and he raced off to see what he could scrounge up for their meal.

Kwan walked down from the second floor. "Well, whatever happened, it appears people were in such a hurry that they left behind all their belongings." In his hands he held several strings of money coins and a pile of jade and gold jewelry.

"What are you doing?" Kira asked. "You can't take those."

Kwan glowered at her. "Why not? They won't be coming back for them."

"How do you know that? What if they do return? You're stealing," she said.

"Kira, don't be stupid," he retorted. "They're all dead. I don't know what happened, but that much I know. All these people were driven into the snowstorm and they're all dead."

"Still, it's not right. I thought you said we had enough money!"

"I'm being practical. The way this trip is going, we will need all the money we can get our hands on," he said. "You're going to have to let your morals slide right now, little sister."

Major Pak entered with their soldiers and the guide. "We've got a five-man rotation on guard duty right now. That'll give everyone a chance to stay out of the cold," he said. "But it looks like the village has been deserted for several days."

He turned to Kira with a questioning eyebrow.

"I need to check the rest of the village to be sure, but I don't think there are any demons here," she said. "This whole place feels like it's been completely abandoned for over a week."

"Odd," he replied. "What could have driven this entire village into the storm?"

"And where did they go?" Kira asked.

Puzzled by the mystery, she walked the length of the room before noticing Taejo's bundled-up form. He sat next to the monk who was dozing by the roaring fire Seung had started. His faithful dog sat at his feet, softly whining in sympathy. Taejo's face was filled with a deep melancholy that wrenched at Kira's heart.

"What's the matter?" she asked, crouching before him.

"This place scares me. I want to go home," he whispered. "I'm tired of traveling so much. I just want to stay in one place and feel safe."

She stroked his head. "I wish the same. But nothing is safe anymore. The world has become a frightening place."

"It's always been that way for you. You were always able to see them," he said. "And no one ever believed you.

But now they know. They all know."

He sat gazing into the fire. "I wish I didn't."

"Better to know and be prepared, rather than ignorant and dead. I never agreed with your father's decree to keep the common people from understanding the extent of the danger. They should have been more prepared," Kira said.

Taejo's eyes brimmed with unshed tears. "I miss him. I miss my father and mother. I miss your parents. Why did they all have to die? Why did our uncle have to die?"

There were no words of comfort she could give him. She had no idea what she could say to ever make this pain better. She opened her arms and embraced him, letting him cry with wild abandon. She felt the pull of her own despair wishing to be set free. Swallowing down her own sorrow and homesickness, Kira concentrated all her energy on comforting her young cousin until finally he fell asleep. She laid him gently before the fire and covered him with her own coat.

Turning around, she found herself face-to-face with Jaewon.

"Will he be all right?" he asked, concern etched in his handsome face.

"He's exhausted and heartsore, like all of us," she said.

Jaewon let out a weary breath. "Life is so much more difficult than we thought it would be when we were young," he said.

"Life was always difficult for me," Kira responded.

"It just keeps getting worse."

He closed his eyes for a brief moment and then reached for Kira. Before he could speak, the tavern door flung open and Jeong stomped inside.

Jeong paced in an awkward circle, snow cascading off him with every step, an alarmed expression on his face.

"I don't understand. I was just here a month ago," he mumbled to himself. "Where could they be? Where would they have gone?"

"Jeong, did you have family here?" Kira asked.

He nodded. "My sister and her family. I went to her house, but it's empty. They didn't even take the family valuables and heirlooms! They would never have left them behind unless it was an emergency!"

Jeong, who was usually so arrogant, was shaken up. "What happened here? What's going on?"

No one spoke. The only people who could answer his question were probably long-dead in the snowstorm.

The blizzard worsened. The wind was so fierce that it blew the snow sideways and the temperature had dropped to a dangerous level. There was no way they could travel in the storm. They holed up in the tavern, taking over the abandoned rooms and stabling their horses. Fortunately, they were able to scavenge for all they needed.

Jaewon found a baduk board and, upon Brother Woojin's urging, began to teach Taejo how to play. Kira was glad that Taejo had something to occupy him.

Boredom was the worst thing for a person who was depressed. She was almost tempted to play herself, but she could not get rid of her chronic headache. At times, it was debilitating and all she could hear was the Demon Lord's voice taunting her.

Come to me, my lovely.

You are so unhappy, aren't you?

Come to me and I will rid you of all your sorrows.

At night, instead of seeing visions, she would hear the Demon Lord whispering to her constantly. Sleep was impossible. And she moved around during the day in a daze of pain.

Outside, as she patrolled the deserted village, she heard the Demon Lord's treacherous voice over the howling of the wind. It urged her into the blizzard. Lights shimmered in the distance. Her feet began to move toward it, away from the safety of the building. The voice stopped but the light beckoned her, promising warmth and safety. It promised her endless sleep. Lulled by a false sense of security, Kira walked in a trance.

Only after she'd walked quite a distance did Kira's senses react. A burning in her chest stopped her in her tracks. She shook her head and reversed. Even through the blinding snow, she was able to see a yellow light seeping through the crevice of a window in the tavern. Slowly she forced herself to navigate the heavy drift, against the driving winds, and entered the building.

Inside, she avoided the others and went to lie down in

her room. Sleep would not come, but she needed to rest her aching head. She began to shake. Had she not snapped out of the strange fog she was in, she would not have stopped. She would have wandered far into the blizzard. They would not have found her.

The next day saw her on patrol duty again; this time she vowed not to listen to the voice. She would stay vigilant. She would not let herself be taken under the Demon Lord's spell.

She was circling the outer boundary of the village when she heard the plaintive cry of a young child.

"Mommy! Mommy!"

The wind had died down, letting Kira hear the child's cry clearly.

"I'm scared, I'm so scared."

"Where are you?" Kira shouted.

The child began to weep again.

It wheeled her around, racing from building to building searching for it. The wind began to howl again, muting the child's voice. Kira kept shouting for the child, following the voice as it led her farther and farther out of town. Until it led her to the end of the village, where the vastness of the snowstorm left no trace of civilization. Already, the path she'd taken from the tavern was completely gone, no trace of her footsteps anywhere.

The lack of sleep, the exhaustion, and the constant murmuring of the evil voice had led her here, to the verge of death. She slowly turned around and could see nothing but the driving snow. The sky, the air, the ground was a sea of white. She heard the cries of the false child rising in a shrieking crescendo, but Kira ignored it. Wind buffeted her, nearly knocking her down. She lowered her head and concentrated on putting one foot in front of the other. Frostbite was setting in on her extremities and she was tiring quickly. She should never have wandered so far from the town center. Exhaustion crept over her and her eyes closed as she swayed on her feet. She just wanted to sleep. Her knees buckled and she slipped down into the snow.

There was another sharp burning sensation in her chest, just like the day before. She placed a hand against her heart and felt heat radiating from the tidal stone.

Get up. Keep walking. You mustn't sleep.

Kira had to slap herself in the face to try and shake off her drowsiness.

Just move your feet; I will guide you.

She rose with great difficulty, her hands pressed against her treasure. The stone was hot against her frostbitten fingers, causing them to tingle with sharp pain. It helped keep her awake as she plowed through the deep snow. Heat was now coursing throughout her body, even her legs. When she moved, snow melted all around her. It was as if she were on fire. Water pooled around her and she could see the frozen ground. No longer cold, Kira was sweating under her heavy coat. She could feel her feet again, although she almost wished she couldn't, they hurt so much. The tidal stone guided her through the storm. Kira had no idea where she was. She kept her eyes on the ground before her. It felt like an eternity of walking before she finally reached the tavern. Relief made her knees buckle as she held on to the wall, exhausted tears sliding down her face.

"Thank you," she whispered to the tidal stone. With one last pulse of heat, the ruby returned to its normal state.

She stood for a long moment pressed against the wall before composing herself and entered the building.

Jaewon came over, his face relaxing with palpable relief.

"Thank the heavens you are back! Why were you gone so long?" Jaewon asked. "Your brother went out searching for you."

"I got a little lost," she said. "The storm is getting really bad. Where is the prince and Sunim?"

"They're sleeping," Jaewon said. "Otherwise they'd be besides themselves with worry also."

Kira noticed a small blade and a carved piece of wood in his hands. "What's that?" she asked.

He shrugged. "Found some wood and a carving kit. Thought I'd try it again."

"How'd you learn to do that?" she asked.

"My father," he said. "It's nice to know I haven't forgotten."

Seung brought over a warm bowl of vegetable stew.

"Eat this, it will warm you up again."

Kira sat gratefully by the fire and ate. Not much later, her brother returned in a foul mood.

"You scared me to death! If you can't be smart about patrol duty, then I'll pull you off," he shouted. "Even Major Pak couldn't find you in that blizzard!"

Kira apologized but didn't mention anything about the hallucinations she was having. She was too scared to talk about it. The one good thing that had come out of nearly getting lost in the blizzard and being saved by the tidal stone was that the voice of the Demon Lord had vanished for now.

That night, Kira decided to pamper herself by bathing thoroughly. Kira opened a small satchel that she always carried with her. It contained a comb, her tooth rag, and a small round cake of precious perfumed soap wrapped in a hemp cloth. In the far side of the tavern, there was a bathing room with a large wooden tub. Kira took with her a hot kettle as well as several buckets of water. By adding some hot water to the cold, she was able to bathe herself with luke-warm water.

First she built up the fire in the fireplace, letting it burn strongly before she began her bathing ritual.

As she lathered her face with the soap's fresh essence of ginseng, honey, and soybean oil, her senses were awakening from the dulled effects of her headache. The pain faded as the voice that had become an incessant drone disappeared. She peeled off her jacket. Underneath, she wore only a quilted cotton bust cover wrapped tightly around her chest. She had not removed it in several days and she was itchy and uncomfortable. She untied the wrap and breathed a huge sigh of relief. Her chest and stomach were marked with deep impressions where the band had cut into the flesh. She rubbed herself down with a small cloth, enjoying the cool water against her skin.

She took out a clean bust wrap and tied it tightly around herself. Using her two remaining buckets, she quickly washed the rest of herself and then her hair and changed into new clothes. When she was done, she washed all her dirty clothes in the buckets and hung them on a folding rack.

Refreshed and happy, Kira sat before the fire and ran her fingers through her hair before using a fine-toothed ivory comb. Her fingers tightened around it and for a moment she pressed it to her chest. The comb was a present from her mother and the one truly feminine item Kira carried with her. She remembered how when she was little, she would sit in her mother's chambers getting her long, dark brown hair brushed and braided. Her mother would sing as she gently worked the knots from Kira's hair.

Mother, that hurts. Why can't I cut my hair off? Then I won't have any knots in it.

Cut off this beautiful hair? I would be so sad, her mother had said. *As long as I am here, it is my pleasure to take care of you, my child. Would you take away my joy?*

No, Mother, I wouldn't do that to you.

Kira opened her eyes and found her hair was almost dry. She must have dozed off by the fire for over an hour. Sitting up, she brushed her hair until it crackled with sparks, causing it to fly about her like silky fine threads of a cob-web in a friendly wind. The rhythm of steady footsteps and a sharp rapping on the door brought Kira's head up. Before she could answer, the door opened and Jaewon stood framed in the doorway.

For the space of a moment, both froze. Jaewon's eyes were locked on to Kira's hair. Self-conscious, she braided it with quick jerky movements. She packed up her belongings and her wet clothing and headed for the door.

"I'm so sorry, I thought you were done hours ago," he stuttered.

"I fell asleep by the fire," she said, brushing past him.

"It's beautiful," he called to her.

She turned around, a puzzled look on her face. "What are you talking about?"

"Your hair," he said with a bashful smile. "It's beautiful."

Kira suppressed a smile, embarrassed and yet happy at his remark.

15

They'd been in Hushan village for over five days before the snow-storm passed and they were finally able to head back onto their route. Jeong the guide was quiet and jumpy. His uneasiness was contagious. There was something unreal and terrifying about the situation they found themselves in.

For five more days, they rode without sighting another human being. Whole villages stood empty. It was eerie.

"We discovered a village ahead." A soldier had returned from scouting. "It's inhabited. We saw several smoking chimneys."

"That would be Numa," Jeong said in relief.

But as they approached the village, Kira sensed something was wrong. She breathed deeply. She could smell nothing, and yet her stomach felt queasy.

"We need to stop," Kira called to the major. They were right outside the village limits, next to a wooden *jang-seung* welcoming them to Numa. Kira observed smoke spiraling into the air.

"I don't like it," she said.

"What is it? Demons?" Major Pak said.

"I don't know. But we can't go in there," Kira said, pointing toward the settlement.

Jindo began to act in a peculiar manner. He kept sniffing the air and circling before stopping and sniffing again. Suddenly, he turned and bounded away.

"Jindo!" Taejo yelled, but the dog kept running.

"I'll go after him," Seung said.

Brother Woojin looked at Kira with a curious expression. "I, too, shall follow the dog." He took off after Seung and Jindo.

Major Pak called Jeong over to ask for a different route.

"Different route? Why? Numa is right there! I can see the smoke from the chimneys," Jeong said in rising agitation.

"We can't go there," Kira answered. "It isn't safe."

Jeong spat on the ground. "Stupid girl! You don't know what you're talking about."

He kicked his horse and galloped to the village.

"Stop!" Kira yelled. "You're going to alert them that we're here!"

The guide didn't listen; instead he kept riding into the center of town, where several buildings showed smoke pouring from their chimneys.

"Alert who?" Major Pak asked.

"I don't know, but we have to leave now!"

"Somebody go get that fool," Major Pak said.

"Forget him! The prince is in danger!" Kira was already turning around and reaching for Taejo's horse, when she was assaulted by the strong scent of demon.

"Pull back!" she yelled. "Pull back!"

The two guardsmen who had gone after Jeong stopped in confusion. Just then, villagers poured from the center buildings and rushed toward them. They attacked the guide first, ripping him apart as they gorged on his internal organs. The guards who tried to escape were also quickly surrounded and pulled off their horses.

Kira heard their screams as she and Taejo raced away, only to find that a group of demon-possessed villagers had circled behind them and were closing in fast.

There were too many. All around them, their soldiers were being slaughtered. Blocked from behind, Kira knew they had no choice but to ride through the village and pray they could come out of it alive. Kwan and Jaewon rode ahead, their swords slicing through the neck of any villager who approached. Kira used her bow to shoot any they missed. But more and more demons were appearing from every corner of the village.

A group of schoolchildren descended upon a soldier and devoured him and his horse. As their small faces contorted into bloodlust, Kira could see the true faces of the demons beneath the child skins.

Kira wanted to scream but she could not catch her breath. Even small children were not safe from demon possession. She knew she had to kill them, but their small faces and bodies shocked her into immobility.

Just then, a young boy jumped at Taejo. He couldn't have been more than eight years old. Kira shot an arrow through his neck. Her emotions dulled even as her skills sharpened. Demons didn't care who they killed. She couldn't either.

She shot several more possessed children as Taejo unsheathed his sword and fought off any who came too close.

Jaewon fought his way over to them.

"Get the prince out of here!" she yelled, as she continued to fight off their attackers.

"Follow me, Your Highness," Jaewon shouted.

Before he could lead them, a villager that had half morphed from its human skin and into its true demon form attacked Jaewon and savaged his leg, trying to drag him off his horse. Kira shot several arrows into its neck, taking it down.

Jaewon surged ahead with Taejo, leading him down

a clear path that cut through the village. Blood flowed down his leg, leaving a heavy trail in the dirt.

Their horses were frightened and hard to control. Jaewon was fast losing his strength.

"Leave me behind," he said, slowing down. "Save the prince. Go now!"

He tried to head back toward the demons pursuing them, but he lost consciousness and began to fall out of his seat.

"I won't leave you!" Kira caught Jaewon by the front of his coat and heaved him in front of her saddle. Freeing his horse, she slashed her sword viciously at the demons that had reached them. Keeping them from Taejo.

"Taejo, you must stay close to me!"

With a desperate cry for help, she urged her horse ahead, keeping even with Taejo as Kwan fought free of his attackers and came to their rescue. He led them toward the end of the village.

She heard Taejo sob in fear. Before them more possessed villagers appeared in ever increasing numbers. Unless there was a miracle, Kira knew there was no hope of escape. Major Pak and their soldiers were probably all dead by now.

She'd never seen so many demon possessions before. How had the demons killed an entire village full of people? There were just too many of them.

All the empty villages they'd passed. All the missing people. Was this the explanation?

The possessed villagers were converging in the far end of the village. More and more appeared, covering the streets ahead and behind them. They were assembling in a wide circle around Kira, Taejo, and Kwan. They were waiting for something, but Kira had no idea.

There was no way to fight them all.

She had failed.

"I'm sorry, Taejo," she said. "I'm sorry, Oppa. I failed you both."

Kwan's lips tightened, but his eyes never waivered from the ever increasing mob around them.

"Please, Noona, whatever happens, don't let them possess me," Taejo said.

"I promise I will not let that happen," she whispered. "But we must fight until our very last breath."

Taejo gripped his sword tight and nodded. A wave of despair threatened to overwhelm Kira as she braced herself for the coming attack.

"Heavenly Father, Heavenly Maidens, please help us now," she prayed.

A half-breed appeared and made his way through the mob. He stood tall, his long black hair worn loose in sharp contrast to his hideous demon visage.

"Tear the others apart but bring the Demon Slayer to me alive!" the half-breed proclaimed.

The demons roared and the mob advanced toward them. As the three cousins desperately fought off the first surge of possessed villagers, sudden shouts and a bold, rhythmic drumming heralded the arrival of an army. Men and women dressed in a variety of colored uniforms were all wearing red headbands tied around their foreheads. The headbands sported a black and gold dragon insignia. They descended on the villagers, wielding their swords with expert precision and clearing a path to Kira's side. Some bore heavy torches that they used to fend off the hordes of possessed villagers.

One of them turned to Kira and yelled, "Head for the mountains!"

Kwan, Kira, and Taejo didn't hesitate. They rode their horses up into the mountains. There they were met by more soldiers with dragon insignias who led them to their campsite.

A dog came rushing to them, his tail wagging madly. "Jindo!" Taejo jumped off his horse and buried his face into the dog's fur.

Brother Woojin and Seung came soon after. Seung promptly turned his attention to Jaewon and pulled him off Kira's horse.

"I don't know how Jindo knew to come here, but it is because of him that we found this encampment," Brother Woojin said. "These dragon fighters were planning to attack that demon-infested village tomorrow but changed their plans once they heard where you were."

"Whoever their leader is, we are truly grateful!" Kira said as she dismounted. "We would have all died down there."

Brother Woojin approached Kira and Kwan. "I urge you both not to overreact when you see who the leader of this group is," he said.

Kira was too worried about Jaewon to pay attention. A couple of dragon fighters helped Seung carry Jaewon's unconscious form to a nearby tent. Kira followed closely asking Seung about the wound.

"It's pretty bad," Seung said. At the tent, a soldier barred Kira from entering, admitting only Seung.

"Young mistress, I think it would be best if you wait outside," Seung said.

Kira wanted to argue, her worry for Jaewon making her nervous.

"Don't worry, I will take good care of him," Seung said.

Faced with his quiet confidence, she agreed and returned to the others.

As she approached Brother Woojin, she pondered over his cryptic remark.

"What did you mean when you said don't overreact?" Kira asked the monk.

Brother Woojin was rolling his prayer beads between his hands, a habit she knew from experience meant the monk was nervous or worried.

"Do you believe that a person can change if he puts his mind to it?" he asked.

"Yes, of course," she said.

"Please don't forget that," he said. He then wandered

over to sit next to the shaken prince and Jindo.

A little while later, a new group of arrivals made it to the campsite. Kira was relieved to see Major Pak but alarmed that only two of their soldiers had survived. They'd lost so many men.

She still couldn't understand how an entire village of demons had hidden themselves from her. What kind of magic had they used? Uneasy, Kira was about to greet the major when the lead rider dismounted and faced her.

There was a loud ringing in her ears and her body went rigid. Kira's mouth hung open but no words came out. And then the sound flooded back in and she heard her own voice shouting. For once again she faced her former betrothed, Shin Bo Hyun.

16

"You're alive!" Kira's voice cracked.

Shin Bo Hyun was the nephew of the traitor Lord Shin Mulchin, who assassinated Taejo's father, King Yuri. Kira's betrothal to Shin Bo Hyun had been sanctioned by the queen before Lord Shin Mulchin's betrayal. It was broken when both Shins' traitorous actions led to the invasion of Hansong.

The last time she'd seen Shin Bo Hyun was at the Diamond Mountains, when he'd captured the prince and threatened to kill Jaewon if she didn't reveal herself. Wielding the tidal stone, she'd unleashed a water dragon that had swept over him and his men with a wild and raging flood. She'd thought for sure he was dead. But here he was, smiling at her.

Shin dismounted and headed toward her.

Kwan stepped in front of his sister and punched Shin hard, knocking him down. Shin's men responded at once, pulling out their swords and menacing Kwan.

"No, no, sheath your weapons," Shin said. "He owes me much more than a punch."

He rubbed his jaw and rose to his feet. Major Pak now stood with Kwan, their anger palpable.

"Come, let us go to my quarters where we can talk in private," Shin said.

"You may have saved us, but we owe you nothing." Kwan spat on the ground.

Kira heard the muttering of Shin's men. Regardless of Shin's past betrayals, he had clearly won over the respect of his army.

"Let's take this somewhere private," she said, putting a hand on her brother's arm.

They followed Shin farther into the woods, his men close behind them. He ushered them into a large circular tent with a peaked roof that had a small chimney. Inside, the tent was warmed by a small stove.

Shin ordered his men to leave them alone. They left reluctantly, making clear that they would be standing outside the tent. He nodded, but his attention was set on Kira. Avoiding his gaze, she walked to the far end of the tent and sat down on a small stool.

"What kind of tent is this?" she asked, fingering the felt fabric.

"It is called a *ger*," he said. "Compliments of the nomadic tribes of Cathay. They are very easy to assemble and very easy to travel with. You will find it essential to have when traveling the northern lands."

"How are you alive?" she asked.

He sat on a floor cushion and stretched his legs in front of him. "It seems the gods didn't want me dead yet. I floated down that river for a long while until it swept me into a tree and I clung to its branches for dear life. By the time the flood passed and I climbed down, I felt more dead than alive. A traveling family of farmers took pity on me and saved me. They were heading north, so I stayed with them, wondering what I was supposed to do with my life now. I never wanted to be a traitor."

"But you are!" Taejo yelled before he dashed over to Kira's side.

Shin sighed. "Yes, I am. Or was, actually. But I didn't think of myself as a traitor for I was loyal to the head of my clan."

"Your uncle was a very bad man!" Taejo yelled, his voice cracking in grief. "He killed my parents!"

"I'm very sorry, Your Highness. I was not in Hansong when it happened. But he was my uncle, and I did wrong. And I'm trying to atone for my mistakes. Isn't a man allowed to make amends?" He glanced at Brother Woojin. "Can a man who rebuilds his life be forgiven?"

"Of course, my son," Brother Woojin said.

Taejo huffed in disbelief, which made Kira smile.

Shin smiled back. "I never thought I'd see you again. But allow me the opportunity to beg for your forgiveness."

Kwan made a disgusted sound. "We will never trust you, let alone forgive you."

"You're a traitor to all Hansong!" Major Pak growled.

Brother Woojin waved his hands in distress. "Please, please stop! He has atoned for his sins and made a new life for himself. We must forget and forgive."

"I think I'll leave that to you," Kwan said.

There was an awkward silence.

"Well, be that as it may, you are welcome to break your journey with us," Shin said. "And when you continue, I will be happy to escort you to Mount Baekdu."

Kwan rounded on the monk in disbelief. "You told him our destination?"

"Yes," the monk replied. "I have no reason not to trust him."

"Well then, you are not as wise as I once believed you to be," Kwan said. With a final glare at Shin, he stomped out of the tent. The major followed close after.

Kira stood up and walked toward the exit when Brother Woojin stopped her.

"I shall take the prince to find something to eat. Please stay and talk with Lord Shin," he requested. "There is a reason our paths have crossed again."

With a bow, he left with the prince, leaving Kira alone with her former betrothed. There was a long awkward pause as Kira avoided looking at his steady gaze. Finally she heaved an aggravated breath and turned to him.

"One thing that is really troubling me," Kira said. "There were so many demons in that village, but I couldn't smell them. I could sense something was wrong, but not exactly what."

"I think it's because they were hiding underground," Shin answered. "We found huge rooms that had been dug under many of the buildings in the village."

Kira nodded. "That's why I couldn't smell them right away, I could only sense something was wrong. But why were you using fire against them?"

"I learned that if you burn all the flesh off a demon-possessed human, it releases the demon. So we set that whole village on fire and went after every single possessed person."

"Are you sure you got them all?" Kira asked.

Shin nodded.

"I have no news of what has happened since I last saw you," he said. "Sunim said it would be better if you told me of what happened. Can you fill me in?"

Kira examined her former betrothed. He was no longer the meticulous nobleman of Hansong. He looked grimy and tired. New scars webbed the side of his face and neck, giving him an older and battle-worn appearance.

"Your uncle left me this parting gift." Kira pointed at her scar. Shin winced.

"And what did you leave him with?" he asked cautiously.

"Nothing—my aunt took care of him herself." Kira answered bitterly. In a low voice, she recounted her aunt's sacrifice, the shaman's death, Eojin's murder, and their subsequent flight from Hansong. She didn't mention her struggle to free her mother's soul from Shaman Ito. It was too personal and not something she would share with him. Thinking of the loss of her mother and her father always brought Kira to tears. She quickly turned her head, unwilling to let her old enemy see her pain.

Shin sat in silence, gazing into the fire that lay between them. When he finally spoke, his voice was low and hesitant.

"When I was stuck in that tree, wondering if I would survive, I kept thinking to myself what I would do over if I had another chance." He stood up and approached her cautiously, dropping down on his knees before her. "And I knew that if I could do just one thing, it was to make amends with you. I am so sorry for all that you have suffered. I don't know how you will believe me, but I will do everything in my power to help you. I, Shin Bo Hyun, will swear my allegiance and those of my men to Prince Taejo and we will fight for him, no matter what."

"Don't be so melodramatic," Kira snapped.

He shook his head and took hold of one her hands,

holding it tight within his own.

"You have no reason to ever trust me but I will dedicate my life to proving to you that I have changed."

Kira was moved by his sincerity. And yet, something held her back. Looking at him brought forth memories of years of teasing. He was a constant of her childhood. She could never reconcile his stated admiration of her with the willful teasing she'd endured at Shin's hands. It irked her that she was so aware of him and of the attraction she could feel between them. It made her uncomfortable. It made her mad.

She jerked her hand out of his grip. As much as he was a part of her childhood, she could not forget who he was and what he had done. His uncle had betrayed Hansong and caused the death of her own parents and her king and queen. Taejo had lost his kingdom and they were now homeless.

While she understood loyalty to one's clan, she could never forgive him.

"Thank you for saving us, Shin Bo Hyun. I owe you my life. I will let the others know what you have said. I'm sure they will welcome the allegiance of your men."

Kira ignored the disappointment on his face and made for the door.

"Kang Kira," Shin called. "I am so very sorry."

She paused to study his handsome face. The court ladies of Hansong had loved to moon over his good looks. But they were all gone. She had a vivid memory of their brightly colored hanboks fluttering in the wind as they jumped from the cliff.

She shook her head and left the tent.

He was responsible for so much death and betrayal. How could there be hope of forgiveness?

17

"We can't trust him!" Kwan was in a rage as he paced the length of their campsite.

"We may have no choice," Major Pak said. "We lost our guide, almost all our men, and our supplies in that debacle."

"I will vouch for Shin," Brother Woojin interjected. "I have seen into his heart and I believe he has changed for the better."

Taejo looked puzzled by the monk's comment.

"Sunim," Taejo asked, "what did you see?"

The monk put his hands together and gazed up to the heavens as he murmured a quick prayer. "I saw that the darkness that had colored his aura is now gone."

Taejo started in surprise. "You never told me that you can see people's auras!"

"It is not something I've ever told anyone besides my own master," he said, "for it is a gift from the heavens and a secret I've guarded for over sixty years."

Kira clapped her hands together. "That's right. You never trusted him before. You knew he was lying when he set that first trap."

The monk nodded. "The young lord didn't always have a dark aura. His was a mix of colors, mostly red. But when we first left Hansong I observed the confusion and darkening of his aura. And when we saw him again, his aura was almost completely black."

"What is my color, Sunim?" Taejo asked.

"You are a bright orange, Your Highness. Like the sun, it tells us you are our future king," he said.

"The major's color has always been a bright blue, signifying his unwavering loyalty, while both Captain Kang and his older brother, General Kang's auras are purple, indicating nobility of mind and leadership." He walked around the campfire and stopped at Seung, who had just arrived from tending Jaewon's wound. "Our young friend here has one of the brightest forest-green auras I've ever seen. And, as we know, he is a great healer. His friend, though, has a blue aura tinged with darkness that worries me."

Seung started. "Don't say that! He's not evil!"

"No, not an evil darkness but more of a deep melancholia. I hope one day he will overcome it so that his aura may shine bright again."

Making his final turn, he faced Kira. "Young mistress, in my entire life, I have never seen a golden aura like yours. I have been taught that such an aura means you are touched by the Heavenly Father."

"I wish more people could see it, Sunim. Maybe then they wouldn't be so afraid of me." Kira smiled. "So this is why you've always had been such a good judge of character."

"It is a gift and I've only divulged it today so you would trust Lord Shin. He is not like his uncle," Brother Woojin said.

A tense silence fell upon the group. Even knowing the monk's abilities, it would not be easy to do as he asked. And yet what choice did they have? They needed help.

Looking at her brother, she realized that he was not quite convinced.

"Oppa, I know you don't like it, but we have no choice. Even though we may not trust Shin Bo Hyun, we do trust Sunim. So let us listen to his counsel on this," she said.

Kwan shook his head. "I cannot agree to this. I cannot trust him. He nearly killed all of us! His uncle killed our father and was the reason for our mother's death. How can you so easily forget this?"

Turning on his heel, Kwan stormed off into the woods.

Kira felt bereft at his abrupt departure. Why did he always run away when she needed to talk to him? Even knowing that Kwan was a brooder and needed time alone to mull things over, Kira couldn't help but feel shut out. She wished her oldest brother was with them. He was so much like their father. If Kyoung were here, he'd know exactly what to do and Kwan would trust him. They all would.

On this one issue, whether or not to trust Shin Bo Hyun, Kira needed guidance. Should they trust Sunim or was it foolish to forget all the wrongs Shin was responsible for?

Kira looked at Major Pak, who shook his head.

"I don't know what to think," he said. "I lost so many men. I would not be alive right now but for Lord Shin. I don't think any of us would be."

With a bow, he pulled out the map that he was always studying, seeking the best route to their destination.

Kira glanced at Taejo.

"What would you have us do?" she asked.

"I trust Sunim," he replied.

"His uncle killed your father and mother," she said.

Taejo flinched. "That was his uncle. And I don't want to talk about it," he said, holding in his tears. "If Sunim trusts Lord Shin, then I will trust him. But I will never forgive him."

Kira was sorry she'd upset him. Leaving him to be comforted by Brother Woojin, she left their campsite to walk aimlessly into the woods. She needed to clear her mind and think. Her heart and mind were in conflict and she didn't have anyone to advise her.

The woods were quiet and dark. Kira found a fallen log and sat down on it, watching a colony of ants gathering food before her feet. She couldn't help but admit to herself that she was glad Shin Bo Hyun had survived. That a part of her had always felt a sort of connection to him. Good or bad, he was someone familiar. Someone she'd grown up with.

But he was also part of the treachery that caused the death of her mother and father. Just the thought of his involvement with his uncle filled her with instant rage.

Taejo was right. They could trust him to a limited extent because of Brother Woojin, but they should never forgive or forget.

18

Kira rose early, enjoying the luxury of having her own personal space. Shin Bo Hyun had set up a small ger just for her, right next to the larger one that Taejo shared with Kwan and Brother Woojin. Someone had brought in a basin of water and a clean cloth. With a sigh of relief, Kira stripped and took the opportunity to wash as much as possible. Even the cold morning air couldn't diminish her pleasure.

When she was done, she exited her ger and checked on Taejo. She poked her head in and saw Taejo and the monk were still asleep under their blankets, while Kwan sat in a corner, cleaning his weapon. With a nod to her brother, Kira decided to search for food.

She noted how close Shin's tent was to her own. Hoping to avoid him, she walked down the mountainside to canvass the area. She noticed a lot of movement in the valley below and headed toward the activity. The sloping woods opened into a large clearing where a small mobile village was living in a tent city. Children ran around gathering supplies while men and women worked at different tasks. Even the elderly sat around campfires, carving, sewing, weaving, and otherwise keeping busy.

As she walked among them, she recognized the cautious reserve with which everyone greeted her. They all knew who she was and were polite but distant. A short woman with a sweet, round face came over and brought her a large white bun, steaming hot and filled with savory meat and vegetables. Kira thanked her and ate it in three bites, enjoying the soft texture of the bread. The woman nodded with a small smile and returned to her cooking station.

Kira watched the women working together, kneading the dough, making the filling, and steaming the buns in large bamboo baskets. Cooking was the one thing Kira had never been exposed to. Living in the royal court meant all her meals had been prepared by the kitchen staff. This was her first exposure to the art of cooking and she was fascinated by it.

"Can I help?" she asked.

The round-faced woman shook her head, instead

pressing another bun into Kira's hands.

Disappointed, she left the women's company, as she realized they were discomfited by her presence. She took her time, eating and enjoying the bun as she walked around the camp noting how everyone was working. Even the children were busy gathering wood and herbs. One child ran by with a basket full of ginseng. It reminded her of Seung. She wondered how Jaewon was doing. Before she could return, she saw Shin Bo Hyun walking through the campsite. Everywhere he went, he was greeted with reverence, as if he were royalty. He responded with kindness and seemed to genuinely care about the welfare of his people.

It was odd to see Shin Bo Hyun acting as a leader of such a ragtag group. Clearly, his people respected and admired him. It was odd for Kira to see such devotion for someone who she could not trust. She didn't know how to reconcile Shin Bo Hyun the leader with Shin Bo Hyun the traitor.

Spotting Kira, he came over with a smile.

"Come walk with me?" he asked.

Unable to refuse him politely, she followed him from the tent city.

"Why do you have all these families with you? Isn't it hard to travel this way?" she asked.

"We rescued these people from a small village called Bahe some hundred li north of here," he said. "It's slow going, but we plan to take them with us to Wunu

Mountain City, where they'll be safe."

"A mountain city? Like Wando?"

He shook his head. "No, it's something you have to see to believe. An entire city built on the top of a mountain."

Kira shot him a disbelieving glance.

He laughed. "The top of the mountain is flat. It's as if the Heavenly Father cut off the peak and left us with an amazing plateau. It is difficult to reach it, but once you are there, it is completely safe."

"How many can live there?"

Shin Bo Hyun tilted his head and thought for a moment. "Seven hundred, maybe. But not everyone lives on the mountaintop. Many villages surround Wunu. My men are constantly patrolling them. When there's danger, we round everyone and bring them into the city."

"How did you come to be in charge?"

"The previous chief of the Dragon Fighters was a great leader who helped me when I was lost. I became his right-hand man. When he was killed in a demon attack, not too long ago, his men came to me and asked me to lead them."

"Why you, a stranger? I don't understand," she said.

"In this crazy world, does anything make sense? Most of them had never seen a demon possession before and didn't know what to do. They'd lost so many men to the demon attacks. When I arrived, I immediately started training them how to fight and how to recognize a demon. I became the chief's strongest fighter. When he died, I was their best hope. We're just trying to survive day by day. That's all we can do."

Kira nodded. Shin Bo Hyun had always been an excellent warrior.

"Since taking over, we've amassed a sizable army of demon fighters," he said.

"You may need to bring your soldiers south," Kira said. "The Iron Army needs all the help they can get to defeat the Demon Lord and his army."

A child ran up to Shin and handed him a piping hot steamed bun. He took it with a smile of thanks, ruffling the little girl's hair as she beamed in adoration.

He offered it to Kira, but she declined.

"I already had a few," she said. "You eat it."

Shin demolished the steamed bun in two bites, wiping his hands on his trousers.

"We were on our way home when our scouts got word of the demon infestation at Numa."

"Lucky for us you were nearby," she said.

"It's not luck. It's destiny," he said. "Don't you see? Our lives are bound. Fate keeps bringing us together."

Kira rolled her eyes, making Shin laugh.

"Do you remember when we were children?" he asked. "The nurses would take us outside to play and we would chase you around, but no one could ever catch you. You were so fast. Once, we thought for sure we had you and you climbed up a tree and stayed there for hours."

"I'm no fool," she said. "You and your friends were terrors."

"Yes, but how does a five-year-old climb the biggest tree in the kingdom? Grown men had a hard time climbing that tree and there you were, scampering to the very top like a monkey."

He shook his head in wonder. "You never did have any fear."

"No, that's not true. I was scared of monsters," she said. The nightmare image of the imoogi appeared in her mind. "You have no idea how scared I was."

"But you never showed it," he said. "I admit that I was jealous of you. We all were."

"Of me? Why?" she asked.

"You can't be serious. You were better at taekkyon fighting at five than most boys were at twice that age. And then when you were seven years old, you were already training with the *saulabi*. And you were a girl! We weren't allowed to start our training until we were ten, and only if we were deemed worthy."

Kira crossed her arms across her chest. "Is *that* why you were always pulling those nasty pranks on me?"

"Well, yes, and also to get you to notice me. You were always off in your own world."

"That's because everyone called me a freak and no one would ever play with me," she said.

"I would have," he said.

They'd reached a creek and Kira bent down to pick up a few stones.

"No, you were the worst of them! Always telling

157

everyone how strange my eyes were and mocking me. I really hated you." She flung the stones into the creek, watching the growing ripples in the water.

Shin sighed. "The things I would do differently if I could only have a second chance. I'm sorry about that. I was a dumb kid."

Kira made a rude noise with her tongue.

"But the truth is, I've always liked you," he said.

"You had an odd way of showing it," Kira said.

"I was happy about our betrothal because not only would I get you, but I would be the son-in-law of the greatest general of Hansong," Shin said.

Kira gazed at him in pity. "My father didn't approve of our betrothal and would never have allowed our marriage."

She bent her arm to throw another stone, when he took hold of her hand and drew her closer.

"The river washed the old me away. Here I stand, a brand-new man. Can't we start all over again?"

Before she could answer, a young man came racing toward them, bumping into Kira hard. Kira would have fallen into the creek if Shin hadn't been holding her.

"Chansu, what is it?" he asked, a slight frown creasing his face.

Chansu gave Kira a hostile glare before answering him. "Chief Shin, the men are back from patrol and have important news to report."

He stared at Shin with an expression of besotted hero worship that caused Kira to hide her grin. She'd seen many young soldiers idolize her oldest brother in the same way. Even though Chansu looked about the same age as Kira, she felt years older than him.

Shin sighed and bowed to Kira. "Will you excuse me while I see to my men?"

As he returned to camp, Chansu stayed behind, looking Kira up and down with a haughty sneer. It reminded her of the way she used to be treated by the nobles at home. As soon as she thought of it, she remembered the sight of the court ladies falling from the cliffs—the colorful silk clouds floating in the Han River. The memory saddened her.

"You're not really his betrothed, are you?" Chansu asked.

Kira was puzzled by his unexpected question and open hostility.

"We were once engaged, but not anymore," Kira replied. "All those who wanted it are no longer with us."

Kira remembered when her aunt and her mother had surprised her with news of the betrothal.

My dear sister, let my daughter get used to this idea, her mother had said. *After all, you said so yourself. She's thought of herself as more boy than girl for all these years. Give her time to consider what it means to become a woman.*

"So you're not going to marry him," Chansu said.

Kira pushed aside the painful memories. "No, I'm not."

"The betrothal was a political arrangement, then?" he asked. "He didn't want it either?"

Kira hesitated. There was an intensity about his gaze that was off-putting.

"No," she replied.

"And you won't be holding him to it?"

"I said no," Kira snapped, losing her temper. She did not like this soldier at all.

Chansu smiled, a look of relief crossing his sly face.

"Come, let me take you to your injured friend—he is asking for you," he said.

Kira couldn't help showing her annoyance. "Why didn't you tell me sooner?" she asked.

"I'm telling you now," Chansu said with a laugh.

He moved quickly through the woods, leaving Kira to wonder at his mercurial mood swings. She glared at the young soldier as he ran ahead. It was not that often that she took such a strong dislike to someone, but Chansu had struck a nerve with her. She pondered over their bizarre conversation and the intensity of his hero worship of Shin Bo Hyun. Chansu made her uneasy.

She knew she could not trust him.

19

Upon their return to camp, Chansu waved Kira over to the infirmary tent and took off. As soon as Seung saw Kira, he hustled over to her side.

"Young mistress, my master is asking for you," he said. "If you could spare a moment to see him—"

"Of course," she said.

Inside the large ger, there were a few rows of injured people lying on straw pallets on the ground. Off to one side by the wall, she found Jaewon covered by a thick blanket. She maneuvered around the other patients and sat down next to him.

Jaewon opened his eyes and smiled at her.

"How are you?" he asked.

"What kind of silly question is that?" she asked. "You're the one who's stuck in a sickbed."

He laughed. "It's just that I haven't seen you since the attack and I was worried."

Kira patted his hand. "Well, as you can see, there is nothing to worry about."

"I'm sorry for getting injured and delaying our journey."

Kira glared at him in mock anger. "You should be! How dare you nearly get killed by a demon and force me to eat all the yummy steamed buns I can get!"

"Steamed buns? I didn't get any—"

"That's because you are sick and can only eat rice gruel," she replied. "But if you get better soon, I might share some with you."

He smiled. "Perhaps just a bite or two, if you are feeling generous."

"Hey, hey! I think you're pushing it there," she said, smiling at him.

He gazed at her with such intensity, Kira felt that same uncomfortable feeling she had around Shin Bo Hyun.

"What's the matter?" she asked.

"They say you are still betrothed."

"What? Who said?"

"The soldiers. His soldiers. They say you are his

betrothed and he plans to marry you," Jaewon said.

Kira shook her head in annoyance. Why were people still talking about their betrothal? "It is true that he was once my betrothed. But not anymore. I have no intention of marrying him." *Or anyone else,* she thought to herself.

Jaewon sighed in relief. "Good. Don't marry him."

She scowled. "I'm not exactly the marrying kind."

"That's not true. You would make a wonderful wife for the right man," he said.

"Ha! That's the problem," she said. "There's no such thing as the right man for me."

"Don't say that, Kang Kira, you are so special. You deserve to be happy."

"Who said I need a man to be happy?" she snapped.

Jaewon was quiet, his lips twisted as if he were looking for the right words to say.

"Perhaps it is just my own feeling," he said finally. "To have someone and not be lonely in life, as I've been for so long. I mean, I've always had Seung, but it's not the same. Sometimes you can be sitting in a crowded room and still feel all alone. I just would love to find someone who would be the mate of my heart."

Kira understood his loneliness.

"That would be nice. But I don't think it happens that often," she said. "Maybe some lucky people meet their soul mate. The rest of us just continue on the best we can, never knowing that there's something missing. We can still be happy enjoying the little things in life. Like the delicious steamed buns that I had this morning. Those made me so happy!"

She grinned at him, but his expression was sad.

"Do you not believe in love?"

She sighed.

"Of course I do, but just look at me." She pointed to her face. "I tend to scare people off."

He reached over to touch her face. "I don't even notice the scar at all—why don't you realize how unimportant it is?"

"I—" Kira stopped, unsure of what to say. The fever was still bright in his eyes, leaving them glassy. A sheen of sweat dotted his forehead. She felt a rush of affection for him—how very dear he'd become to her.

"I have no right to speak of a future with anyone when my own is so uncertain. I can offer you nothing. And yet, I know that I would do anything for you, if you needed me. I will always be there for you," he said. "Promise me that you will remember this. That you can always rely on me."

He gripped her hand tight within his.

A pain stabbed at her chest, a tightness she was unfamiliar with. Overwhelmed by the awkwardness of her emotions, Kira nodded jerkily and rose to her feet.

"Try to get some rest now," she said. "I'll check on you in the morning."

As she exited the ger, she placed a hand over her chest, massaging the soreness that lingered there.

She was back in the cavern facing the lava pit. It was empty and yet she could feel a pulsating presence that drew her closer.

"Come to me," it demanded.

She knew who called her and yet she had no choice but to approach. Her feet dragged, but her body moved forward. She was at the edge of the lava pit, her eyes riveted on the growing fiery mass that rose before her. The heat was becoming unbearable. Molten lava poured off gray-black skin as red pupils gleamed at her.

"Come to me."

She tried desperately to fight it, her feet scrambled against the edge of the pit. Kira's whole body shook. She would not let him take her. She would fight him.

"No!" she shouted. She flung her hands up, trying to keep the Demon Lord away, but instead, she found her body being drawn to him. Her hands touched his leathery skin and began to burn. Screams tore from her as she felt herself consumed by the lava.

Someone was shaking her hard.

Sitting up, Kira rubbed her bleary eyes and saw Shin in the dim light.

"I was walking outside when I heard you moaning. I thought you were sick, so I came in to check on you," he said. "Are you all right?"

She folded her arms around herself. "It was just a bad dream."

"Must have been one awful dream," he said. "It was hard waking you."

He leaned forward to brush her hair from her face, his fingers lingering over the long strands.

Uncomfortable, she slapped his hands off.

"Stop it," she said.

"I'm sorry." He straightened up. "Do you want to talk about it?

Kira shook her head.

"Sometimes it helps to talk about your nightmares so you can fall asleep again."

She thought of the last time she had shared her dream with Jaewon. It was odd to realize that had it been Jaewon sitting beside her, she would have gladly talked about her harrowing vision. These two men invoked such different responses from her. She felt comfortable with Jaewon; she could talk to him about anything. But Shin Bo Hyun, who she'd known all her life, filled her with tense discomfort. Sitting in her ger alone with Shin felt strangely disloyal.

"I'm all right," she said. "Thanks for checking up on me."

They were both silent for a long moment. Shin was stiff and unlike himself as he gazed down at his hands. He cleared his throat before speaking again.

"If you would like some company, I can sit with you,"

he offered. "That way if you have another dream, I can wake you."

Kira shook her head. "I'd rather you didn't."

Disappointed, he stood up and looked around the ger. He seemed reluctant to leave her.

"I know we've had our differences in the past, but now we are starting fresh," he said. "I'm here for you. I want to help you."

"Shin Bo Hyun, if you want to help, then take your army and go fight with my brother to stop the daimyo," she said. "That's the only thing I want."

"Then that's what I'll do," he said. "Because I would do anything for you."

With a gallant bow and one last smile, he left her ger, leaving her in a state of troubled confusion. His words were identical to what Jaewon had spoken earlier. How could two such different men say something so similar? She didn't like the sense of obligation it imposed on her. This was not something she wanted to deal with. Frustrated and annoyed, Kira fell into an uneasy sleep.

20

After several days of rest, Jaewon was finally ready to journey again. Kira tried to keep Shin from escorting them, but he refused.

"I will see you safely wherever you need to go," he said.

Since they needed the extra protection of his guards, Kira could not object. But Jaewon made his unhappiness and distrust of Shin painfully clear. Jaewon did not like when Shin would approach Kira and would find reasons to interrupt them or hover nearby. The only person more annoyed than Jaewon was her brother Kwan, who forcibly placed himself between his sister and Shin at every chance. It was all too much for Kira. She was already so confused by all of the emotions that were raging through her. But the hostility among the three men gave her a headache.

The only relief Kira had was knowing that Chansu would not be coming with them. The young soldier pleaded with Shin to let him come but was turned down. Chansu made no attempt to hide his anger. It was clear that he blamed her for taking away his beloved leader.

"If anything happens to Chief Shin, I will come after you," he vowed.

Kira smirked at him. "You can try."

He shot her a nasty glare before storming off. Kira wondered what she'd done to garner such dislike from him. This was not just the normal prejudice she had endured over the years. His hatred was personal and she didn't know why.

"How long will it take to reach Mount Baekdu?" she heard Taejo ask.

"If we are lucky and the storms hold off, it will take us another five days," Shin replied.

Five more days! Kira didn't think she could stand them for five more minutes. Her emotions were confusing her. Never before had she been in the position of being the center of attention of two such different men. She still didn't completely trust Shin, but Jaewon's blatant animosity toward him was irritating. It was easier to avoid them both.

On the third day of travel, Kira sensed something different. A niggling feeling in her gut told her danger was near.

She opened all her senses and noted the hint of demon that was getting stronger.

"Demons are on our trail," she told the others.

"From what direction?" Shin asked.

Kira pointed to the west, in the direction they had come from.

"We need a decoy," Shin said. He looked over their group. "We'll send two of my men with the packhorses north while we head south and then return to our original route."

Kwan and Kira conferred for a moment and agreed.

They quickly split up the groups and followed through with their plans. Kira's group, led by Shin and six of his soldiers, left first, riding south along the Yalu River before heading back onto their chosen route. The other group would wait as long as it could, messing up the trail, before heading north.

Another day passed and Kira knew the decoy hadn't worked. That sick sense of impending doom still followed, along with the foul stench.

A sudden movement caused Kira to let loose her arrow. An imp shrieked and fell into a black pool of its blood. More rustling in the trees followed as Kira shot several more arrows, killing three more imps.

"We've got to pick up the pace," she said.

They were riding alongside the Yalu River, weaving in and out of the forest line. The urgency with which she pushed the others was hampered by the wet, muddy terrain of the riverbank. It was no use. She sensed how close their pursuers were and she knew they were not demon-possessed humans but something worse. She knew she was right when she noticed how odd Jindo was acting. The big dog would often growl and then whimper.

"Taejo, I need to put Jindo up with you," Kira said.

Her young cousin stopped, and Kira quickly lifted the heavy dog onto his horse. Jindo was shivering with fear and kept his head turned, staring at something they couldn't see.

One moment there was no one behind them, and in the next, large creatures were charging after them at incredible speeds.

"What are those things?" Shin asked.

"Half-breeds! Half human, half demon. They're stronger and faster than demon-possessed humans and a lot harder to kill," she said. "Move! Move now!"

She launched herself onto her horse and urged it forward.

With a howl, a half-breed leaped at the rear guard, pulling him down in a haze of blood mist. Their supply horses broke free and raced off in terror. They were too close.

"Get in the river!" Kira yelled.

"That's crazy! We won't make it!" Shin pointed at the

roaring rapids, where huge ice boulders, rocks covered with ice, flew by.

The horses reared in terror, one flinging off its rider before running into the woods, only to be sliced to shreds by a half-breed.

As if sensing that the worse danger came from behind, the rest of the horses allowed themselves to be led into the dangerously flowing river. Their horses tried in desperation to swim with the rapids, but they were all being swept downstream. One of their soldiers was swept into the current and pulled into the middle of the river, where he was instantaneously crushed by a massive ice boulder. Kira guided her horse after them. Grabbing the bag with the tidal stone, she asked it for calm waters. Immediately, the flow of the water in which she stood slowed. The others gathered around her.

"Can you calm the entire river so we can cross?" Kwan asked.

Kira shook her head. "The problem is those things."

In the middle of the wide river, large and small ice formations were crashing into one another within the rapids. Some were jagged and pointed ice blocks, while others were frozen clusters of debris.

"I can control the water but not the rocks. Where we are now, I can direct them away from us, but in the middle of the rapids—" She shook her head. "There's far too many. I don't think I can divert them all. We can't dodge them. They would crash right into us. It's too dangerous."

"You must at least try," Kwan urged.

Kira focused on the river and tried to calm a path through to the other side. The water stilled, but the churning rapids upriver still sent the ice debris crashing into the calm water. Kira diverted the flow of the rapids toward the other side of the riverbank, but this sent a series of ice debris crashing into the trees and ricocheting into the river. Waves crashed over their heads before Kira could calm the water again.

They were now floating as a group in the one calm section of the river. Their legs were ice-cold from the freezing water. She could see the fear on everyone's faces. Brother Woojin rubbed his prayer beads between his fingers and chanted, while Taejo and Seung hunched down in their saddles. Poor Seung was shaking. It touched her to see how Taejo was trying to comfort the older boy.

As their horses swam, the half-breeds kept pace with them along the riverbank. Approximately thirty of them lined the river. Their long flowing black hair and pale faces looked almost human, but their eyes gave them away. They were large and completely black, lidless and unblinking. In her mind, she was in her nightmare again, watching the daimyo create a half-breed. She could still hear the agonizing scream of the young man who'd been sucked into the demon. Looking at the half-breeds now, she perceived no sign of any humanity left.

"What are they doing?" Jaewon asked, his voice beginning to sound weak.

She flashed him a look of concern. He was still not fully recovered from his wounds.

"Don't you remember your lessons with Sunim? They're half demon, so they can't survive in bodies of water," she said. "They can get wet, although I'm sure they don't like it. But a moving body of water will send their demon souls straight back into the underworld."

Two leaped into the river, trying to jump on them. But they fell short, floundering in the water, and steam rose in clouds from their bodies before they disappeared from sight.

Kira gave a derisive laugh. "And they're not too bright, either."

"It's no use. We have to return to shore," her brother said. "We'll all freeze to death if we stay in here."

A half-breed took a running leap and landed on one of Shin's men who had floated too close to shore.

Kira waved her arm over the water, sending a huge tidal wave at the half-breeds. The wave swept several of them into the river, but not enough. Within minutes, they were regrouping again, wet and furious.

"Don't do that, Kira!" Kwan said coughing up water. "You'll drown us all in the process."

She saw that her actions had soaked everyone and nearly sent Brother Woojin into the pathway of the ice boulders. Only Kwan's quick thinking had saved the monk. Infuriated, Kira grabbed her bow and arrow and began to shoot as many half-breeds as she could, downing seven of the creatures. The remaining half-breeds screamed and raged in protest. But still, there were too many of them.

Shin turned to Kira.

"Our horses are tiring. They won't last much longer," he said.

She knew he was right. They couldn't stay in the water anymore. She reached for another arrow, when Shin stayed her hand.

"You don't have many left—you need to make each one count. My men and I will charge them; you give us covering fire and then get out of here," he said.

Kira's lips tightened as she recognized the sacrifice he was proposing. She reached for his hand and pressed it tight between hers before releasing him.

"I told you I would do anything for you." He ran a cold finger against her cheek and gave her his sideways smile. "It was good to see you again, Kira."

Moments later, he and his men charged into the middle of the half-breed horde. Kira and Kwan felled as many creatures as they could with their remaining arrows as Major Pak led the others out of the river.

Kira watched as Shin fought like a possessed man in the thick of battle. His horse was cut down from under him, and he rose up with two swords, moving so quickly that he dispatched several half-breeds before they could blink. She'd never seen anyone so magnificent. Two half-breeds turned toward them. Shin charged after them, gutting one and catching the other by its long hair before slicing its throat. For a brief moment, Kira caught Shin's eyes and saw him nod before he continued to battle the half-breeds.

"Kang Kira! Sweep them into the river now!" Major Pak shouted.

"I can't! It'll take Shin Bo Hyun and his men too!"

"They might have a better chance in the river!"

Just then she saw that the half-breeds had killed most of Shin's men and were heading toward them. Shin was surrounded but still fighting valiantly.

"I'm sorry, Shin Bo Hyun," Kira whispered.

With a flick of her wrist, Kira sent a tremendous wave of river water gushing between her and the attackers. Ice boulders slammed into the half-breeds and the entire riverbank was flooded. There was no sign of Shin or his men.

As they rode away, she could hear the echo of Shin Bo Hyun's battle cries ringing in her ears and her heart ached with a surprising grief.

21

Since leaving Shin Bo Hyun behind, Kira was very quiet. Once again she was responsible for trying to drown him. He'd survived the flood before; could he do it again?

Why would he sacrifice himself? She kept praying to the heavens that he survived. This time, the idea of Shin dead was actually upsetting her. She didn't want to think of him or his sacrifice at all. Why did he do it? Why did his men unquestioningly follow him into certain death? It was difficult for her to reconcile the actions of Shin with her memories of the man. And yet, whoever he had been was no longer who he was. The idea that this new man could be gone tormented her.

The ache in her heart made it hard to breathe. Confused by her thoughts and the ever-growing pain, Kira kept to herself.

All of Shin's guards were gone and only one remained from their original contingent of fifteen soldiers. They'd lost their supply horses and no longer had their tents to protect them from the weather. The snowstorms had stopped but the wind that whipped through them was bone-chilling. One night they slept in a cave, another night in an abandoned farmhouse. But the last two nights were spent sleeping in the cold, huddled close together near their campfire.

Their supplies were dangerously low when they spotted a small village. Kira took the lead with Kwan right behind her. There was no sign of demons, but something seemed wrong. She detected a whiff of an unusual scent that was hard for her to identify. It wasn't human, but it wasn't demon. And yet it had a demon-like feel to it. Sort of how shaman magic always smelled slightly of demon.

The only sign of life came from a large tavern at the center of the village. It glowed with a hospitable light and they could smell the inviting aromas of an elaborate feast.

Kira was wary.

"What is it? A demon?" Kwan asked.

"I'm not quite sure what it is," said Kira.

"Then it isn't a demon," Major Pak cut in.

She was about to disagree, but she paused. It wasn't

something she could put her finger on. She didn't know what it was. "I just don't know," she said.

"Then we will enter, but cautiously."

Kira spotted the flash of bright reddish-orange tails in the periphery of her vision.

Foxes. If foxes were living here, then it meant that it was a good food source for them. She hoped that whatever they were feeding on wasn't human.

When they reached the tavern, Kwan fell off his horse in his haste to enter the establishment.

"Oppa!" Kira shouted. "Don't go in!"

Without acknowledging her, Kwan ran into the building. Major Pak and his soldier had dismounted and were headed toward the doors. Even Jaewon and Seung seemed entranced as they slid down from their horses. Only Taejo and Brother Woojin seemed unaffected by the pull of the strange magic.

As she dismounted, Kira could hear Jindo's fierce growls. Looking down at the white dog, she was unsurprised to see his hackles raised, his fierce gaze glued to the tavern doorway.

Kira turned to Taejo and Brother Woojin. "Stay here. Whatever you do, do *not* enter the building. Understand?"

They both agreed, Taejo looking on with wide-eyed concern.

"Keep Jindo close by your side but let him go if you hear me calling for him," she said.

Kira grabbed Jaewon and Seung by their coats and

slapped them hard on the back of their heads. Turning them around, she pushed them over to Taejo.

"Guard the prince!"

She ran past the other men, reaching the doors before anyone else could enter the premises. Drawing her sword, she stood before them, blocking the door.

"I'm afraid I can't let you go in," she said.

Dazed and confused, the soldier stopped, but Major Pak still tried to pass her.

"Major Pak!" she called. She observed the effort it took him to control himself. "There's strong magic here. You must return to the prince and guard him."

Pak shook his head hard, slamming a fist to his own forehead. Grabbing the other soldier by the arm, they returned to the prince's side.

Leaving them behind, Kira entered the tavern. She was deluged by the overwhelming odor of burning incense, mingled with the different scents of tantalizing food. Underneath it all was the rotten stench of death and decay. Her head pounded from the sensory overload. Wiping a hand over her burning eyes, she sighted her brother kneeling before a woman dressed in a flowing hanbok of red and gold silk. Her face was that of a beautiful woman with sharp, narrow features, but when she turned to look at Kira, her true form showed clearly. Her eyes were a bright amber with flecks of reddish gold shot through the vivid irises. The woman was not human, but a kumiho, a nine-tailed fox demon.

Her brother was enthralled by her beauty and under its sway.

Kira's first instinct was to kill the kumiho, but something stayed her hand—a memory of an old tale that her father had once told her. It had been about a soldier who had fallen in love with a kumiho. When the kumiho was slain by the soldier's brother, the soldier had fallen into a deep madness from which he never recovered.

She could not kill the kumiho yet. Their only hope was for her brother to recognize the kumiho's true identity.

Kira approached slowly, her sword raised.

"Why do you threaten me like this when I sit here before you unarmed?" the kumiho asked.

Kwan leaped to his feet. "Kira, are you crazy?" he sputtered. "Put your weapon down at once!"

"Oppa," Kira said in a low voice, "you know who I am and what I do. Do not let the magic confuse you further."

Kwan looked perturbed. He stared at the kumiho. "Are you telling me that she is a demon?" he asked uncertainly. "No, that can't be right. You're wrong for once."

But he looked unsure. Kira stood before him.

"I will prove it to you," she said.

"Don't hurt her!" Kwan thundered.

Kira nodded. Walking to the door, she opened it and called for Jindo. With a savage growl, Jindo raced into the room and charged at the kumiho.

The kumiho screamed and transformed into a fox,

cowering in a corner, its eyes the same amber color as those of the woman it had just appeared to be. Kira grasped Jindo by the scruff of his neck and held him back, not wanting to have him kill the creature.

Kwan gasped. "A kumiho!"

He staggered in disbelief. "You were going to seduce me and then eat my heart!"

With the kumiho revealed, the enchantment over the place was lifted and truth was revealed. The tempting feast of just a moment ago was now nothing but old bones and garbage. The place stank of rotted flesh. In a corner lay a huge pile of bones and the belongings of dead men. So deep were the piles that it was clear the kumiho had killed at least a hundred men.

Kwan began to retch.

He reached for his sword. "You foul creature!"

Kira stayed her brother's hand, staring at the fox, which was hissing and yipping in fear. Its nine tails bristled in alarm, fanning behind it in vivid color. There was something pitiful about the creature.

No, please don't kill me. I can help you!

The voice came from inside Kira's head. Surprised, she pointed her sword at the kumiho.

"Get out of my head!" she yelled.

Please, I can only speak to you this way in my true shape. But I can help you.

"Help us? How?"

Escape from the demons.

Kira studied the kumiho and wondered if she was being foolish to risk accepting its help.

I can help you, I promise. But we must move quickly. Already the abominable ones are closing in.

Kira asked her brother to leave with Jindo and wait outside with the others.

"I can't leave you with that creature!" Kwan shouted.

"Just wait with Jindo by the door. I will be fine," she said.

Once they left, the kumiho reverted to her human form.

"You have demons right on your trail. Even now as we speak, they are heading toward this village." The kumiho spoke with a languid air of certainty.

"How do you know this?" Kira asked.

"I have the ability to see brief visions of the future. They give me an idea of what is to come," the kumiho said.

"How close are they?"

"We don't have much time."

Kira knew the half-breed pack would be after them again, but she had no idea how to evade them. She pushed aside the thought that Shin was probably dead.

"We need to get to Mount Baekdu," Kira said.

"I can help you. I can take you to the River God's underground lair," the kumiho said. "No human knows of its whereabouts and it is protected by the River God. The demons cannot follow you there."

Kira felt a surge of hope. "You can take us there and get us safe passage?"

The kumiho raised a delicate hand. "I will help you by telling you what you must do when you see the daughters of the River God, but you will have to bargain with them alone."

"But how can they help us? What do I ask them?"

"The River God's palace is deep underwater and can only be reached by their special underwater boat. If you are able to strike a deal with the maidens, then you can use their boat to take you close to Mount Baekdu. However, although they are cousins of the Heavenly Maidens, they are not alike. The River Maidens are indifferent to the welfare of humans. They are more likely to kill you than help you. But I will tell you the secret of how to receive a boon from them. That is the most I can grant you."

"It is enough," Kira said. "And in return, what is it you want?"

"To be human, like you," the kumiho responded.

"But that's impossible!"

"Nothing is impossible. The gods themselves blessed the Ungnyeo and changed her bear form to that of a woman. I want that, too, to be human. To have a soul."

"You think eating the hearts and livers of human men will change you?"

The kumiho was silent. After a long pause she closed her eyes and breathed deeply. Kira felt a push, as if someone had tapped her on the head. The next moment, images flashed before her eyes. The beautiful kumiho seducing men, pleading with them to accept her for who she was. The men eagerly agreeing until she transformed into her true shape, then recoiling in horror or attacking in anger. The kumiho killing the man she'd loved and eating his heart and liver as tears poured down her face.

Kira was appalled and yet moved by the scenes she saw. The kumiho seemed to feel something similar to human emotion.

"I thought eating human flesh would turn me into a human, but it has been a lie. It leaves me thirsting for more blood. And all it does is heighten my fox senses."

"So, again, I ask you. What do you want from me?" Kira stared into the kumiho's beautiful eyes, trying to gain an understanding of the creature.

"I want you to show me what it feels like to be a true woman."

A surprised laugh left Kira's lips.

"And how can I possibly do that?"

"Let me into your mind."

Kira recoiled. "No!"

"I offer you safety in exchange for sharing your memories. Where is the harm?"

"How can I trust that you will help us?"

"You must decide one way or the other," the kumiho said. "I promise that I will keep my word. But I will also offer you something else. You travel a dangerous road.

A look into the future, a window into seeing what is to come and perhaps the choices facing you; this is the special gift I will give you."

Kira was unsure what to do. The kumiho had already killed many men, probably by pretending to be a tavern owner. Could Kira trust that she would not do this again?

"I am done with this life, I can promise you that," the kumiho said. "I will seek another way to become human."

If the half-breeds were close by, Kira had no choice but to take the kumiho up on her offer.

"I will agree, but you must take us to safety first and then I will let you into my mind," Kira said.

"Now it's my turn to ask how I can trust *you*," the kumiho said with a slight smile.

"You can't, but you have my word. And the knowledge that I could kill you here and now."

The kumiho's eyes filled with a mixture of sadness and humor before she inclined her head in agreement.

"Then you must follow me closely," she said.

They exited the tavern together, joining Taejo and the others. As soon as Jindo saw the kumiho, he began to growl. Ignoring him, the kumiho morphed into a nine-tailed fox.

Everyone gasped at the metamorphosis.

"Do not harm her," Kira ordered. "The kumiho is helping us."

"Young mistress, do you feel that is wise?" Brother Woojin asked, a worried frown wrinkling his face.

"Can't you see her aura?" Kira asked.

Brother Woojin shook his head. "Creatures of the otherworld do not have auras," he said.

"Then for once, I ask that you trust me," Kira said. She looked each member of the group steadily until they all agreed.

Follow me. Kira heard the fox's voice in her head again.

"If you betray us, I will shoot you through your heart," Kira said. "Know that you will not escape my arrow."

The kumiho shook its fox head at her sadly. *You asked your men to trust you; now I must ask the same of you.* Kira heard in her mind again. The kumiho lifted its head and sniffed the air. *We must fly. The abominable ones are almost here.*

Kira ordered the others to follow, giving them no chance to argue with her.

The kumiho ran ahead, its nine reddish-orange tails whipping behind it like flags in a heavy wind. Kira stayed right on its tracks as the others rode close behind her. They wove through the thickest part of the forest and over rough terrain. The colorful tails flew ahead, but ever visible, until finally the kumiho stopped beside a steep granite rock face. It pawed at a small crevice for several seconds. A grinding sound filled the air as the face of the wall parted, forming a narrow opening.

"Where are we?" Jaewon asked in wonderment.

"This is the hidden entrance to the River God's domain," Kira answered.

Release your horses here, the kumiho said.

They all dismounted and released their horses.

Before entering the cavern, Kwan pulled Kira aside. "How do you know this isn't a trap?" he asked.

"I don't know how to explain my feeling to you. All I know is that my heart tells me to trust her," she said.

Inside the cavern, they found the tunnel was lit by eerie phosphorescent lights, similar to what Kira had seen in the cave behind Nine Dragons Waterfall. When the last of them stepped inside, the rock face slid shut. Major Pak and his soldier lit torches, as the glow within the cavern was too dim to see by.

The kumiho led them down into a narrow passageway that headed farther underground. They walked single file, Kira behind the fox, then Kwan, Taejo, Jindo and the others. No one spoke as their steps echoed within the tunnels. To their surprise, they heard the sound of water lapping on a shoreline. As they reached the end of the tunnel, they found themselves in a thick forest. It was the most extraordinary vision: an underground forest, no different from any they would find above land except that when they looked up, instead of the sky all they saw was a rocky cave interior. They walked through the woods until it opened into an enormous cavern, where an underground river flowed. The forest ended at a beautiful sandy beach with an elaborate gold pavilion.

Shafts of sunlight filtered down from small holes in the high ceiling, bringing fractured light into the cavern and glinting off the sparkling stones and iridescent pearls that covered the pavilion.

The kumiho morphed into her human form.

"This is where I will leave you," the kumiho said. "When darkness falls, the daughters of the River God will dine together in their pavilion. Stay hidden in the forest. Do not step foot inside until they invite you in. When you enter, bring only yourself and the prince. You may eat or drink anything they offer the both of you. However, when the princesses offer any of their food or drink to your men, do not let the men partake. Otherwise they will be beguiled and will want to stay with the river princesses forever."

Kira nodded, listening carefully.

"Are they not like the Heavenly Maidens at all?" she asked.

The kumiho laughed. "Just because they are related does not mean they are similar. Be very wary of them. They are capricious and dangerous. You must capture one of the princesses and hold tight to her, no matter what happens. She is pure magic and can change into any form. If you manage to hold her until she tires, then will she grant your wish. Be warned, it will come with a price. You must willingly give up something you treasure to her," the kumiho said.

Kira bowed deeply. "Thank you. You have saved all of us."

"But now I will claim my prize," the kumiho replied.

Nodding, Kira sat on the cool sand before the fox girl.

She gazed into the kumiho's jewel-toned eyes, noticing how the reddish gold flecks seemed to enlarge and take over the irises. The kumiho placed her hands on Kira's head and pushed into her mind. Kira reached for her tidal stone and held her thoughts firm, not allowing the kumiho to overwhelm her. It was a strange sensation, as if someone was thinking along with her. Slowly the kumiho's mind began to seek images of the life Kira had led. Her life from when she was a little girl began to fly through her brain in rapid succession. The kumiho sighed in pure satisfaction—soaking in the emotions of love, jealousy, hate, sorrow, anger, and envy. She was particularly interested in the memory of Kira's first meeting with Jaewon and her recent emotional turmoil over Shin Bo Hyun. The kumiho seemed to be curious about the guilt and sorrow that Kira had experienced. She lingered over the memory of Jaewon's impassioned declaration to Kira from his sickbed.

Thank you, the kumiho's voice whispered in her head. It felt almost like a caress. *Now it is your turn.*

Images flooded Kira's head.

She saw her brother Kyoung rallying a huge army. She heard them chanting his name and then saw him leading them toward a large plain overlooking the shore. The ocean was filled with Yamato ships. She saw Kyoung fighting in a battle against half-breed demon soldiers.

Then there was the complete darkness of an underground cavern, shadows dancing and fighting all around her. Ghosts, spirits, and demons in a shadow world. Danger and agony. A question posed by a shadowy creature and a demand from another. She saw an explosion of fire and then the beautiful sight of pure white *chollimas*, winged horses, flying through the air.

The connection was abruptly cut off and Kira was left wishing she could keep the image of the chollimas with her forever. She contemplated the beautiful foxy features of the girl kumiho, who gazed at her with eyes that seemed almost human. As she watched, the face shifted, growing furry and pointed as the kumiho transformed into its normal body.

"Wait!" Kira called. "What is your name?"

I would like you to call me Nara, the kumiho said.

"Thank you, Nara. Thank you for saving us."

With a nod, the fox fled, its nine luxurious tails flowing behind it.

22

As night fell in the underground cavern, Kira found that it was not quite as dark as she'd feared. The cavern ceiling was covered with luminescent crystals that shimmered against the reflecting water. Her group had camped themselves in the woods behind the pavilion. Taejo was propped up against a tree next to Seung and Brother Woojin with Jindo sleeping by his side. The cave was cold but not as bad as outside. Kira unfastened her coat and took off her nambawi, sticking it into her bag.

Kira's thoughts kept returning to the kumiho. Like Shin Bo Hyun, here was another being who confused her. Although she should abhor the rampant murder that the kumiho had committed, what she really felt was pity and a sad sort of understanding. The kumiho wished for a human nature that was at odds with her animal one. And yet there were facets of the fox demon that were almost humanlike. It was what made Nara so appealing to Kira. There was something about her that Kira liked. She wished the kumiho well, and hoped that one day their paths would cross again.

Not too long after, unseen hands lit lanterns within the pavilion, and she watched in shock as platters of food began to appear upon the long tables inside.

The water began to surge forward as if a large tidal wave were upon them. From the crystal waters flowed small, jewel-toned dragons that rose onto their hind legs and morphed into beautiful women. They were dressed in flowing silk dress robes of emerald and gold that bared their shoulders, arms, and midriffs. Jewels covered their arms and necks, and gems winked inside their belly buttons. Their hair was jet-black and left flowing down, nearly to their feet. Their skin varied in color from pale white to light brown, but all of the maidens' eyes were a vibrant green.

The women walked across the sand, laughing and chatting as they headed to the pavilion. When they reached the pavilion door, the lead maiden stopped.

"Sisters, I believe we have visitors," the maiden said.

"I smell men, several of them," another replied, peering about her coyly.

"Show yourself now," the maiden commanded, "or I will flood the area and you will all surely drown."

Kira revealed herself first and motioned for the others to join her.

"My ladies, we are on a mission set for us in part by your cousins, the Heavenly Maidens. We must seek the Dragon King's treasure at Mount Baekdu. But we are in mortal danger from half-breed abominations that hunt us," she said. "We seek your help."

"We do not involve ourselves in the problems of humans," the head maiden said with a dismissive air. She turned to enter the pavilion but the other sisters lingered, staring at Kira and Taejo with fascination.

"Sister, do let them in! We haven't had human company in so very long," she beseeched.

"Yes, do let them in," chimed in the other sisters.

The oldest snapped her teeth in a very dragon-like way. "Men are not allowed in the pavilion, must I remind you, dear sisters?"

"That is fine," Kira interjected. "My men can stay outside. Only the boy and I will join you, if we may."

The younger sisters whined in protest, but the oldest smiled in approval.

"Very well—enter and share with us your troubles."

Kira and Taejo followed the sisters into the pavilion and sat at the very last seats at the long table, which was filled with exotic delicacies from the sea.

"Come and eat with us," the oldest sister invited.

Taejo filled his plate with the food before him and devoured his meal with no concern about what he was eating. Unlike her cousin, Kira was intrigued by the variety of food. Chewy noodles made of jellyfish with horseradish, broiled octopus sliced into thin slivers and sautéed in a peppery sauce, steamed whole fish of a species she'd never seen before, and crabs the size of a small dog. Everything was wonderful and yet peculiar. She listened to the sisters chatter as they ate their meal, and wondered at the banality of their conversation, given the urgency of her situation. They talked of their hair and complexions and their dresses and jewels. They could not have been more different from the Heavenly Maidens. They were as different as their habitats.

"Now, let us turn our attention to our guests," the oldest said. "What is it you wish from us?"

"We merely seek safe passage to Mount Baekdu," Kira answered.

"That we cannot do." The maiden was adamant. "We do not take humans into our domain unless you plan to stay with us forever."

"Can you show us a route through these caverns that we can take, then?" Kira asked.

The maidens all began to laugh.

"Not unless you are part fish," the youngest and smallest of the maidens said. "Several li from here, the cavern becomes entirely submerged by this river."

She leaned over to pat Kira consolingly on her arm.

Quick as a wink, Kira seized hold of the young maiden and wound the maiden's hair around both of her hands. There was a shriek of fury before the maiden began a series of metamorphoses. Kira found herself wrestling with a furious dragon that morphed into a slippery octopus that instantly changed into the largest eel Kira had ever seen. But through each change, Kira kept a tight hold of the maiden's hair, which seemed to remain the same no matter what she transformed her body into. The maiden continued to flash in and out of forms until she began to tire. Returning to her natural body, she collapsed into Kira's arms, sobbing uncontrollably.

"You win," she said. "I shall grant you one wish. Anything you want. But in return you must give me something you value!"

"I have your word?"

"Yes, now release me, you fiend!"

Kira let the maiden go. As soon as she was released, the maiden ran to huddle with her sisters.

"How dare they treat me like an animal! I say we kill them both now!"

"No, kill the girl but keep the boy. He'll be a handsome addition to our palace once he grows up," another sister said.

Before Kira could reach for her weapon, Taejo jumped to his feet and held his sword to the throat of the nearest maiden.

"Is this how you keep your promises? Is your word

meaningless?" Taejo spoke with a fierceness that belied his age. "Try anything on my cousin and I'll slice your head off!"

"No one will be harmed!" The oldest maiden had risen to her feet, her face a mask of fury. "You have my word on behalf of us all. Now release my sister!"

Taejo glanced at Kira, who nodded. Slowly, he withdrew his sword and sat down. Kira didn't change her expression, but she was so proud of him.

"We cannot take you all the way to Mount Baekdu, but we can take you as far as we can," the oldest maiden stated. "What will you give my sister in return for this boon?"

Kira thought over her possessions. There was so few she truly treasured, but those few she could not part with for anything. She began to worry about the sacrifice when the youngest maiden made her own demand.

"I want her hair!" she screamed. "She ensnared me by my own hair. It is only right that I have hers in return."

The sisters began to nod in agreement.

Kira didn't hesitate. Grabbing a sharp knife from the table, she cut off her long braid and handed it to the youngest. All the maidens crowed in delight.

"Now her hair will match her face," the youngest said with a malicious smile.

Free of the heavy weight of her braid, Kira could feel her hair puffing around her head. She glanced into a long mirror that hung inside the pavilion walls. Her hair had curled up all around her face into loose waves like brown wriggly snakes.

Realizing that the maiden wanted to see her upset by this action, Kira forced herself to show an aggrieved expression. But inside, she was relieved that she would not have to give up something of more value to her. What did she care about her hair? Eventually it would grow again, as hair always did.

The oldest maiden stood up and clapped her hands, gathering her sisters around her. With a languid wave of her hand, she indicated for Kira and Taejo to follow them. They exited the pavilion behind the maidens.

Outside, Kira recognized the bewitched expressions on the faces of the men, even Jaewon's, as the maidens went past them. Jindo growled softly as they passed him, causing the oldest maiden to hiss at him. The large dog jumped in alarm and hid behind Seung, quivering in fear.

The youngest maiden circled their last soldier with a look of intense concentration. His expression was the most besotted of them all. Kira felt the hair on her neck stand up, but before she could issue a warning the oldest maiden began to chant by the riverbank. The water began to froth, then it heaved up a submerged structure, shaped like a gigantic turtle. It was made of a lacquered wood that was intricately carved and decorated with pearl inlays and studded with gems. At the stern of the ship, facing them, the doors split open wide like a clamshell. Inside there was a lavishly decorated room, as plush as anyone would find in the palace at Hansong. The carpeted floor was covered with thick cushions and the walls were decorated with beautiful paintings, hung in between lit lanterns that brightened the room.

"We use this conveyance when our cousins, the Heavenly Maidens, come to visit us at our underwater kingdom," the oldest maiden said. "It should serve your purposes well."

Before they could enter the turtle-shaped boat, the youngest maiden darted around Kira and threw her arms around their last soldier's neck. Quickly morphing into her dragon form, the maiden roared and dragged the frightened man into the water. Jindo raced forward, barking angrily at the turbulent water.

Everyone was too stunned to react. The last of Major Pak's men was now gone. The oldest maiden gave Kira a little smirk.

"Don't worry, he will be fine," she said. "You'd better hurry if you want this ride. It will take you as far as it can and then you are on your own. Good luck."

One by one, the maidens turned into dragons and dived into the water.

"Let's go," Kira said.

They all entered the boat. As soon as everyone was safely onboard, the door closed and they began to drift with the current.

"The maiden said that the cavern is all underwater," Taejo said with a hint of nervousness, "but it won't leak since this is for the Heavenly Maidens, right?"

"We'll soon see," Kira said.

"What will happen to that soldier?" Taejo asked.

Brother Woojin said a quick prayer to the heavens before answering. "I once heard an odd tale of a man who was taken by the daughter of the River God. He lived happily in the underwater palace for what he thought was a couple of years. One day he started to worry about his elderly mother. He asked to return to the human world to see his mother once again, but when he arrived, he found that no one knew him and his mother had been dead for nearly one hundred years."

"What happened to him?" Taejo asked. "Did he return to the underworld palace?"

"He couldn't," Brother Woojin replied. "He was said to wander the riverbanks calling for his lost love, until he died of a broken heart."

"Well, that was a cheery tale," Jaewon remarked. The boat picked up speed, causing Jaewon to pale.

"How will we know when we are underwater?" he asked.

The turtle boat took a sudden dip that caused them all to fall onto the cushioned floor. After the dip, the boat steadied.

"That must have been it," Kira said. "At least it isn't as rough as our ship ride."

Jaewon still looked uneasy, but he agreed. "My stomach doesn't feel like jumping out of my mouth right now. Perhaps I'll survive."

He sat up and touched Kira's head.

"What happened to your hair?" he asked, staring at her short hair in astonishment.

"Forfeited for this ride," Kira said with a smile. "It was a cheap price to pay."

She touched the poufy hair that curled all about her face. "I guess I look ridiculous."

"You look fine," Kwan said. He glared at everyone as if daring them to contradict him.

There was a rush of words as they all began to compliment Kira's hair. Self-conscious, she leaned against the padded wall and lowered her head, letting her hair swing forward and cover her face.

"Well, this is as good a time as any to break for our meal," Seung said. He began to prepare their meager supplies. There was only a handful of dried squid pieces left. Kira and Taejo refused to take any, allowing the others to eat all that they had brought. Seung shared a piece of squid with Jindo, who licked Seung's face gratefully. Within minutes all their food was gone and their water skins were empty.

"Let's hope we find your clan close by," Kwan said. "We are in dire need of supplies."

"But in the meantime, we should rest while we are warm and safe," Kira said.

The gentle motion of their underwater ship was soothing, and pretty soon everyone had fallen into an exhausted sleep but Kira and Jaewon.

"Your hair really does look pretty," Jaewon said.

She ran her hands through her hair. "You don't have to say that. I don't mind losing it."

"I don't mind either," he said. "I would never have known that your hair was so wavy. It suits you. You look less intimidating."

"Well, that's no good," Kira said. "I liked being scary looking."

"Now you have to settle for being charming."

Kira made a gagging noise. "Don't call me that. I'll get mad, and you know what happens when I get mad."

Jaewon raised his hands in surrender. "I'm so sorry. You are not charming! Please don't hurt me!"

They lapsed into a long, comfortable silence. Kira was starting to feel sleepy when she heard Jaewon speak.

"He was a good man," Jaewon said.

Kira looked at him in surprise.

"What?"

"Your former betrothed," he said. "Regardless of what he'd done in the past, he died a hero."

"Don't say that!" Kira snapped. "He might not be dead!"

The look Jaewon gave her was sympathetic. "It would take a miracle."

"Yes, but I thought he was dead before, and he wasn't. I'm not going to make the same mistake again," she said. "He's a great fighter. He could have survived."

"If he did survive, would that change your opinion of him?" Jaewon asked.

"I don't understand—"

"You said you wouldn't marry him. Does his sacrifice change your mind?"

She didn't know how to respond. This was not a question that she wanted to think about, especially not knowing if he was dead or alive. A fresh wave of grief filled her, not just for Shin Bo Hyun but for everyone she'd lost. Throwing up her hands, she leaned against the wall and closed her eyes.

"I don't know," she said. "I don't know what to think anymore."

The quiet was broken by Seung's thunderous snores.

"He sacrificed himself to save you," Jaewon said. "He was most definitely a worthy suitor."

Ignoring his words, Kira settled down among the soft cushions and tried to fall asleep.

She was trapped inside a dark cave that had no exits. She stumbled around in circles, pounding on walls, screaming for someone, anyone to hear her. But she was truly a prisoner. Her body was heavy and she had trouble walking. All she knew was that something precious had been taken from her. And she had to get out in order to get it back. She would do anything to get it back. She threw herself against the crack in the wall, feeling the rock give. Her massive body felt slow and lethargic, but she could feel anger giving her strength. Over and over she threw herself against the wall, reveling in the cracks. Laughing as the wall began to break free.

Kira woke up when she felt the movement of the boat change from a quick but level pace to a slowly rising one. She felt the tilt and sway that signaled their landing, and then watched as the doors swung slowly open. She was still bleary and confused from the strange dream. It was not like any vision she'd ever had. She knew that it was a warning of what was to come, but it was as if it had happened to someone else. To some*thing* else. She just didn't understand what it could mean. It left her feeling completely out of sorts and off-balance.

A cold blast of wintry air filled the boat, clearing her head.

She quickly woke everyone up and picked up her bags. Jaewon was the first one out, closely followed by Jindo. They were on the snowy banks of the Yalu River, in the shadows of the mountains. In the distance, she took in the magnificence of Mount Baekdu, the great white-covered volcanic mountain. Once they were all outside, the River Maidens' boat closed itself up and submerged into the water. Kira watched the ship disappear with some dismay. The hours that they'd spent on the River Maidens' boat had been the safest any of them had felt in a long while.

A tremor of apprehension upset her stomach. She had no idea what to expect, but she feared the worst.

23

They walked through the snow-covered landscape, searching for Seung and Jaewon's clan. With the beginning of the fourth month the weather became milder, allowing the sun to shine through and melt some of the blinding snow. Even the wind seemed to let up. The worst of the winter weather was behind them. This made hunting easier, and Kira and Kwan were quickly able to shoot some rabbits and fowl.

Seung dug up edible roots and tubers from the snow, to supplement their meal. Kira was awed by his ability to cook simple meals that tasted good. They didn't go hungry, but Kira longed for a bowl of hot rice.

The closer they got to Mount Baekdu, the quieter Jaewon became. He was tense and withdrawn and began to eat less and less, refusing to speak of what was troubling him. Kira worried that Jaewon would make himself sick before they reached his clan.

Early in the morning of the third day of walking, Kira sensed strong shaman magic in the vicinity.

She scouted the area first, finding a new village of roughly built houses and farms and barnyards filled with animals. In the center of town there was an expansive communal kitchen area, where many women stood around chatting and cooking. Small children played in the melting snow and ran through the open stalls filled with woodworkers, weavers, blacksmiths, and other tradesmen. It was a bustling village, noisy and boisterous, where everyone seemed to have a purpose.

The magic that was protecting the village was very strong. Whoever their shaman was, he was a good one.

Returning to the others, she quickly told them what she'd found.

Seung beamed in delight. "That must be our clan! We have the best shaman in all Kaya! Possibly of all the Seven Kingdoms."

"Seung, you think we have the best of everything," Jaewon chided.

He stood staring off into space, his nervousness obvious to all of them. They all waited quietly, watching to see what Jaewon would do.

He let loose a shaky breath and put an arm around Seung. "Come on, old friend. Let's go find your family."

As they arrived in the village, they were met with immediate suspicion and reserve. Small children dropped their toys and ran for their parents. The friendly chatter of the women at the open-air stoves died down. Everyone turned and ogled the newcomers. One of the villagers approached them cautiously.

"Who are you?" he asked.

"Master Song, don't you recognize us?" Seung asked with a bright smile.

The man froze in place, his mouth opening and shutting like a carp.

"Chief Kim Jaeshik! Chief Kim Jaeshik!" The man ran stumbling across the village center, racing for the largest house.

Kira wouldn't have thought it was possible for Jaewon's face to get paler, but she was wrong. His complexion now rivaled the snow-covered ground, and his uneasy expression made Kira nervous for him. He looked as if he might faint.

Only Seung looked happy. The villagers who had been so quiet at their arrival were now yelling his name in joyful surprise. They embraced Seung and dragged him to a nearby hut. They banged on the door and shouted for the occupants to come see their surprise visitor.

Minutes later, happy shrieks filled the air as Seung was surrounded by a group of people who hugged him in a flood of tears and laughter.

Kira and the others still stood by Jaewon's side. The villagers bowed to him with respect and curiosity, but none tried to talk to him yet. It was just as well—Kira didn't think Jaewon could have spoken to anyone.

From the large hut across the village center, a man emerged.

Jaewon closed his eyes, his face a mask of fear and guilt. For a moment, Kira thought he would bolt. She put a hand under his elbow, steadying him as he rocked on his heels.

The chief's jaw convulsed several times as he stood where he was, gazing at his son with a fierce expression. There was a strong resemblance between the two men. Jaewon's father was a tall, broad-shouldered man whose sculpted features were an older version of his son's. No one seemed able to move; the air was tense and quiet.

Kira pulled Jaewon forward, making him walk across the square to meet his father. When they were a horse length from the chief, Jaewon stopped and refused to move any closer. The chief watched them closely.

"So, you have finally returned to us," Chief Kim said. His voice was raspy and deep.

"Father." Jaewon's voice cracked. "I've come home to take my punishment. I know that you can never forgive me. But I'm sorry. So sorry."

Chief Kim made a harsh sound. "Did I raise a son who runs away from his troubles?"

Jaewon's head bent lower, and tears coursed down his cheeks.

"I was wrong, Father, I was scared," he whispered. "I didn't believe you could ever forgive me."

"We lost two sons that day," Chief Kim said. "How could you do that to us?"

Jaewon flinched.

"I am so sorry."

"How can you be a leader if you run at the first sign of trouble? How can you become a good man if you reject your family? How can you be my son?"

Jaewon fell to his knees and hung his head in shame.

As much as Kira wished to stop Jaewon's pain, she knew she could not interfere. She folded her arms across her stomach, saddened by his ordeal.

"Jaeho died because it was his fate. But you chose to desert your family and your clan. You turned your back on all of us and that is your greatest sin."

The chief's words echoed in the silence. Jaewon was almost doubled over, his hands pressed against the snowy ground. After a long moment, he pushed himself up.

"You're right. I can never expect you to forgive me. How can I when I can't forgive myself? If I could, I would gladly give my life for Jaeho's and end my wretched misery."

He bowed deeply. "I know that I can ask for nothing, but can you let Seung return to the clan? He left only because of his loyalty to me, but it is time he came home. However, I will not burden you with my presence any longer."

The silence stretched for such a long moment, Kira became agitated. She was ready to interrupt when the chief spoke.

"So you would abandon us again!"

Jaewon froze, his face showing his uncertainty.

"Father, what is it you want me to do? Tell me and I will do it," he said.

"I want my oldest son to come home to me!"

Jaewon choked on a sob. He ran forward into his father's embrace. Father and son hugged each other tightly.

"My son, my son," the chief said over and over.

Kira blinked away her tears. She was awash in emotions. As happy as she was for Jaewon, she was overwhelmed by her own grief. At that moment, she missed her parents so much that she felt a physical pain in her chest. She struggled hard to contain herself.

Suddenly, the door behind them was flung open and an older woman, dressed only in her bedclothes, came storming out. Her hair was tangled and dirty and her face was a mix of grief and tormented fury. Several women tried to intercept her, but she pushed and hit and screamed at them. She broke free and came racing toward Jaewon.

"Murderer!" she screamed, and pointed at Jaewon. "He murdered my baby!"

She ran forward and began beating Jaewon with her fists. Alarmed, Kira pulled the woman off of him as Jaewon muttered "Mother" and "I'm sorry" over and over.

"No! Don't call me that! Don't you ever call me that!" Jaewon's mother spat on the ground. "You are no son of mine."

She turned and slapped Kira hard on the face. "Don't touch me, evil one! I should have known he would surround himself with the likes such as you. Stop looking at me, soul eater. I won't let you take me. I'll kill you!"

With a shriek Jaewon's mother raised her clawed hands at Kira's eyes. Jindo rushed at the woman, barking furiously. Kira wrapped her arms around Jindo and clamped a hand around his mouth, keeping him from attacking Jaewon's mother. She felt the crazed woman's nails gouge deep into her cheek before she was pulled off by the chief. Holding his wife by the waist, he carried her thrashing body away, her unholy screams ripping through the stillness of the crowd. Only then did Kira let go of Jindo, allowing him to lick her hands in comfort before returning to Taejo's side.

Kira saw Jaewon's ashen face, an expression of horrified agony distorting his good looks. She put a hand up to her cheek and realized it was wet with blood.

"This was a terrible mistake. I should never have come," he whispered.

With a sudden turn, he ran from the village. Seung rushed after him, calling his name, but Kira didn't move. She stared in stunned disbelief at the closed door of the chief's house, where Jaewon's mother continued to shriek.

24

Brother Woojin shook his head as he, Taejo, and Kwan came to stand by Kira's side.

"This is so sad," he said. "It is worse than I'd expected."

Taejo was angry. "I don't understand it. Why is his mother so mean? How can she be so cruel?"

The monk placed a gentle hand on the prince's shoulder. "She is not of her right mind anymore, Your Highness. We cannot judge her."

"Still, it's not right!"

Kwan ignored their talk. Instead, he grasped Kira by the chin and examined the painful gouges on her face.

"This needs to be cleaned thoroughly," he said.

Kira nodded, not trusting herself to speak. He hurried over to the women near the open pit to ask them for some clean water and cloths.

"Noona, it looks really bad," Taejo said. "Does it hurt?"

Kira shook her head absently, her attention captured by the sharp gaze of an old man. He had the eyes of a hawk and a long white beard. She could sense his power even from across the village square.

"Brother Woojin, who do you think that is over there?" Kira asked, motioning to the old man.

The monk peered over and crowed in delight. "Why, he has a beautiful violet aura! He is filled with magic! He must be the village shaman, and a very powerful one."

Kira wasn't surprised. She gave him a deep bow of respect and watched as he approached.

"It has been an unfortunate welcome for you all," he said. "My sincere apologies. The chief's wife has not been well since the loss of her youngest son. You must forgive her."

Kira was in no mood to forgive anyone, but she inclined her head in agreement. "Were you surprised that Kim Jaewon was able to find you?"

"Of course not," the shaman replied. "He's always known of these hereditary lands of ours—the lands of our Puyo forefathers. Once he heard of the evacuation, he would have had no doubt of where we would relocate. This was once an ancient city called Gaema. Now there's

214

nothing but the old city wall and some building foundations." He pointed to the large ruins of stone buildings that marked the outskirts of their village.

"We now have built our home here in what we call Northern Wagay village," Shaman Won said. "We may no longer be in Kaya, but Kaya will always be with us."

Kwan returned with a wet rag, but the shaman stopped him.

"Please, come to my home instead and let me treat her wounds," he said. "I am Shaman Won Ji-Mon, and it is an honor to meet the Demon Slayer in the flesh."

They followed the shaman to a large wooden hut with a straw thatched roof. Inside, the room was cozy and warm.

"Please take off your outer garments and sit," the shaman said.

The dirt floor was covered with layers of woven straw rugs. They piled their coats in a corner and sat on the ground.

"Master, how is your house so warm? There is no *ondol* flooring or stove," Taejo asked.

The shaman gave a knowing smile. "It is my magic and Mount Baekdu. It's not just a mountain, it is also a volcano."

Taejo's eyes widened in dismay. "How can you live here, then? Isn't it dangerous?"

"Perhaps it is inactive," Brother Woojin said.

The shaman shook his head. "Oh no, it is very much

active, my friend, which is why there is so much power here. For now, we are safe. One day it will indeed erupt again, but that day will not come for many years."

He brought over a small wooden bowl with a paste that smelled of ginseng, ginger, and something less pleasant. Kneeling before Kira, he smoothed the concoction over her cheek with a wooden spoon. The pain relief was immediate as the medicine cooled the burning of her wound.

"Thank you, Master," she said. "That feels much better already."

"Then I shall give you some to take with you," he said.

When he was done, he rose to his feet and spooned the salve into a small leather bag, which he wound tight and brought to Kira.

"I have been impressed by the protective wards that have been set up around this village," Kira said. "It would seem that most travelers would pass right by, as if the village would be invisible to them."

"I come from a family strong with magic. My family has guarded our clan for generations," Shaman Won said. He then pointed at the mountain beyond the village. "Ever since we came here, in the shadow of Mount Baekdu, the Whitehead Mountain, my powers have increased threefold. The magic is strong here."

The shaman pointed to the four corners of the village. "This entire area is under a misdirection spell, something I could not have done back at home. It's not just a repellant, for that would indicate that something was here. Rather, the spell causes them to avoid this area, which is how we are protected."

"How far does the magic extend?"

"Approximately twenty li around the village," he answered. "The spell also works on humans, but to a lesser extent."

"But how do you trade and survive?" she asked.

"We send all our trade to Wando or Jilin. There's no reason for anyone to seek us here," he replied. "Besides, we will not settle here forever. This is only our temporary home until we can return to our beloved Kaya."

The shaman seemed so confident.

"How are you so sure?" she asked.

"Because I have seen it," he replied.

Kira examined the shaman with sharp interest, noting the absolute sincerity with which he spoke.

"Please tell me what you have seen, Master," she said.

"I have seen you," he said, his eyes boring into hers. "I have seen you in battle. I have seen the prince being crowned king. I have seen peace."

"And how are you so sure that this is the true future?" she asked.

"I don't know for sure," he replied, "but I believe it."

"And what if I fail?"

"Then there is no future for any of us," he said.

His words drove her to her feet. Grabbing her coat, she ran out into the cold, propelled by a fear of failure.

Her chest was tight and her breathing agitated. She didn't want people depending upon her. She didn't want to be responsible for failing. Her job was solely to protect the prince.

And that is how you will save everyone, my little tiger.

Kira raised her face up to the bright blue skies. "Father, are you still watching over me?"

Grief brought hot tears to her eyes as she waited to hear her father's voice again. But she heard nothing except the sound of approaching footsteps. She wiped her tears and looked to see who it was.

Chief Kim walked slowly with his head down, his expression troubled. When he spotted her, a smile appeared on his face.

"You are the Demon Slayer," he said. "And you are a friend to my son."

Kira bowed. "Yes, sir. I'm proud to say I am."

"I'm glad to hear that. For he has been in need of good friends." He looked up at her with kind eyes. "Will you do me a favor? Will you find my son and bring him back? I plan to have a celebration for his return."

Kira was surprised. "But what of his mother?"

The chief heaved a great sigh. "She will not disturb us for the rest of the night. It will be safe for him."

Skeptical of his words but unwilling to turn down his request, Kira bowed and left the village. She'd been worried about Jaewon and had been on the verge of looking for him herself. Not too far from town, she ran into

Seung. He brightened when he saw her.

"Young mistress! You are just the person my master needs to see," he said. "He will not talk to me, he is deeply wounded. But I'm sure you will do him much good."

"Where is he?" Kira asked.

Seung pointed at a clearing at the other end of the woods. "He's not that far from here. He's by a small pond, sitting on a rock. You can't miss him."

Kira thanked him and weaved her way through the forest. When she found him, he was working on his wood carving.

"What are you making?" she asked.

He didn't look up. "Nothing."

Kira climbed up the rock and sat next to him, noticing how he tensed up at her nearness.

"Are you all right?"

"No."

"Do you want to talk about it?"

"No."

"Your father asked me to come and get you," she said. "He is really happy to see you again."

"I can't go back."

They sat in silence, listening to the sharp flick of Jaewon's knife as it scraped at the wood. Kira blew on her hands to warm them up, watching a cloud of frosty air rise up. She thought about what she had witnessed, and relived seeing the torment on Jaewon's face as his mother attacked him. She may have lost her parents, but she never doubted their love for her. The pain she felt for her own loss was now directed toward her friend. She couldn't imagine how he must be feeling.

Impulsively, Kira leaned over and hugged Jaewon around his shoulders, resting her face against his. Jaewon went completely still, and then he dropped his knife and wood and embraced her. Burying his face into her shoulder, he began to shake uncontrollably. He pulled her closer and hugged her tight, as if afraid to let her go. Kira held on, knowing how badly he was hurting and wishing she could take his pain away.

They stayed locked together for a long time. His tears slid down her neck, wetting her jacket, but she didn't move. Here, finally, was his release. He wept with hoarse sobs that brought answering tears to Kira's eyes. He held on to her as if she was the only thing real in the world.

She was no longer cold; heat cascaded through her. Sudden awareness of him caused her to shiver.

"You're cold," he whispered. He lifted his face to look at her.

Kira shook her head and swiped at his tears with her right hand. He turned his head to kiss her fingertips. Feeling a bit awkward, Kira scrunched up her face and swatted at his nose, laughing at his surprised expression.

Jaewon gazed at her with a tenderness that sent a rush of warmth up into her cheeks. Flushed and uncomfortable, she tried to free herself from his embrace.

"Don't," he whispered. "Please don't push me away this time."

His arms tightened, drawing her face right up to his. "I don't think I could bear it if you left me right now."

Kira tried to speak, but her mouth had dried up. She found herself staring mesmerized at his lips as he inched closer, until he breathed a soft sigh and placed them softly on hers.

She tasted ginger and honey, and something masculine and intoxicating. And then she lost any ability to think as he moved his mouth over hers. All she knew was that her body was aflame with the desire to get as close as possible to him. Her hands crept up his back and dug into his thick hair, grasping and pulling as the kiss turned more urgent. Dizzy and in shock, she pulled away and buried her head in her arms.

Her blood was still pounding in her ears when she felt the gentle brush of his hand on her hair.

"Don't be mad at me," he pleaded. He tried to pull her arms apart to sneak a peek into her face.

With a garbled curse, she straightened up and ran her hands through her short hair. Her face felt flaming hot.

"Are you mad at me?" he asked again.

"Yes."

"Don't be mad."

"Shut up."

He poked her in the ribs. "Please don't be mad." He poked her again.

Kira twisted his finger.

"Ow, all right, are we even now?" he asked with a pained look.

"I'm fine," she snapped. "I'm just cold. My behind is frozen and it's all your fault."

"Why don't you sit on my lap, then?" he asked.

Kira whirled around to glare at a grinning Jaewon.

"Why don't I punch you in the face?" she growled.

He pulled an exaggerated frown. "Are you still going to hit me when I'm a weak old man?" he asked.

"Why do you think I'd still be hanging around you when you are old and feeble?" Kira cocked an eyebrow at him.

He lay back on the rock, folding his arms behind his head. "I believe that my purpose in life is to stay by your side and irritate you."

"Then you will probably never make it to old age," she retorted.

"At least I will die happy," he replied.

Kira rolled her eyes and glared at him. "Are you never serious?"

His smile faded as he sat up and he stared beyond her, toward his village. Kira felt instant remorse. For a few moments there, he'd forgotten about his troubles. Impulsively, she reached over and held his hands.

"Then your new life is with me," she said. "I'll just have to explain to the chief that as much as he would want you to stay, you are on a mission with us and I cannot spare you."

His eyes searched hers with a desperate longing that hurt her to see.

"You would want me to be with you?" he asked.

Kira sighed dramatically. "I am stuck with you. Your life is intertwined with mine. Didn't the monks foresee it? I will just have to keep you busy so you don't drive me crazy."

Jaewon leaned forward, rested his forehead against hers, and closed his eyes. "Thank you," he whispered.

They returned to the village together. Jaewon was quiet but content as he walked close by her side. Kira wished she didn't feel so embarrassed. She had to force herself not to shy away from him when his arm would brush against her own, aware of how fragile his emotional state was. As uncomfortable as it was, she would never do anything to hurt him.

The chief met them as soon as they arrived. He'd clearly been watching for their return.

"Young mistress, why don't you and your brother go with our hunters and catch us some game to supplement our village feast tonight! Game is plentiful in this area, and you will enjoy the hunt." The chief put an arm around Jaewon's shoulders. "I would like to talk to my son and learn all about his travels."

Kira looked around and saw Taejo in deep conversation with the shaman.

She hesitated. She didn't want to take Taejo hunting given the danger they were in, and she was unwilling to leave his side.

"The prince can stay here in the village," Chief Kim said. "He will be completely safe. Shaman Won is the most powerful shaman in the Seven Kingdoms. It was because of his warning that we were able to flee from our village before the invasion. You can trust him."

Kwan came up to them, bowed to the chief, and passed Kira her weapons.

Kira gave her brother a questioning look. Kwan glanced at the prince and nodded. "He'll be fine," he said.

They hunted for two hours and returned with a boar, rabbits, and a brace of grouse by lunchtime. The women descended on the hunters, ordering them to skin and clean the game as they prepared to cook. Not long afterward, the village was awash in the aromas of delicious roasting meats and spicy stews from open pits in the village green.

As the sun set, all the villagers came to the large square. They each walked by the chief's residence and offered a bow of respect to the closed door before taking their place by the fire. Kira sat staring at the door herself, wondering what Lady Kim was doing and how the chief could be so sure Jaewon would be safe.

"Don't worry, young mistress, there will be no complications tonight."

Kira blinked in surprise and turned to face a dimpled woman with kind eyes who handed her a bowl of rice porridge.

Kira took the bowl with a nod of thanks. "But how do you know she will not come out?" she asked.

"Shaman Won has given her some herbal medicine that will keep her sedated until morning. Our young master will not have to worry," the woman said with a bow of her head before retreating.

Kira demolished her porridge quickly and watched the crowds. She found it fascinating how everyone congregated around the huge central campfire that warmed them in the frigid night. It would be more comfortable to take the food and eat inside, but no one was willing to miss the reunion of the chief and his son, and the stories they were bound to share. Spicy boar and cabbage stew were passed around in wooden bowls, while rice mixed with beans and meat was served with an assortment of vegetables.

She walked over to where Taejo, Brother Woojin, and her brother were sitting nearby the chief and Jaewon. Kira felt a strange bashfulness when her eyes met Jaewon's. His eyes were warm and his smile sweet before his attention was pulled back to his father. Kira sat next to her brother with a happy sigh, avoiding Kwan's suspicious gaze.

"Why are you smiling like that?" Kwan asked. He

leaned forward to gaze at Jaewon, who was absorbed in conversation with his father. "You look peculiar."

"What are you talking about?" Kira asked, her cheeks flushing under his sharp eyes.

"See, like that! I've never seen you do that. You look all soft and unlike yourself." He was examining her as if she were an exotic insect that had crawled onto his leg.

Kira put her hand on his face and shoved him hard.

"Leave me alone! You're making me lose my appetite." Jumping up, she walked over to the other side where Seung's family was spread out. They welcomed her with shy greetings and handed her a wooden bowl of spicy boar and cabbage stew over rice. Kira fell in love with the spicy stew. She'd never eaten anything like it before. It was garlicky and peppery and stimulated her taste buds. The boar meat was so soft it melted in her mouth, while the vegetables added texture and flavor. She wolfed down two large bowls before she was content.

Everyone sat close together, wrapped up in furs and blankets, their laughter coming out in great clouds of cold air. After a while, the chief stood up, waved his hands for attention, and asked Seung to share their adventures with the village. Seung stood happily and recounted all that had happened with great gusto. He was a born storyteller, describing Kira's meeting with the Heavenly Maidens as if he'd been there himself. He told of the queen's heroic sacrifice to the weeping of the villagers, and crowed over Eojin's triumphant march into Hansong to loud cheers. But when he reached the part of Eojin's murder and their subsequent flight from Hansong, the villagers stilled, listening in rapt attention.

"Where must you go now?" someone asked.

Seung turned to Brother Woojin, who took over the narrative. "We must head to Mount Baekdu and find the hidden entrance to the shadow world."

"Sunim, that is impossible. No human can ever pass through that entrance," the shaman said. "How do you plan to get to their world?"

Brother Woojin looked like he was at a loss.

"I was not aware of this," he replied. "What can we do?"

The shaman sighed. "I have a feeling you will not like the answer, but I will commune with the spirits and ask them what can be done." He ordered his two young apprentices to gather up his supplies and return quickly.

A few minutes later, the boys returned with a heavy leather bag, a large gourd, and a long staff laden with bells at its tip. The shaman stood and approached the fire.

He retrieved a small pouch from his inner pocket and began to chant as he sprinkled the contents into the fire. Continuing to chant, he shook the staff at the fire. An apprentice brought him the gourd. The shaman unstopped the gourd and tipped the white liquid into the fire. Kira recognized it as earth's milk, a magical substance that all shamans used. Only shamans knew the secret ingredients that it contained. While Kira had no idea what made it magical, she did know that it would take a shaman a month to brew the earth's milk to full potency.

The fire raged high, letting off an intense heat before dying down again. The shaman continued to chant, raising his arms high in the air as he shook his bells hard above him.

Shadowy figures danced within the fire, and then a shadow darted from the fire and entered the shaman's body. Kira jumped to her feet, her hand reaching for her sword. The shaman's eyes rolled back into his head and his entire body began to jerk and shake before finally collapsing. Kira approached carefully but sensed no demon presence.

The shaman levitated from the ground, his feet dangled above their heads. His eyes were bright and feverish and his smile seemed tinged with insanity.

"Demon Slayer! I see the Demon Slayer before me!"

Kira stopped in alarm. The voice coming from the shaman's body was different, higher and manic in sound.

"Who are you?" she asked.

"She's asking who I am—who am I?" He giggled, clapping his hands together in glee. "Should I tell her? Should I?"

Kira had no idea who he was talking to. Had another spirit inhabited the shaman's body?

"Master Won, are you still there?" she asked.

"He can't talk to you! He's busy," the spirit said. "You can only talk to me. What do you want? What do you want from me?"

Before she could answer the spirit tilted his head, as if listening to another person. "What? She wants to go to the shadow world?" He burst into insane laughter. "Yes, let's tell her! And then we can keep her. Yes, we will keep her and she can never leave!"

He cavorted around in a macabre dance, his body flying through the air.

"Come to the shadow world, Demon Slayer, but leave your physical body behind," he said. "The portal is through the fire. You must enter the fire. We can't wait to meet you there."

There was another burst of raucous laughter before Shaman Won's body began to twitch again and the black shadow flew back into the fire. The shaman collapsed to the ground, and as his two apprentices raced over to attend to him, Kira kept staring at the flames. What was that creature? And could its words be trusted?

Several minutes later, Shaman Won stood up onto shaky feet.

"What did I say?"

Kira quickly explained all that the spirit had revealed. The shaman looked unhappy.

"It is as I feared: the only way into the shadow world is to become a shade yourself," he said.

Her brother reacted in shocked anger. "What are you talking about? That's impossible!"

"No, it's not impossible. There is a way, but it is very dangerous and has never been done before," he said.

"No! Absolutely not!" Kwan shouted. "What kind of danger are you sending my sister and cousin into? I thought they were entering a cavern inside the mountain. What is this shadow world?"

"That which you seek lies in the deepest cavern within Baekdu. No living thing can enter it, for it is the entrance to the land of the shadows and is guarded by the haetae," the shaman said.

Kira's hand flew up to the pouch she always wore around her neck. Her fingers traced the outline of the little haetae figurine her father had given her. The thought of seeing the mythical fire-eating dog in real life thrilled her. The haetae had been her father's favorite creature because it was the guardian of justice and protector from disasters. Her hand tightened over the pouch. She missed her father terribly.

"The only way to enter the cavern is by passing as a shade yourself," Shaman Won continued.

"You mean we have to be dead?" Taejo asked.

"Death is one way. Another way is to leave your body and let your spirit enter the cavern and pass by the spirit guards."

"Is that even possible?" Kira asked.

"Of course it's possible. But it is very dangerous," the shaman answered. "If you are not careful, you can be imprisoned there forever."

"What do you mean? How?"

"The ritual is done at the darkest point of the night.

Your incorporeal form must return to its physical body before the first rays of the sun touch it. Otherwise, your body will die and you will remain a shade for all eternity."

The shaman shook his head. "There are so many dangers in this. Are you sure you must enter the land of shadows?"

Kira turned to Brother Woojin, who nodded unhappily.

"I have no choice," she said.

"Then we must prepare to go to the foot of Baekdu Mountain, and we will need protection," the shaman replied. He looked old and exhausted. "I must rest in order to prepare for what I must do. May the heavens help us."

All the villagers who had sat in spellbound silence were now released by the shaman's words. They chattered loudly as they gathered their things and returned home. Only Kira and her group remained unmoving. She recognized the fear and worry on their faces, but it was Taejo she was most concerned for.

"If we are late, then we will die," Taejo whispered.

A shiver ran down her spine at his words.

That night the men were placed in an empty hut at the edge of the village. The chief went to stay in the hut with the others, not wanting to be parted from his son. Kira had no choice but to sleep in the chief's cottage, in the spare room.

The room was as warm as the shaman's house, but sleep wouldn't come. There were too many troubling thoughts that kept her mind in a stressful whirl. Since she'd been in North Wagay Village, she'd not heard the Demon Lord's voice at all. While she was grateful for the reprieve, she had to wonder why. He must know where she was going. Therefore, she would be walking right into a trap. How was she to protect herself? How was she to protect Taejo?

Tired and yet wide-awake, she lay staring at the slivers of moonlight that peaked through the shuttered window when she heard the unmistakable sound of footsteps. She could hear the heavy snores of the female caretaker, who was to watch over Lady Kim, and was the only other person in the house. Kira rose to her feet and crept over to the long bamboo curtain that hung over the opening to her room. Through the slats, she saw Jaewon's mother open the front door and walk out. Kira quickly pulled on her boots and her heavy coat and followed the chief's wife. She was already halfway across the square and moving fast. In the moonlight, Kira spied something shiny glinting against the woman's full skirt.

Dread coursed through her body. This would not end well. She'd been told Lady Kim had been given a second dose of the herbal medicine to ensure that she would not awake through the night. But somehow she had fooled them all. And she had been listening to their conversation because she moved with absolute certainty toward the last hut.

Kira began to run as fast as she could after her.

"Lady Kim—" Kira began, trying to catch her attention, as she reached a hand to grab her arm.

The woman whipped around with an outraged scream and stabbed Kira in the shoulder.

"Get away from me, demon! You won't stop me from my vengeance!"

Searing pain momentarily blinded Kira as she pressed her hand to the wound. Then rage pushed aside the pain. Kira bellowed for her brother as she tackled the older woman from behind and disarmed her.

Doors flew open all over the square as people exited from their homes. They found Kira sitting on top of a screaming, spit-spewing woman.

The door to the last hut opened as Kwan and Jaewon dashed past the chief's form. Only Kwan came to Kira's side, Jaewon froze as soon as he saw his mother, an expression of grief-stricken horror on his face before he returned to the hut, gently leading Taejo inside. His father gave him a consoling pat on his shoulder before he closed the door and came to Kira's side.

"You are hurt," he said. "Quickly, Shaman Won, you must take care of her wound."

Kwan and the shaman helped Kira up. Lady Kim staggered up to her feet and attacked the chief.

"How dare you help the demon witch and ignore me, your wife! How dare you keep me from my vengeance!" She screamed as she pounded on his chest.

The chief became enraged and shook her. "Be silent, woman! Must you destroy the last of our sons?"

She was instantly silent and unmoving. She remained in that position for a long moment before spitting in the chief's face.

"I have no sons," she said. "And you are not my husband."

Profound grief warped the chief's craggy old face.

"Because of you, I must say good-bye to my only son, for he cannot stay here," he said. Without another word he dragged her protesting form through the crowd.

Kira continued to glare at Lady Kim's struggling form. Kira did not feel pity for the crazed woman. What she felt was a deep anger. Lady Kim's grief had turned into hatred so warped that she no longer recognized the son she still had left. Kira could not understand a parent who could favor one child over another. As difficult as her life had been growing up, Kira had never doubted the love of her parents and had never felt that their love for her was less than that of their love for her brothers. She couldn't imagine how a parent could close their heart off to their own child. Her heart ached in sympathy for Jaewon and his father. Because of his mother, Jaewon was not safe in his own village, and his father would lose his son once again.

25

In the morning, Chief Kim called a meeting with the shaman.

"Due to the unstable nature of Lady Kim's mind, it would be best if you were to leave as soon as possible. I understand that this is a dangerous task that you must undertake," the chief said. "I wish you did not have to do this, but Shaman Won tells me there is no other way."

The shaman nodded gravely. "Where we are going, we cannot take horses," he said. "The trails are too narrow and the terrain too rough as we maneuver through the mountain valleys. It will take us many days to hike to the foot of Whitehead Mountain."

"Why do you call it Whitehead?" Taejo asked.

"It is to constantly appease the mountain gods," the shaman explained. "We praise the mountain for being covered with snow in the hopes that it will stay that way. As long as we can call it Whitehead, we are safe in its shadow."

"How can you know that?" Taejo asked.

"My magic is tied to that of the mountains. As long as my magic stays strong, I know that we are safe," the shaman said. "But I am concerned about your safety, Your Highness. Perhaps it would be safer for you to stay here in the village."

Before Taejo could even begin to protest, Brother Woojin cut in. "He is part of the Dragon King prophecy, our future king, and so he must go. We do not know what would happen if he were not with us."

"Ah yes, the prophecy. Seven will become three, three will become one, one will save us all. Bunch of nonsense if you ask me. Who is the one? Prince Taejo?"

"He is the future king, and Kang Kira is the Dragon Musado," Brother Woojin said.

"Then Kang Kira is the one," Shaman Won said.

"No, they are both part of the prophecy," Brother Woojin countered.

The shaman shook his head. "Can't be. The prophecy says one, not two."

"Yes, but our first head monk, Master Ahn, is the one who foretold of the savior. That the 'one' of the prophecy refers to a royal descendant of the Dragon King—the

Dragon Musado, a warrior who will unite the kingdoms and save us from the Demon Lord."

"So then she *is* the one," the shaman said.

"But the Heavenly Maiden told Kang Kira that she must protect the prince, as he is the heir to the Dragon King's throne. He is the future king," Brother Woojin protested.

The shaman looked at Kira, who nodded.

"That is true," she said.

Shaman Won glared at the monk and made a rude sound. "Is it so hard for you to accept that a girl is our savior? Do you not recognize her worth? Can you not give her the true respect she is due?"

Brother Woojin was taken aback. "I do respect young mistress very much."

"No, you are blinded," Shaman Won cut in. "Even recognizing that the girl is the Dragon Musado, your mind seeks a more acceptable interpretation. That she is only part of the prophecy instead of the only one. She is only relevant to you as the prince's protector. But what you fail to recognize is that everything is irrelevant without her. The only person who truly sees her worth is young Kim Jaewon."

Everyone was quiet, stunned by his words. Only Jaewon looked unsurprised.

"Young Musado, I speak the truth, for I have told you what I have seen. You must believe in your own worth. They would sacrifice you to save the prince, but what they don't realize is that there is no future without you. You are our savior."

Kira didn't know what to think of his words. They seemed harsh and condemning of Brother Woojin and she didn't believe he deserved it. Before she could object, her brother stepped forward.

"Master Won, I must disagree with you on one thing," Kwan said. "I would never sacrifice my sister, and I do believe in her with all my heart."

"Me too!" Taejo said. "I do believe in Noona! And I know she is more important than me!"

Kira shook her head. "That's not true! Don't say that." She rounded on the shaman. "Tell him it's not true. He is very important! He is our future king!"

"Yes, he is very important," Shaman Won said. "But you are more so. There can be other kings, but no other Musado."

He sent a long pointed glance at Brother Woojin, letting his words sink in before continuing.

"Now then, we must have additional guards for our journey. We cannot rely solely on my magic."

"We lost all our soldiers on the way here. Major Pak, my sister, and I are all we have left," Kwan said.

The shaman and chief shared a troubled look.

"The strongest of our men and I will accompany you," Chief Kim said.

"No, chief," Shaman Won said. "You cannot come with us. We are bonded by my magic. Even though I leave, the village will still be protected through you. But if we both go, our people will be defenseless."

The chief subsided, unhappy with the turn of events.

"I will send our strongest men on the journey," Chief Kim said.

"And we would welcome them," Kwan answered.

The chief rounded up six men, clearly hunters who knew how to wield a bow and arrow and a spear. But they'd never dealt with demons before.

Kira approached the shaman with her concerns.

"Master, these men can be of no help in a demon attack. They'll get slaughtered."

"That is why time is of the essence," he replied. "And if we find ourselves in great need, I have special magic that I can use in case of a dire emergency. But it is dangerous, as it will deplete me of my magic."

"Then that's not helpful," Kira said. "Without your magic, how will you get us to the shadow world?"

"That is my fear," he said. "But I may be able to replenish my magic at the mountain."

"So you're not sure if you can?" Kira asked.

"Young mistress, I am not sure of anything," he replied.

Kira couldn't worry about that. Instead, she prepared for their journey. Their supply bags were packed tight with food, water, and tents. Kira reloaded her arrow case and checked all their weapons.

Jaewon and Seung's departure was very different from

the last time they left their families. Instead of disappearing without a trace, they were saying their good-byes to tearful family members.

The chief held Jaewon by the shoulders, his forehead pressed against Jaewon's as he bid his son farewell.

"You are my son, you will always be my son. My pride and joy," the chief said. "Wherever your travels take you, know that you carry my heart with you."

"My mother—" Jaewon started and then stopped, his throat constricting against his own words.

"Look at me, Jaewon," Chief Kim said in a firm, no-nonsense voice. "That person is not your mother anymore. She's an empty shell of a person filled with only hate. When Jaeho died, her mind became too ill to handle the tragedy. It twisted into this new entity that lives only in the past and cannot move forward. I barely recognize her anymore."

"Will she never recover?" Jaewon asked.

Profound grief crossed his father's face. "Sometimes I will get a glimpse of who she used to be, and for a moment, I have hope. But then she disappears and leaves behind this person I don't know. But you must look to your memories. Only there is she still alive."

"Forgive me, father," Jaewon whispered.

"There is nothing left to forgive," the chief said. His tears fell down his weathered cheeks. "Be well, my son, and may fortune cross our paths again soon."

Kira was grateful for the chief's emotions. Already

she perceived the healing that had begun in her friend. The dark sadness that always seemed part of his life had lifted. It wasn't completely gone and she doubted it ever would be, but there was a lightening of his soul that even she could see.

Their parting reminded Kira of her last conversation with her own father, when he'd given her the little hae-tae statue. How proud he had been of her. She could see his face, his smile. Thoughts of her father threatened to overwhelm her. She turned aside to wipe her eyes and saw the serene smile on Brother Woojin's face.

"Our friend's aura has begun to shine a little brighter now," he said with a happy sigh. "And maybe the darkness will fade completely one day with your help."

Kira flushed at his words and went to check their supplies. Her feelings for Jaewon were complicated, a matter she didn't like to think about too deeply or too often. What she wanted from him most was his friendship. She wasn't sure she was ready for anything else, just yet.

The warmer weather had melted a lot of the snow in the surrounding area. Hiking was easier as they traveled the mountain trail during the day. But as night fell and they got closer to the mountain range, the ground was covered with heavy snow again, impeding their progress.

That night, they set up camp near the snowy bank of a narrow creek. Shaman Won used his earth's milk around their campsite, warning everyone to stay within the protected area. Where the earth's milk touched the ground, it left a faint glistening in the snow. They huddled around the campfire as they ate their dinner. When Jaewon moved to sit next to Kira, Kwan cut him off with a glare. Ever since the first night at North Wagay Village, Kwan had gone out of his way to keep Jaewon from being alone with his sister. Normally, Kira would be annoyed by his high-handedness, but not this time. She was confused by her emotions. Just thinking about their kiss would bring a high flush to her cheeks. The comfortable friendship she'd had with him was now marred by a tension caused by her awareness of him as a man. She didn't like it. She wanted to go back to the way things were.

Kira's nerves had been strained ever since leaving the village. Once again a sense of impending doom overwhelmed her so much that her dinner lodged in her throat. And the voice of the Demon Lord had returned in full force. While she was in North Wagay Village, she'd not heard the voice at all. Now she realized that it was probably due to Shaman Won's protective spells that she'd had such a reprieve. Since leaving the village the voice mocked her, threatened her—promising the most horrible death. It was so clamorous, she could not hear her own thoughts.

She stood up, unable to eat, and began pacing. Her nose sensed the danger first. She whipped her head around and saw a Wagay clansman approaching with a dagger in his hands. She saw the shimmer of demon magic as the man's face revealed what was hidden underneath. Kira grasped her sword and sliced off his head in one move. In the next moment, there was an explosion of movement as a dozen half-breed demon soldiers appeared through the trees.

The clansmen were easy targets. Two were down before Kira could take her first shot. She retaliated by shooting five demons in a row.

The campsite was in chaos. Everyone was fighting a half-breed. In one-on-one combat, they were extremely hard to kill. Kira did what she could, shooting her quiver empty. Her last arrow pierced the face of an oncoming half-breed, and was left protruding from its jaw. Using her sword, Kira aimed straight for its neck. But it was quick, dodging her blow and kicking her in the chest, sending her crashing into a tree. The half-breed seized her by her hair and laughed. Kira jerked the arrow out of its face and shoved it deep into its throat.

She heard a scream and her heart stopped. Taejo and Brother Woojin were facing a monstrous half-breed, when Jindo flung himself at the creature. Kira saw the slash of the creature's claws as it raked Jindo's side. The big dog fell bleeding to the ground. Racing up behind the half-breed, Kira pierced it through its neck, killing it.

With a wild sob, Taejo knelt by Jindo, who was badly injured. But he was not the only one. Major Pak had severe chest and leg wounds. Kwan and Seung were by his side, trying to stanch the bleeding.

Of the six clansmen, only two had survived. Jaewon was dragging the dead out of their campsite, a dazed expression on his face.

Why had their protective ward failed? She looked for the shaman and found him standing within a circle of three dead half-breeds, steam rising from their charred faces.

"What happened?" Kira asked.

Shaman Won shook the gourd that held the earth's milk. "I wasted half its contents on them," he said.

"How did they break through your barrier?" she asked.

"It had to have been one of the men, the one you killed first. He must have left the safety of the circle and become possessed," he replied. "Since he'd been allowed within the ward in the first place, he was able to break the barrier when he returned."

The shaman gazed at the destroyed campsite, a bleak look on his face. "Are there any more of them?"

"Not nearby," Kira answered. "But that was just a scouting group. I'm sure there's a larger faction after us."

"Now more than ever, we will need strong magic to protect us."

"It hasn't done such a good job yet."

"Then I have no choice but to use my strongest magic," he responded. "Without it, we won't make it to Whitehead."

"But you said that magic would deplete you. How will

we get to the shadow world then?"

Shaman Won faced her. "If we die before we get there, we'll never know, will we?" he countered.

"Good point," Kira said. "What can I do to help?"

"Let me think what I need to do as I reinforce our barrier," Shaman Won said.

Kira returned to Taejo and Jindo. Seung was applying pressure on Jindo's wound. Blood stained the snow, looking black by the light of the campfire.

"Will he survive?" Taejo asked.

Seung didn't answer, tying a strip of cloth tightly around the middle of the dog's body.

"We need to get him someplace warm or he will die," he finally said.

He lifted his eyes to meet Kira's. "The same goes for the major."

Alarmed, Kira ran over to Major Pak. Kwan and Jaewon were tightening the bandages around his wounds.

"I'm sorry, young mistress," Major Pak said. "I've failed you and the prince."

"Don't be ridiculous!" Kwan snapped.

The major was terribly pale. He'd lost a lot of blood. He'd have to return to the village or he'd die.

She approached the shaman as he finished reinforcing their protective barrier.

"We need to get Major Pak and Jindo to the village," she said. "But it's too dangerous. We would run right into the half-breeds on our trail."

"What we need is our own army," Shaman Won said.

"That would be a nice trick," Kira said. "I'd like to see that."

"Me too," he replied. "And I think I'm ready."

"Ready for what?"

"To use the deepest shaman magic that I know."

Shaman Won crouched down on the ground, collecting rocks and branches and other hard objects. "I've never tried this spell before, but it may be our only choice."

Kira looked at him with deep suspicion. She could never shake her innate distrust of shaman magic. It seemed too close to demon magic. "What is it?"

"I want to create our own army to protect us," he said, "one that is virtually indestructible. Help me collect a pile of objects. It can be anything! A bowl, a stick, a rock, anything that is hard. But don't leave the perimeter."

"Will it work?" she asked.

"I don't know. And it will render me helpless, but we still need to try."

Too tired to question him, Kira, Jaewon, and the remaining two villagers collected rocks, twigs, pieces of bark, chopsticks, and even bowls, which they piled high in a large stack before the shaman.

"More!" Shaman Won demanded. "Bring me everything you can."

By the time they were done, the area within their campsite was a barren wasteland picked clean of everything but dirt and snow.

"We will need the blood of a maiden to bring them to life," the shaman said. He turned to gaze at Kira. "Preferably the blood of a warrior maiden to give them strength and intelligence."

"Take what you need," she said.

The shaman began to chant and shake his belled staff around the huge pile of objects. He poured all that remained of earth's milk over them. After several moments, he beckoned Kira to approach the pile. Grabbing her hand, he sliced open her palm with his dagger. Kira grimaced from the sudden pain. The shaman held her palm over the pile and let the blood drip onto a wooden bowl. He continued to chant steadily under his breath.

The blood hissed and steam filled the air. A shimmery glimmer encompassed the object. With a sudden popping sound, the bowl jumped off the pile and began to transform, unfolding itself into a misshapen body with long arms and short legs, a stout chest, and huge head. Kira could not believe her eyes. She turned to see the reaction of the others. All of them wore identical expressions of shock and wonderment. Shaman Won had turned the bowl into a *dokkaebi*, a goblin. Kira gaped in awe at it and was stunned when the dokkaebi's enormous mouth gaped back at her. With a grunt, it capered off to ogle at a frightened-looking Seung.

Shaman Won covered more items with Kira's blood. A series of popping sounds, like fireworks, caused Kira to flinch. Before her stood a small army of dokkaebis, each slightly different from the other. The ugly, ill-formed creatures were short and stout, with hideous goblin faces. They were dressed in beige, belted jackets and matching trousers. One ran up and yanked Jaewon's hair, while others turned cartwheels, crashing into one another and starting fights.

More dokkaebis were made until Kira didn't think she had any blood left in her to give. The last object left was a small rock, but no more blood would squeeze from her cut. Kira leaned over and picked it up, feeling dizzy in the process. She smeared the blood on her hand all over the rock. It immediately began to transform. Startled, Kira dropped the rock as it morphed into a dokkaebi the size of a small child and scurried away.

There were at least three hundred dokkaebis packed tightly together before them. Shaman Won stuck his fingers into his gourd to coat them with the remnants of his earth's milk. Then he picked up a stick and began a low chant as his hands twisted and pulled at the wood. There was a green glow around the stick as it grew larger and thicker, until it transformed into a long heavy cudgel. The shaman thumped it on the ground seven times. All the dokkaebis froze and gazed with hungry longing at the weapon.

"Use your magic!" the shaman roared at them.

He hurled the cudgel into the air, and several dokkaebis made wild grabs for it, screaming, "Another! Another!" The first dokkaebi to grab the club slammed it down with a mighty thump. Instantly a new one sprouted from the ground. That dokkaebi cast aside the original cudgel and snatched up the replica, howling in glee. The shaman's magic stick was passed from dokkaebi to dokkaebi, a rhythmic thudding filling the air as new cudgels were formed. Once every dokkaebi had an exact replica, the original was returned to the shaman.

Even the littlest dokkaebi carried a huge club.

"Dokkaebi army!" Shaman Won shouted, catching all their attention. "This is your creator." The shaman pointed at Kira. All the dokkaebis bowed in unison.

"When she calls you, you must always show yourselves. You will protect her and whoever she wishes with your lives," the shaman continued.

The dokkaebis grunted and pounded at their chests.

The shaman turned to Kira with a tired smile. "They have a demon nature, but they're not demons and will protect you or die trying. You will not see them. They will hide from sight, but know that they will always warn you of danger and fight for you. Why don't you address them now?"

With that, he fell to the ground in exhaustion. Kira knelt by his side, but he waved her away, pointing to the dokkaebis.

Kira faced the waiting crowd.

One dokkaebi came over and bowed reverently in front of Kira. It was the smallest one, which had formed last. Not knowing what to do, Kira bowed back. This caused the dokkaebi to smile in delight, its long fangs glistened as it stroked her arm in an affectionate display that surprised her. She patted his head, which caused the other dokkaebis to laugh and clap their hands.

"Dokkaebi army, I thank you for your support. I need you to help protect Prince Taejo," she said. Walking over to where Taejo still knelt by Jindo's side, she helped him rise to his feet. "This is the prince and he must be protected at all costs. Will you help me?"

The dokkaebi army howled in agreement.

Kira smiled. "I also need some of you to help guard these men and this dog as they return to their village. May I have a few volunteers?"

Six dokkaebis stepped forward, thumping their cudgels. She turned to the shaman. "Will that be enough to keep them safe?" she asked.

The shaman nodded. "They are not the target anyway—you and the prince are. But one dokkaebi has the strength of ten strong men. They will be fine."

"Then let's get them to safety."

She faced the dokkaebis again. "Keep them safe and then return to us."

With Jaewon and Kwan's help, Kira and the two villagers made makeshift litters from heavy branches and their blankets. The stronger villager would pull Major Pak, while the other carted Jindo. Seung would go with them to help carry and take care of their wounds. It made sense to send the villagers home. They'd been very shaken up by the demon attack, and Kira didn't want their deaths on her hands. When told they would be returning home, their relief was palpable.

Kira spent the rest of the night retrieving arrows, cleaning and sharpening those that were not damaged. She knew she would need every single one of them.

The group taking the injured left at the first rays of sunlight.

Seung stopped before the prince and tried to reassure him. "Don't worry, Your Highness. I promise I will do all in my power to save Jindo."

Taejo wiped at his tears and nodded his thanks. He hugged Jindo one last time before walking over to Kira and burying his face in her shoulder.

"I feel like I'll never see him again," Taejo whispered.

There was nothing she could say to make him feel better. The road ahead of them was far more dangerous than the one behind.

26

The closer they got to Mount Baekdu, the colder and icier it was. Although it was not snowing, travel was slow and treacherous, and a wrong step could send a person tumbling into a deep ditch filled with snow. They were constantly battling the wind and their own fatigue. They had to set up camp earlier each day in order to rest their legs and warm themselves. Pitching their tents was difficult with winds that hurtled through the valleys and drove the snow into their faces.

The only dokkaebi they ever saw was the little one, who had bonded with Kira.

He would appear at camp, bringing a fresh kill for

their supper: rabbits, several black grouse, and even a small deer. He didn't talk but would smile in his gruesome manner, his long fangs glinting. He would dig up potatoes and other roots—even finding a gold mine of ginseng, the medicinal herb that Seung was so fond of. She woke up one morning to find a large piece of honeycomb in a bowl next to her bedroll. When she tried to thank him, the little dokkaebi would pat her arm and purr like a large cat before running off.

"You've made a friend," Jaewon said with a laugh.

"Guess I don't scare him off," she replied.

Jaewon reached over and patted her arm, just as the dokkaebi had. "You don't scare me off either."

A reluctant smile crossed her face. "I'm glad," she said.

Whatever strain Kira had felt toward Jaewon since the kiss had dissipated. Once again she felt comfortable in their friendship. It also helped that the dokkaebi was always around, keeping Jaewon from being alone with her. Kira developed a great affection for the dokkaebi. He returned that night and slept curled up at her feet. Despite his appearance, he had all the mannerisms of an animal but could understand human speech.

She didn't know why, but when the little dokkaebi was near her, she couldn't hear the voice of the Demon Lord.

The next night, the wind had died down and the snow lay peacefully around them. Kira warmed herself by the campfire. The little dokkaebi lay at her feet, eating a raw squirrel.

"What's your name?" she asked.

The dokkaebi gave her a questioning look.

"I don't think they have names," Brother Woojin answered. "But you can name him yourself."

Kira leaned her chin on her hand, gazing at her dokkaebi friend. He was rolling on the ground in front of her, chewing on the end of his cudgel while taking playful swipes at Kwan, who growled at him.

"He acts more like your pet than a guard dog," Kwan observed.

"He's no dog." Kira laughed. "More like a bear cub."

The dokkaebi rolled over and leaned on Kira's legs. She scratched his head as he made small sounds of contentment.

"I'll just call him Gom 'cause he reminds me of a bear."

Jaewon nodded. "He sure has the claws of one."

Gom yawned wide, exposing the cavernous depths of his mouth.

"And the mouth of one, too!"

As they laughed, Gom smiled in perfect harmony.

Taejo winced at the reminder of his missing dog. Kira put an arm around his shoulders and squeezed him tight. "Don't worry. Seung is the best. He'll take good care of Jindo."

Taejo nodded, but the worry was still deep in his eyes.

* * *

They trekked through the dense, snow-covered forest before reaching an open field. Mount Baekdu rose over the heavy mist. They were almost there when a hideous screeching sound reverberated against the mountains. Kira stopped in her tracks as her nose picked up the scent of demon.

"Gom," Kira said urgently, "call the dokkaebis!"

The little dokkaebi pounded his cudgel on the ground. The dokkaebi army rushed from their hiding places and surrounded Kira and the others in tight circles seven layers deep. Demon half-breeds appeared and swarmed them. Kira had never seen so many in one place. There were at least a hundred half-breeds. The daimyo had been very busy.

The dokkaebis surrounding them stood with their backs to her and their clubs held high. Within minutes the battle ensued. The dokkaebis in the outer ring of their circle smashed in the heads of the half-breeds, killing them with one blow. Several half-breeds retaliated by grabbing hold of a dokkaebi and tearing him apart, until he transformed into broken pieces of wood. Even his cudgel vanished.

Kira was horrified. Seeing her dokkaebis destroyed felt personal to her. They'd been made from her blood. She made a move to leave the protective circle, but the dokkaebis pushed her back.

"Have you gone mad? Where are you going?" Jaewon asked in shocked incredulity.

"They're being slaughtered! I need to help them!"

"It's their job to protect you! Let them!"

Within their circle, they were all safe. Kira hoped little Gom was safe. The first two outer layers of nearly sixty dokkaebis had fallen to the half-breeds, but the half-breeds had been reduced by more than half their number.

Whenever Kira saw a dokkaebi in trouble, she used her bow to take down their enemy. Finally, the dokkaebis killed the last of the half-breeds. They howled in victory and rapidly dispersed. Only Gom remained. Kira watched as the little dokkaebi collected arrows, which he brought over to her side with a lopsided grin.

"Thank you, Gom," she said.

He scooted off, continuing to collect arrows for her.

Shaman Won urged them on.

"We are almost there," the shaman said. "Let's go quickly."

The last leg of their trip was uneventful. She couldn't sense the presence of any demons or half-breeds. It should have felt safe after so many weeks of being followed, but it didn't.

She couldn't help but wonder—where were the demons? Did they know where her group were headed? Would they be ambushed? The sudden quiet was uneasy.

They finally reached the foot of Mount Baekdu by early afternoon. The shaman used the remnants of his powers to set up a protective barrier.

"Without my earth's milk, this barrier is weak, but

it will warn us of nearby intruders. We must rely on the dokkaebis to protect us while we are here," the shaman said.

"Will you be able to speak to the spirits without the earth's milk?" Brother Woojin asked.

The shaman nodded. "The barrier between the realms is in Whitehead. I can call them easily here."

Starting a great fire, the shaman performed a ritual of the dead. Within minutes, three shades entered the body of the shaman. It was alarming to hear the different voices emanating from his mouth, his facial expressions changing with each. One was that of a frightened old man, the second of a madwoman, and the last of someone filled with great evil.

"Do not seek this land." The old man's voice quavered and was weak. "Save yourselves! Go back!"

"Shut up, stupid!" The madwoman shouted. "Let them come, let them come!"

"Is it safe to continue our journey?" Kira asked.

The madwoman cackled. "Depends upon your definition of safe."

The old man cut in. "It is not safe!"

"Be specific—what's not safe? Are there demons around us now?" Kwan asked.

"There are no more demons! They are all gone! All gone!" The madwoman began to mumble and laugh.

"Is that true?" Kira asked.

The shaman's face shifted between several

expressions until the sad face of the old man settled in. "She is correct," he said. "That is why you must stay here!"

"Interesting," Brother Woojin mused. "I wonder what is going on?"

The shaman's body rocked with raucous laughter. This was the evil one. The sound of his voice made Kira grit her teeth, the hairs on her arms standing on end.

"Fool! The Demon Lord does not have to attack you any longer when he knows where you are headed. You enter the land of shades. It is his domain. He will ambush you there!"

Gom growled and tried to hit Shaman Won with his club. Kira tackled Gom and held the little dokkaebi as the evil laugh echoed all around them. As the shaman collapsed, Jaewon caught him before he could fall into the fire.

"What did he mean by that?" Kwan demanded. He turned to Brother Woojin. "They are walking into a trap? They shouldn't go!"

Taejo was trembling. "Do we have to do this? Isn't there any other way?"

Brother Woojin looked helpless. "All we know is the jeweled dagger is in the shadow world." He sent Shaman Won a pleading look. "Is there any other way?"

"There is only one entrance to the land of shadows and it is guarded by fire-breathing haetae who are the protectors of the gates. Their duty is to ensure that no shades enter the land of the living and no living enter the land of the dead. They take their duties very seriously."

Kira thought of her own haetae figurine, which she kept close by her always. They were the keepers of justice.

"Young mistress Kang, the tidal stone can't help you there. It won't be with you—it will be with your body. You will need to rely on your wits, and the ability to trust correctly," Brother Woojin said.

The thought of danger without any adequate defense frightened Kira. She didn't know if she could trust herself, let alone any who she might encounter in the land of shadows. She'd only ever learned to rely on her fighting abilities.

"But if I'm a shade, how can I bring back the jeweled dagger? And how am I to fight the dragon?" she asked.

"You are the Dragon Musado," Brother Woojin said. "The dagger belongs to you. Once you claim it, it will be yours."

"But the dragon—"

"Perhaps you are not meant to fight the dragon with weapons," he said.

Kira couldn't believe what he was saying. "Well then, what am I supposed to do? Fight him with words?"

"Maybe." The monk shrugged his shoulders. "No one knows what will happen, but you are meant to do this. The only thing we can do is pray to the heavens."

"No, I can't just rely on prayers, Sunim. I think it would be best if I go alone," Kira said. "I can't protect the prince if I have no physical form."

Brother Woojin looked upset. He was rolling his prayer beads between his hands and seemed to be praying.

"Sunim," she called him again. "Please let me leave the prince behind."

Several long minutes later, the monk opened his eyes and sighed. "As much as I wish to keep him safe, this journey is one he must take with you if he is to become our future king."

Kira ran a frustrated hand through her short hair. How could she keep the prince safe, knowing they were walking into a trap? How could this be right? As she watched the shaman prepare for their next step, she'd never felt more helpless in her life.

27

"In order for me to keep you both safe during your journey, I must replenish my powers," Shaman Won said. "Here at White-head Mountain, the magical current flows strong and deep. If I allow my spirit to flow in it, I should become revitalized."

"How long will it take?" Kira asked.

"No more than a few hours," he replied. "You will be safe with the dokkaebis."

He climbed up the mountain and disappeared from their sight. While he was gone, Kwan and Jaewon tried to keep Kira and Taejo from going.

"I don't like this at all, little sister," Kwan said. "You

will have no weapons, no way to protect yourself or the prince!"

"I agree with your brother," Jaewon said. "This is insane! Don't go."

It was up to Brother Woojin to try and reason with them, for Kira could not refute their arguments. She listened to the dispute but remained quiet, too worried to have the energy to challenge them. If they were to obtain the second Dragon King treasure, they had no choice. Walking away would mean letting the Demon Lord win. And that was not something she could allow.

The shaman returned at sunset.

"It's amazing. Even though I don't have any more earth's milk, my power is strong here. Stronger than it has ever been," Shaman Won said. "Your bodies will be safe. Now you must lie down directly before the fire, feet first. When you feel a pulling sensation in your midriff, don't fight it. Let it pull your spirit from your body."

Kwan turned to the shaman. "You can't send them in there defenseless!"

"They won't be defenseless," the shaman replied. "They will be able to seek help as long as they choose wisely."

"What does that mean?" Kwan's frustration was making him short-tempered. "I'm tired of cryptic messages that say nothing! Just tell me this: Can my sister navigate the shadow world, find the jeweled dagger, and return safely?"

"I don't know, but she must try."

Before the argument could start anew, Kira took Gom's club and slammed it on the ground. "Enough already!"

The others observed her with wary concern. Kira gave Gom his weapon, and the little dokkaebi patted her arm while making small whimpering sounds.

"We have to go," Kira said. "If we want to defeat the Demon Lord, we have no choice."

The hissing sound of the Demon Lord's voice whispered through her mind, causing her to shudder. *You are coming into the darkness. So close, so close. Soon you will be mine.* It didn't matter if his voice was real or part of a madness that was taking over her mind. The fear that always afflicted her at the thought of the Demon Lord nearly overpowered her. How could she do this? How could she go where he was bound to set a trap for her?

Suddenly, it was hard to breathe, her breath coming in short and rapid spurts. Her heart was pounding as if she'd climbed a mountain. Panic filled her as she walked blindly ahead. The muffled sounds of the others calling her came as if from a far distance.

Someone gripped her by the shoulders. Her eyes refocused on Jaewon's concerned face.

"If I could go instead of you or the prince, I would," he said. "But there is no doubt in my mind that you are the only person who can fulfill this prophecy. You will succeed. I have absolute faith in you."

For a moment, his image blurred, and it was no longer

Jaewon but her father who stood before her, his deep voice providing her with the assurance that she needed.

I believe that one person can change the world. Whether he is the Musado or a girl with a tiger spirit. . . . There is no one else in the world like you. . . . You were meant for greatness.

Her father's words from long ago filled her, pushing the insidious voice of the Demon Lord out of her mind. It gave her strength again. Her eyes cleared and Jaewon stood before her.

"Thank you," she said.

Kira and Taejo lay down on the cleared ground where the shaman had placed blankets to protect their bodies from the frozen ground.

"Remember, you must return to your bodies before the sun rises, otherwise you will be trapped in the shadow world," Shaman Won said.

He then focused all of his attention on the fire and began to chant, ringing his bells in an odd but rhythmic pattern. He began to dance, swaying in great, sweeping movements as he capered about like a monkey. The chanting and the rhythm of the bells sent Kira into a trance as she watched the smokeless fire begin to leap high into the sky. Tiny figures were dancing within the flames, beckoning to her.

Kira felt a tugging at her gut that became more urgent. It yanked her up and out of her body, leaving her staring down at her physical form. The sensation of floating was bizarre and liberating. Her spirit was light and airy yet with substance—not firm, but something between water and mist.

A moment later, she saw a ghostly form rise from Taejo's body. He floated up to her, his eyes wide with shock.

Are you all right? Kira asked. She paused in surprise. *That's so odd. Did you hear me speak or was it only in your head?*

Taejo's lips moved, but she heard his voice directly in her head. *You are speaking to me in my mind. It's so odd.*

Kira wondered if he could hear her thoughts or only what she wanted him to hear. When he didn't respond to her thoughts and she could not hear anything else from Taejo, she realized he could hear only what she meant for him to hear.

Look at me! I'm see-through! Am I a ghost? he asked.

We're not dead, Kira said. *These are just our spirits.*

Looking down at the others, she saw the fear and worry on the faces of Kwan and Jaewon as they hovered over Kira's and Taejo's bodies. Brother Woojin and Shaman Won were both praying. They had no idea that Kira and Taejo were now shades floating above them. She hoped the heavens would listen to their prayers.

Once again she felt the strong tugging in the pit of her stomach, pulling her toward the fire.

Come, we must get going, she said. She and Taejo were sucked into the fire, where the dancing figures leaped in wild abandon, but they didn't feel the heat. If anything, she felt a clammy coldness.

At the bottom of the fire, a burning chasm appeared.

Stay close, she warned Taejo as they were sucked into the deep cavern.

They left the flames behind and flew through a long, spiraling tunnel. The walls around them were dark and shiny, as if coated with an oily substance. Soon they were in absolute darkness, but Kira could still see Taejo's form next to her.

Don't be scared, she said. *I'm right next to you.*

She saw him nod and grab for her hand. His shadowy hand had no real substance, but she felt his touch.

Their free fall slowed as the tunnel began to turn sideways. Their feet touched down on ground, but they were still being pulled. At the end of the tunnel, they reached a sheer drop. Far below, Kira discovered a shimmering pathway at the bottom of the cavern floor. It seemed to be moving toward a faraway opening. Taejo looked frightened and uncertain.

"What are we supposed to do now?" he asked, and then looked surprised. "I heard my voice this time."

Now that they were in the land of shadows, they could talk aloud again.

"How curious," Kira said. "But no matter, we have to get down there. Follow me."

She stepped off and began to float toward the cavern floor. As she got closer, she realized it wasn't the pathway that was moving but the thousands of shades that were traveling on it. They were young and old, women and men; some were dressed in clothing that Kira had never seen before, and with facial features and hairstyles she didn't recognize. There were dark-skinned people and fair-haired people, reminding her of the inhabitants of lands the Heavenly Maidens had told her about. These were shades of people from all around the world.

A small figure of a young girl floated by, plaintively calling for her mother, while farther ahead Kira could hear the weeping of a woman. These were all tormented shades, taken from life before their time and ensnared in this world. Their faces bore testimony to the awful nature of their deaths. There were no happy souls here. In this world, the dead were cursed.

The path led to a gigantic entranceway. On either side stood a monstrous haetae.

Kira let out a long breath at the sight of them. These were the real thing, not just cute figurines. The haetae were humongous creatures with heads disproportionate to their bodies. They had large bulging eyes and flat snouts over fearsome muzzles filled with huge curved fangs that jutted from their mouths. When they roared, they belched a stream of fire that reached ten horse lengths in range. They were magnificent. The one on the left was aquamarine, with a darker shade of blue on its long, flowing mane. The other one was a fiery red all over, from burning mane to the tip of its tail.

"They're so beautiful," she said.

Taejo made a sound of disbelief. "No way! They are

the scariest-looking things I've ever seen!"

The haetae oversaw the procession of shades passing through the entranceway, their eyes sweeping over all of them. Kira had no doubt that if they had come in their physical bodies the haetae would have burned them to ashes. They were indeed dangerous and formidable beasts.

They walked past the haetae and into the land of the shadows. Kira was shocked to find that she was shaking with cold. They'd left their physical bodies behind, so they shouldn't feel anything. But upon entering, she felt cold and empty.

"Where do we go now?" Taejo asked.

Kira took a moment to take in their surroundings. They were in a vast cavern, at the end of which were a series of tunnels. She watched as the shade of an elderly man seemed to be pulled through the cavern and into a tunnel at the far right. It was as if the tunnels were sucking the shades down various paths.

Terrible frustration rose in her. How in heaven's name were they to find the dagger? They didn't even know what it really looked like. One thing she knew: she didn't want to get sucked down a tunnel randomly, without knowing where it went. There had to be a way of knowing where everyone was going. Many shades were milling around the middle of the cavern. Perhaps she could question them.

"Excuse me." Kira gestured to the shade of a young girl. "Where are you going?"

The girl turned to face them, and Taejo wheeled back in alarm. Half her face was missing, as if bitten off. She looked at them with empty eyes before floating off.

Kira wished she was anywhere but here in this ungodly land of the dead. She pushed her way through the crowd of shades, her essence passing right through theirs. But they didn't like it, moving out of her way with muttered curses and groans of dismay. For Kira, it felt odd, almost invasive, but it got her through the crowd. Taejo kept close behind her.

Moments later, they found themselves before a grouping of six stone statues of men. She was shocked to see the statues moving as if alive. Each shade passed through a statue before heading down a tunnel. She realized this was a way for her to gain some information.

"I think we must enter one of these guardians, just like the shades are doing," she said.

Staring at the statues, she discerned that each wore a very different expression on its stone face. The first looked fierce and angry, his gray stone eyes seemed to glow with a never-ending fury. The second statue was one of a tortured being of such suffering, Kira could only stare in horrified sympathy. If she had to guess what the next three statues represented, they would be ignorance, greed, and pride, so fitting were the expressions on their stone faces. But it was the sixth statue that Kira gravitated toward. Its calm face looked on the verge of asking a question, filled with a doubtful inquisitiveness that seemed so human to her. Not many shades passed through the fifth and sixth statues. The fifth statue seemed on its surface the happiest of them all. But it was such a prideful happiness that it intimidated Kira. As if she was unworthy of attaining such happiness.

They moved before the sixth statue and waited.

"Kira," Taejo whispered. "The statue is staring at us."

She looked up to find the statue's stone eyes boring into hers. Bowing before it, she began to speak, when she was rapidly sucked into the statue. It was suffocating. And then she felt the mind of the stone statue prod through her own, questioning her place there. It was not painful but it was very heavy, as if a weight was pressing down on her brain. It tired her and made her feel sluggish.

Where is my cousin? Kira screamed the thought in her head.

He is safe, do not fear, the statue said. *But neither of you are dead. I can feel your connection to your bodies. Why are you here?*

I seek the jeweled dagger, she thought to the statue.

The stone man was silent for a long while, picking at certain memories in her head that she could sense by the flash of memory before her eyes.

Why do you seek the Dragon King's treasure? he asked.

To fight the Demon Lord.

The stone man seemed to be mulling over her response.

I can't help you find it, but I can give you a clue. What you seek is hidden and yet in plain view. You must be careful to recognize truth from lies and follow your heart in order to obtain it.

Who has it? Kira asked.

The stone man remained quiet.

Can you at least direct me to the right way?

You chose me for a reason. Follow that reasoning and choose your course.

Kira stepped out of the stone man and faced the tunnels directly behind them. Taejo floated up to her.

"What happened? You were in there for so long! I was worried," he said.

She nodded absently, still looking at the tunnels. "He said to follow my reasoning. I chose him because he seemed the most human." She looked at the tunnels.

"What do you mean?" Taejo asked.

"He seemed curious. Even when he was picking through my thoughts, he was very interested in me," she said.

She looked at the tunnel entrances before them. There were six in all, and very different. One gleamed red and pulsed with heat, while another shone with a shimmering golden light. The others were various degrees of darkness, but the last one was placed high above the others. It was no lighter or darker than any of the other tunnel entrances, and yet it had a harder pathway to it. It made her curious.

"I think that's the one," she said.

Nodding, she waved at Taejo. "Come on, let's go!"

28

The tunnel took them into what looked like a large assembly room filled with low desks placed on straw mats. On each desk was a scroll, calligraphy brushes, and a silver ink stone. Most of the desks had a white-robed student sitting cross-legged before it, practicing their brushstrokes. At the front of the room there was a large papered wall where hanja characters appeared mysteriously.

"'I do not open up the truth to one who is not eager to get knowledge,'" Kira read aloud.

"Confucius," Taejo said.

Kira nodded, watching the careful brushstrokes of the students at their desks. But where was the instructor? She walked the length of the room but could find no doorway. Puzzled, she wondered what she was missing. Looking to the front of the room, she watched as the writing on the wall disappeared, erased by an invisible hand.

A new poem appeared, each brushstroke made by a master hand.

Starlight asked Non-being,
"Master, do you exist or do you not exist?"
There was no answer.
So Starlight stared into the deep void, looking for Non-being.
All day long he looked, but could see nothing.
He listened, but could hear nothing.
He reached out, but could grab hold of nothing.
Starlight then said,
"This is too much! Who can attain this?
I understand the idea of being and non-being.
But I cannot understand the non-existence of non-being.
And then if in fact non-being does exist,
how is this even possible?"

—Chuang Tzu

"What does that mean?" Taejo asked.

Kira shook her head. She didn't know this poem, but it seemed vaguely familiar to her. A philosophical conundrum like the type her father would pose to her during her studies.

"It doesn't make sense. There is no non-being, only the absence of being," Taejo said. "So how can there be an absence of nothing? It's a contradiction."

"It is the message within the confusion that we must decipher," Kira said. "The absence of nothing, the non-being. They are both labels that should be meaningless but have somehow been given meaning within the confines of this poem."

At her words, all the people who had been busy writing on their scrolls turned their heads toward her. Their brushes were poised in the air as they waited for her to continue. Unnerved by their dark, unwavering gazes, Kira paused to think carefully. She somehow knew that what she said next would be of grave importance.

"What is reality? Is a non-being reality? Or is it a false construct? Made into being by a meaningless label?" Kira mused to herself. "Starlight has created a non-being simply by calling it such, thereby bringing into existence that which did not exist. But there lies the problem. Just because something is labeled does not mean it is real. Therefore we must beware of the false construct."

A loud sigh filled the room. The students nodded and returned their attention to their scrolls. The poem on the wall vanished. In its place, a door appeared and opened.

Calling Taejo to follow her, Kira rushed for the door.

"I don't understand," Taejo said. "Why did your words open this door?"

"Because it was the answer they were waiting to hear," she said. "It's a message to us to beware that all is not what it seems here."

"Because we are in the land of shadows?"

"Exactly."

The door led down a hallway similar to that of Wando palace. A wind blew loudly, sending vivid silk curtains of red and yellow billowing all about them.

Abruptly, the wind died and the curtains parted to reveal two different passageways. Both were well lit, but the passage on the left was noisy with laughter and the sound of voices.

Then they heard her voice. It was the queen, Taejo's mother, calling to both of them.

Before Taejo could move, Kira spoke sharply to him. "No, I can't allow you to go this way. You and I both know that she is dead. We won't find her here. She is in heaven with our ancestors."

"But what if she's here?" Taejo said. "What if her spirit was cursed here? We have to know!"

A new voice joined the queen's, causing Taejo to shout. "That's my father!"

He started to float down the tune.

"Taejo! Remember the poem: this is not reality, this is a demon-made illusion. Will you once again put your selfishness above the importance of our mission?" Kira pointed to the scar over her eye.

Taejo recoiled as if slapped in the face. "I'm sorry," he whispered.

She felt bad. It was cruel to remind him of how his stubborn insistence had led to the scar, which Kira would always have. But there was no choice.

As she urged Taejo down the other passageway, she heard her mother's voice.

"Little tiger, where are you going? Come to me, my child. I have missed you so much!"

Taejo glanced up at her, but Kira shook her head fiercely. "It's not real!"

"It's not real, it's not real." Taejo repeated the words with a grim determination as they entered the silent passageway on the right.

Once past the ghostly voices, they were shocked to find the kumiho standing before them in her human form.

"Not only did you choose wisely, but you passed your first test," Nara said. "I would not have been able to help you if you couldn't reach this point."

"But how can you be here?" Kira asked. "Are you real or are you a shade?"

"I'm not a shade. I can cross over into this world in my physical body. I'm here to help you."

Kira was still confused.

"But why?"

Nara smiled. "You and I shared a connection. Through that connection, I learned what it was like to be human. I've longed for that again. To feel the human emotions that you shared with me: compassion, hope, and love. I found myself wanting to help you. So here I am, in this terrible place."

It was difficult to process. Part of her was happy to

see Nara again. She had liked her. And Kira knew that they needed all the help they could get in order to survive. But she also wondered if she was being stupid to trust her, a fox demon, someone who had killed hundreds of men over the centuries. She didn't even know if Nara was real or just a figment of her imagination. What if she was part of the trap set for her and Taejo?

"To be honest, I'm at a loss," Kira admitted. "I want to trust you, but I don't know if I should."

Nara inclined her head. "Fair enough," she said. "But remember your own answer. What is real and what is false. Here in this world, you must be able to answer this question."

The kumiho then nudged at Kira's mind and sent her a memory of Jaewon's fervent confession of his feelings to her. Kira was embarrassed. She remembered that it was one of the memories that Nara had been so interested in during their memory exchange.

"Remember, I am real," she said.

A strong impulse surged through her and Kira decided to listen to her heart and trust the kumiho again. "We would very much appreciate your help."

"Good, then follow me," Nara said as she morphed into her nine-tailed fox form. "In this world, I can speak in both of my forms, as the rules of the living don't apply here."

Kira thought it odd to hear Nara in her fox form speaking directly to her.

"The demons are so stupid," Nara continued. "They

set up two traps for you, in pride and greed. They tend to lump all humans together as greedy or arrogant. You missed them by picking curiosity. Now they will have to regroup and try to trap you in the tunnels. The one you just passed is an echo. It is not a specific trap for you—it is there to torture any who pass through the tunnels. Echoes are always of the voices you've loved and lost, drawing you into a pitfall from which you would never be able to escape. It is wise to be wary of them. But more important, we must stay ahead of the demons at all times. That is why I'm here, to help you navigate the tunnels."

"Where are we going?" Taejo asked.

"To find the cavern of overwhelming sorrow and seek guidance and protection from someone there," she answered.

"Who are we looking for?" Kira asked.

Nara looked around for a moment and morphed into her human form as she faced them. She pressed a finger to her lips and pointed to their surroundings. Turning into her fox form, she proceeded down the tunnel.

They entered an elaborate maze made of embroidered walls, with vivid scenes stitched in bright silk threads. As Kira gazed at a wall, the scene began to move. Demons gorged on humans, while foul creatures were released from the depths of the earth to destroy the world.

Nara growled at her, breaking the spell Kira had fallen under.

"This is what will happen if the Demon Lord is not

stopped," Nara said before proceeding down the maze. Kira tried to put an arm around Taejo, who stood horrified by her side, but her insubstantial arm just passed through him.

"We will stop him," she said. Taejo didn't look convinced.

They followed the kumiho, who moved expertly through the many twists and turns of the labyrinth.

"Where are we?" Kira asked the kumiho.

"This is a maze that traverses all the caverns of the underworld," the kumiho said. "An entrance for each of the caverns is hidden here."

The pictures got darker and more violent the farther along they ventured, until their path twisted into a downward spiral. Nara had them stop well before the decline. Screams and moans bellowed from its depths.

"That is the cavern of damnation. If you enter that domain, you will never escape," she said. She led them toward another section of the maze, with shimmering walls covered in jewels. At the end of a long corridor, there was a gilded door that seemed to shine with a golden light.

"That is the cavern of greed. There is a trap set for you both there," Nara said. She approached the door cautiously and pressed an ear to it. After a long moment, she returned to their side. "They're still there, which is good for us. It means they don't know where we are yet."

She continued to lead them through the maze, past

several more doors, then stopped before a pitch-black door.

"Listen closely. You will need the guidance of long-dead kings. I will open this door, but it is up to you to call to them and ask for their support. Only with their help will you find what you seek. But hurry—time is passing quickly. And whatever you do, don't enter that door!"

"What do you mean? Call to who? And how?"

"Think of one taken too soon. At the hands of a curse. Call him by name."

The kumiho's ears pricked as she heard the sounds of a terrible commotion. Turning human, she unlatched the door and swung it open.

"They know you're here and have missed their traps," she said. "Hurry now! You haven't much time. I will try to distract them."

With a flash of her nine tails, Nara disappeared.

Kira turned to Taejo. "She means King Eojin."

Taejo's mouth drooped in dismay.

"What's the matter?" Kira asked.

"I'm afraid," he said. "I'm afraid of what I'll see."

"Don't be," she said. But he continued to quiver with fear.

"It has to be you," she said. "The bond between you both is strong. That's why you're here! He will come to you. I'm sure of it!"

Before he could do anything, they heard a barking from behind them.

Taejo started. "Jindo!"

He spun around in excitement before catching himself. "No, it's not real. He's not here."

Facing the door again, he closed his eyes and ignored the continued barking. "No, Jindo, you aren't here. The demons are trying to confuse me. But I know I'll see you soon."

The barking became frenzied. Taejo took a deep breath and shouted, "King Eojin! Uncle! If you are here, please help me. It is Taejo."

There fell a complete silence as they stood before the empty doorway. Then a blast of wind assaulted them, whirling their shadowy forms about as if they were leaves in a cyclone. Kira found herself pressed against the wall farthest from the door, Taejo next to her. She felt as if a chill had entered her body, causing her to tremble. The smell of demon magic assailed her senses. In the darkness of the open doorway, a black presence materialized.

"Who dares to disturb me?" A deep voice spoke from within the swirl of black that was forming into the shape of a man. "Who speaks my name and recalls my suffering?"

In a riot of movement, the blackness raced out of the doorway and pulsed before them. They recognized the voice of King Eojin, but the form before them was grayish black from the poison of the cursed blade. This was why he stank of demon magic, Kira realized. What had killed him was now a part of him.

Taejo and Kira bowed in deep respect before rising to face the dead king.

"Uncle, it is I, Taejo, come to ask you for your help."

"Taejo? Yes, the little prince of Hansong—what brings you here to this wretched place? I see your cousin is with you as usual." The shade king nodded at Kira, who bowed deeply. "You should not be here. This is a very dangerous place for you."

Eojin's face came clear and Kira could not contain her shock. His once-handsome face was distorted with pain, sorrow, and anger. His skin was a mottled inky black, and his eyes were a pale gray around large, dilated pupils. The contrast was appalling to see.

"My king! What happened to you? Why do you look so . . . " Taejo trailed off as Eojin's ravaged face flickered in and out.

"It's the curse," Kira whispered to him.

"Cursed, a foul, wretched creature am I!" Eojin's form was flickering madly. "I am imprisoned here for eternity! Never to see my wife and children! My father and mother or my sisters!"

"No! Please, I'm sorry. So sorry," Taejo pleaded. "We're going to save you. King Eojin, have no fear, we shall save you from this place."

Eojin's flickering stopped and his tortured counte-nance looked at them once again. "Swear on this!"

"I swear," Taejo said.

"No, not you! The Demon Slayer. I ask you to swear that you will free me or join me here for eternity." Eojin's terrible eyes burned into Kira's soul. She hesitated. How could she swear this?

"Kira, we must save him! You must swear!"

"But how?"

"By killing the daimyo and destroying the Demon Lord. Only then will I be set free." Eojin's pale eyes gleamed a macabre red.

"I'll do it!" Taejo said with grim determination.

Kira sighed and then clamped her hands over her ears as Eojin's voice thundered. "Swear this, Demon Slayer!"

"Yes, I swear on my soul that I will break your curse!" Kira shouted.

The shrieking subsided and Eojin stood before them, his red eyes fading to disturbing paleness.

"Then I will help you."

"Where can we find the jeweled dagger?"

"A treasure in the shadow world? There is only one place it can be. Fulang's cave," he replied.

"Fulang is the dragon's name?" Kira asked.

"Yes, he is the guardian dragon of all hidden treasures," Eojin said. "He is the keeper of the world's most precious stones and metals. If the dagger is here, then he must have it. But do not trust him. He speaks in lies."

"Can you take us to him?"

Eojin nodded. "But we must hurry. I can sense the

demons drawing near and they are calling for you both."

His shadowed hands reached for their arms. Kira was shocked to find that he had somehow managed to solidify them. With a mighty pull, he began to fly.

The speed with which Eojin barreled down the hallways of the maze was dizzying. Her head was spinning from the sudden twists and turns, and she felt vaguely sick. On Eojin's other side, Kira saw Taejo covering his eyes with his free hand.

They came to a jarring stop, causing Kira to collapse against Eojin's shadowy form. She touched his arm and was stunned to find him nearly solid.

"How can it be possible?" she asked.

He turned his terrible eyes to her. "This is why you must release me from this curse. The longer I stay in the shadow world, the more like a demon I become. If you don't save me, then I will become a full demon and it will be too late."

"What are you now?" she asked.

"I am your best hope," he replied.

He released their arms, and Kira felt herself become insubstantial once again. Taejo was staring at their uncle in alarm. It was how she felt herself. If Eojin was turning slowly into a demon, then could he still be trusted?

"How do we know we can trust you?" Kira asked. "How do we know you are still our uncle?"

Eojin began to laugh. He moved with lightning speed and clutched them by their throats, causing them to feel substantial again. Kira's heart beat in her mouth as she stared up at the pale gray eyes, which held no emotion whatsoever.

"I have demon magic. I could kill you here and now. All it would take is for me to squeeze you to death," he said. "Your physical bodies would perish without your souls and both of you would be trapped here with me."

Kira could hear Taejo gasping as he tried to reason with their uncle. "Please, Uncle! Don't forget who we are. We are your niece and nephew. I am the son of your youngest sister. Remember your sisters!"

Eojin released them and cried in anguish. "This is not who I am. I'm not a demon. I'm still a man. I will not be taken like this. I will fight with all my power. With all my being. I will fight this! I will not be your servant!"

He screamed in rage and gathered energy that churned like lightning and clouds between his hands. He hurtled the mass into the maze, destroying the walls in the process. Eojin stood still as a statue before them.

"Whether or not you trust me, your choices are limited. Right now, you must come with me, for the demons are on their way," he said.

Stepping through the gaping hole in the wall, he beckoned to them. "Stay close," he said.

They followed him, cutting through the destruction he'd wreaked in the labyrinth.

But Kira was worried. Eojin had demon-like abilities. She had thought it was the lingering effects of the cursed blade that she sensed, but now she realized it was him. He had demon magic. So how could she trust him?

Nothing seemed real here and yet it was imperative that she sort reality from a demon construct. What was the truth?

Fact one, Eojin had been killed by a magic blade cursed by the Demon Lord himself. Fact two, Eojin's shade was imprisoned in the underworld, unable to rejoin his ancestors and family in heaven. Fact three, their uncle was a good man who would never harm them.

But what was unclear was whether or not he was really turning into a demon.

Is he a man or is he a demon? Or is he neither? And what did these labels mean anymore in this world? Did the rules of the living still apply here?

If he was truly a demon, he could have destroyed them and kept their shades in the underworld. That he didn't do so made Kira believe he was still Eojin. Still their uncle.

They could hear an unearthly howling from a distance.

"The demons are coming. We must hurry."

He grabbed them again and flew through the broken walls until they reached a gaping hole in the middle of the labyrinth. Down the hole they went, into a cavelike tunnel that was dark and damp. All along the sides of the walls, hundreds of imps crawled toward them, shrieking in excitement. Eojin bellowed, blasting the imps into the air with the force of a hurricane gale until the passage was clear again.

"They will not follow you into the dragon's lair," Eojin said. "Fulang has slumbered for centuries. Even the demons don't wish to disturb his sleep. It would behoove you to find your treasure without waking him."

Eojin's speed decreased as they moved deeper into the labyrinth, the tunnels growing narrower with sharp turns. No imps or demons were seen in this part of the underworld. There was no sound at all, no wind even to stir the air.

When they reached the dragon's lair, Eojin stopped in the passageway.

"I can go no farther with you," he said. "Remember your promise, Niece. Remember me." With that he disappeared.

Taejo stared into the emptiness that Eojin had just occupied.

"Noona, no matter what happens, we must end his curse," Taejo said. "We cannot fail."

"We'll do whatever it takes—"

"No! That's not good enough!" Ghostly tears flowed down Taejo's face. "We will save him or I will die trying!"

29

They entered the dimly lit passageway. It was muggy, the air thick and hard to breathe. Giant stalactites and stalagmites loomed above and before them, bunched closely together. As they wove their way around them, they came into a larger cave that glittered with the glory of piles of gems and gold. But lying within the beautiful treasures were hundreds of skeletons. Kira noted armor and weapons like she'd never seen before.

"If this is a place you can't enter in your physical form, then how come there are all these dead people here?" Taejo asked.

Kira had been wondering the same thing herself.

Skeletons littered the floor. Turning a corner, they entered a great cavern filled with what looked like all the world's treasures. Gold coins and jeweled crowns and necklaces were placed carelessly over more unusual items like a golden chair, jewel-studded cabinets, an elaborate gown made entirely of pearls, and cups and dishes so ornately jeweled that they would have no utility what-soever.

Taejo stood gawking at the treasures for a long moment.

"This is impossible," he said finally. "How are we sup-posed to find anything here? It'll take years!"

He kicked at a giant emerald lying on the ground, only to have his foot pass right through it. "And even if we do find it, how are we to take it from here?"

Kira shook her head, at a loss for answers. She found herself floating to the remains of a soldier whose skele-tal hand clenched a longbow and a quiver filled with arrows. The bow was straight and very different from her curved horn bow, but Kira was sure she could shoot it. She reached over to touch the bow, but could feel nothing.

The majority of the dead held swords of various kinds. One held a sword so large that Kira wondered if the man had been part giant to be able to wield such a weapon. How had these warriors entered the underground cavern with their weapons when she and Taejo hadn't been able to bring anything?

Kira tried to look through the mounds of treasures, but without any ability to sift through them, it was no use.

A rumbling sound filled the air. Kira and Taejo froze in place until the sound faded.

Kira followed the echoes to the back of the cavern and was struck dumb by the sight before her: a massive blue dragon, large wings folded to its side, was coiled tight and asleep. The dragon lay on a bed of gold and jewels that sparkled against its gleaming scales.

Kira couldn't take her eyes off the creature, fascinated by the iridescent quality of the blue scales edged with gold. A few of the dragon's scales were scattered on the floor of the cave. Without thinking, she reached down and picked one up to study it more closely.

The scale was harder than any armor and yet a thing of incredible beauty. It wasn't one shade of blue but several that seemed to swirl together in harmony. She didn't know if it was possible, but the scale seemed to be edged with real gold. Kira remembered hearing long ago that dragon scales were pure magic. Looking at this one, she knew it was true.

"How are you doing that?" Taejo asked, appearing at her side. He leaned down to pick up a scale, but his hand passed right through it. Frowning, he tried to take it from her hand and failed. "What magic are you using?"

Surprised, Kira dropped the scale. "I wasn't using any magic. I wasn't even thinking about anything except that scale."

Taejo looked at her in shock. "But you're not a shade anymore!"

She realized he was right. Her body was heavy again, substantial, her feet firmly planted on the ground. She could even smell the acrid odor of otherworldly magic in the cavern.

Kira bent down and picked up the scale again.

"It *is* magic," she said.

She put a hand to her chest and felt the tidal stone in the tiny bag she always carried against her heart. It was there with her now. Realizing this meant she had a way to get the dagger and protect them from the demons, she quickly shoved the scale into her jacket, underneath her belt, and picked up a few more scales.

Holding one up before Taejo, she had him try again. "Focus all your attention on the scale and nothing else."

Taejo nodded and furrowed his eyebrows as he tried to grab the scale. Slowly, his hand began to solidify.

"I did it!" he cried. "I touched it."

He tried again several times before finally succeeding.

"I've got a dragon scale!" he crowed.

Kira covered his mouth with her hand. Only at that moment did she realize how loud they'd been speaking. An eerie sensation of being watched filled her gut with dread. She was staring into the large black eye of a fully awake and alert dragon.

30

The dragon rose to his full height, unfurling his golden wings so that they seemed to fill the entire cavern. He let out a jaw-cracking yawn and stretched his entire body before lying down again.

"Is it already time for me to kill another human champion?" he asked. He looked around and tilted his head. "That's odd. The door is still sealed shut, therefore it must not be time yet. So how did these two delectable humans get in here?"

He sighed. "It's a pity you don't speak dragon, as I will be obliged to kill you and never know how you got in here."

"We do understand you!" Kira yelled quickly. She covered the dragon scale in Taejo's hand with her own and shoved it into his jacket before stepping forward.

The dragon recoiled in surprise. "I have never conversed with a human before," he said. "This will make for interesting dinner conversation! I am in sore need of entertainment. Champions are never any fun. For all their bravery, they die quickly."

"Champions?" Kira asked.

"Yes, human champions," the dragon said. "That's what I thought you were at first. But I see I am mistaken. You are just a human girl and a human child. You can't be anyone's champions."

"Clearly you are very wise," Kira responded. "But what do the champions do?"

"Every one hundred years I open my cave to the world above. I never know where it will lead. And I don't much care, except when it opens up far north." He stretched. "I detest the cold.

"But I do know that the opening will lead me to whatever I happen to desire. So I venture into the human world and hunt for my treasures, wherever they may be, and return to my lair. But there are always humans who claim I've stolen their treasure and come to slay the mighty dragon. As if an army of humans could hurt me! Foolish men! I am Fulang and I am invincible!"

Kira bowed low before the dragon. "Lord Fulang, it is you who I seek. I am the Dragon Musado and I come to you to fulfill the Dragon King's prophecy by claiming the jeweled dagger."

"You? A human girl? The mighty Musado?" Fulang laughed with great gusto.

Kira waited patiently until the dragon stopped wheezing. "How else was I able to enter your lair?" she asked.

The dragon sat up and gazed down at Kira from his imposing height.

"The girl speaks in riddles," he said to himself. "Intriguing."

He brought his head level with them.

"There is a simple test to see whether or not you are who you say you are, girl." Reaching behind him, the dragon pulled out a large chest filled with jeweled daggers of all kinds and placed it in front of Kira. Kira felt her tidal stone flare up in an immediate response.

"If you are truly the Musado, then it should be easy for you to find the real dagger," he said. "Careful. If you choose incorrectly, then I will eat you."

His eyes gleamed red with excitement. "I haven't had a human meal in a hundred years."

Kira sorted through the box, carefully examining each item. She placed a hand over her chest, letting it rest on the tidal stone. There was no response. She dug harder, wondering why the tidal stone had reacted earlier if the dagger was not in the chest. But it was to no avail.

"It's not here," she said.

"Are you sure?" Fulang asked. He gazed at her from

eyes filled with malicious amusement. "You don't want to be wrong, now."

Something drew her closer to the dragon. Her eye were drawn to the glimmer of his razor-sharp claws. One of his middle talons was elongated, jewels studded the base, making the dragon look like he was wearing an elaborate ring. The tidal stone began to pulse against her chest.

What you seek is hidden and yet in plain view. You must be careful to recognize truth from lies and follow your heart in order to obtain it.

"You have it," she exclaimed. "It's a part of you? How is that possible?"

"That's because it's mine," the dragon said. "It's always been mine and no one can take it away from me!" He stabbed the dagger claw into the ground, causing it to tremble.

Alarmed by the tremor, Kira held on tight to Taejo as the entire cave felt ready to fall apart. The dragon removed the claw from the ground and the tremor stopped. He slowly sank down to the ground, bringing his head to their level.

"But perhaps I can strike a deal with you, girl Musado," he said. "Let me eat this boy for a snack and I will give you all the treasure you can carry."

Kira pushed Taejo behind her and armed herself with a sword from the nearest skeleton. "I will kill you before I let you touch him."

"Wonderful!" He laughed. "A battle before dinner. It'll help my digestion to get a little exercise. I'll just have to save him for dessert, then. But I'll be merciful and kill you first, if you tell me how you entered my lair."

"You answer my question, dragon," she replied. "How did the jeweled dagger become part of you?"

"It was always a part of me, foolish one! I am the great Fulang!"

"That's not true, now, is it, Cousin?" a new voice drawled.

Kira was shocked to see Nara, in her fox form, sauntering toward them.

"Good evening, Cousin," Nara said. Her nine tails seemed to flame at their very tips and her normally amber eyes shone a deep red.

The dragon snorted, leaving rings of smoke to envelope them. "You are no cousin of mine, fiend," he said.

The kumiho smiled, baring sharp teeth.

"We were made from the darkness and the same elemental fire. As much as you may deny it, we are indeed related," she said.

Nara paced in front of the dragon, her nine tails waving behind her like a large burning fan. The dragon swatted at them in irritation.

"What is it you want, fiend? My patience is nearly at an end!"

"You were not meant to keep the jeweled dagger, Cousin. You were only meant to guard it, but when you learned of its power, you coveted it, didn't you? So greedy were you that you even removed your own claw and replaced it with the dagger so that no one could steal it. And then you used it to close up your lair, opening it only when your greed caused you to seek out new treasures." She flicked her tails over a pile of treasures, causing it to come crashing down. "You've abused the power of the Dragon King's treasure, and you will pay for your arrogance."

She stood still right before the dragon, her tails floating lazily under his nose.

Fulang rose to his full height and spread his wings. Both Kira and Taejo shrank back in fear.

"You dare to lecture me, the great Fulang? I will tear you limb from limb!" His bellows echoed through the cavern.

Nara gave Kira a pointed look and then she heard the kumiho's voice in her head. *Now is your chance to take the dagger. It is his source of power. If you cut it off, you will weaken him enough to escape. But you must act quickly.*

Kira was stunned by Nara's words. How was she to cut off the claw without getting them both killed? Was she crazy to listen to the kumiho?

You must be careful to recognize truth from lies and follow your heart in order to obtain it.

"You'd have to catch me first," Nara mocked. "Somehow I doubt you can. Look how fat and lazy you've gotten."

The dragon roared and raised his claw to swing at the kumiho. Nara sprang into the air and landed behind him. As Fulang turned his head toward the kumiho, Kira made a split-second decision and charged forward. Raising the sword high, she sliced it down on the dragon's middle claw, where the dagger sat. Fulang let out an unearthly scream as black blood gushed from the wound. Kira snatched up the dagger claw, stuck it into her belt, and raced away from the thrashing creature.

"I'll kill you all!" Fulang bellowed.

Fire blazed bright and hot as an inferno appeared behind them. Kira pulled Taejo by his arm and raced around the corner. The kumiho was waiting for them.

"This way!" she shouted.

They followed her through the vast cavern, past the armored skeletons. Kira scooped up the bow and arrows as they raced by. Nara ran toward the front of the dragon's lair. The passageway narrowed until they reached a solid wall with no exit. Kira felt an immediate sense of déjà vu. She knew this wall. She'd dreamed of this wall. She could almost feel herself slamming her body against it.

"Quick, use the dagger! Stab it into the wall. That is how Fulang enters the human world. But you must close it quickly behind us."

Kira stabbed the dagger into the wall. It trembled and an opening appeared.

"You will all die!" Fulang howled. Kira could hear him moving his heavy body around, seeking them.

Nara and Taejo squeezed through the opening. From behind, Kira heard the dragon fast approaching. Grabbing an arrow, she aimed for Fulang's eye and fired. He screamed in pain. Kira pulled out the claw and pushed her way through the opening after the others. As soon as she made it through, the opening closed up entirely. The wall shook with the vibrations of the raging dragon throwing its body against it, leaving Kira with a sense of growing dismay she didn't comprehend.

31

Kira inspected the bloody claw. Leaning over, she began to clean it off in the soft snow. The handle was made of pure jade, covered in gold that was studded with rubies, emeralds, and diamonds. Now in her hands it no longer looked like a claw. Clearly it was the Dragon King's jeweled dagger. She'd found the second treasure.

She looked over to where Taejo and Nara had collapsed onto the snow, gazing up at the side of Mount Baekdu. A rosy tinge lightened the horizon where dawn was beginning to break.

Kira stood up and bowed to the kumiho.

"Thank you for all your help," she said. "But I don't

understand why you came when it was so dangerous for you."

Nara cocked her head and watched Kira from black eyes that were sharp and clever and sad. Morphing into her human form, Nara stepped forward to gather Kira's hands between her own.

"You are the only one who has ever treated me like a human and not a monster," she said. "You were the only one willing to share your memories with me. From your memories, I finally understood what it was like to be human."

"We are connected now, aren't we?" Kira asked. "I know now that I can trust you. I feel that we can be friends."

Nara smiled, her eyes lighting with genuine happiness. "I have never had anyone call me friend," she said. "I would like that very much."

"If you ever need me, all you have to do is ask and I will help you," Kira said.

"The same is true for me. We are bonded," Nara replied. "And so I want to tell you something. I know that you think you are the Musado only by default. Because your cousin did not choose the ruby when the turtle offered it to him. But know this: I would not have helped your cousin secure the jeweled dagger. It was because of you that I came back."

She turned to Taejo and gave him a small bow.

"I mean no offense to you, my prince, but it is your

cousin who was always meant to be the Musado," she said.

Taejo smiled. "I am not offended at all. I agree."

Nara nodded and turned to Kira.

"Now I will give you one more gift."

She leaned her forehead against Kira's and closed her eyes. The first vision was of her brother, Kyoung, preparing for battle in his tent. Then he stood on a high cliff, watching as ships landed on the beach and an army of demon soldiers raced across the sand.

Is this happening now? Kira asked.

Soon, Nara responded.

Where is he? Kira asked.

On a far southeast corner of the Jinhan coast where the demons are amassing. Nara allowed the vision to pan over the ocean, where hundreds of ships could be seen in the distance.

How can I help him when I'm so far away?

The kumiho sent her a new vision of majestic winged horses flying through the air with riders on their backs.

How can I find them?

They are right above us, Nara said. She looked up at the top of the mountain.

Nara grasped Kira's hands one last time before changing into her fox form.

Farewell, my one and only friend.

With a last look, the kumiho bounded into the forest, her fiery tails waving in the air.

Kira stared after her, watching the red tails disappear.

She was saddened to see Nara go.

"Where are we?" Taejo asked.

Kira sniffed the air. She could smell the smoke of a nearby campfire.

"We're near our camp," she said. The sun was now peeking over the horizon. "We must hurry."

Before they'd gotten very far, Kira heard a wheezing sound, followed by loud panting. And then Gom flew out of the bushes and tackled Kira around her legs. He grunted happily as he grabbed Kira and Taejo by their hands and began to drag them forward. As they walked, the remaining dokkaebi army materialized and grunted in greeting, waving and bowing at them. They were making so much noise, it was no surprise when the rest of their party appeared soon after.

Kwan was the first to reach them, his eyes wet with tears. "I thought we'd lost you both!" he said as he hugged Kira and then Taejo tightly.

Jaewon ran up to Kira and embraced her.

"Is it really you?" he asked. He touched her face with a gentle caress. "There's that bandit scar."

Kira shoved him hard.

"Yes, it's really you!" He laughed and hugged her tight, letting her go only when Kwan gave an enraged shout.

"Ya! Kim Jaewon! Do you want to die?"

Jaewon raised his hands in apology and backed away, letting Kwan berate him for touching his little sister.

"Enough!" Kira said. "I'm glad to see you both, too."

She turned her attention to Brother Woojin, who was examining the prince with relieved concern.

"I'm sorry we didn't return before the sun rose. You must have been terribly frightened," Taejo said.

"It's not that," Kwan said. "Over an hour ago, something really strange started to happen to your bodies, and then you both disappeared. First Kira and then you. We thought you were dead."

Brother Woojin shook his head. "I didn't. I had faith that you would both be all right."

Kwan snickered. "Which is why he turned white as a ghost and prayed and chanted nonstop."

As they chattered in relief, Shaman Won came up quietly to Kira and pressed a firm hand on her shoulder.

"I'm so glad to see you made it safely," he said. "Sunim has forgotten my words already and is focused solely on the prince, but I know that you are the real reason we are here."

"Master, it's not just that. Sunim has been the prince's tutor since he was a small child. He is like a son to him. What I see is love," she admonished.

Shaman Won touched his forehead in a respectful gesture. "You are not only a great hero, but a kindhearted person. I admire you immensely."

Kira repeated the gesture with a bow. "And I you, Master. Thank you for all that you have done to help us."

"It is my honor," he replied.

"Now," Shaman Won said in a raised voice, "why don't

we return to camp and let them tell us all the details?"

Taejo nodded. "Plus, I'm starving! I hope you have lots to eat!"

There was a cheerful grunt from Gom before he took off into the woods.

"I think that means we'll have something to cook for you," Jaewon said with a grin.

His words were prophetic. By the time they trudged their way through the snow, Gom was waiting patiently for them with two rabbits.

As they prepared their meal, Kira began to recount all the events of the shadow world

"The kumiho shared a vision of what is going to happen soon. The daimyo has sent hundreds of ships with demon soldiers that will land on the southern coast of Jinhan. Our brother and his troops will be slaughtered if we don't get there soon."

"Impossible! It will take us months to return to the Iron Army," Kwan said.

"Perhaps not," Kira said, thinking about what the kumiho had shown her. "We've one more place to go."

"Where?"

"Up," she said.

Jaewon scratched his head and looked uneasy. "Isn't Baekdu a volcano? Will we be safe climbing up there?"

"It's been inactive for the last hundred years," Kira said. "We should be fine."

"But what do you think you will find up there? It's

still winter in the mountains. Everything is covered in snow and frozen over. It will be too treacherous," the shaman said.

"There's something up there we need to find, but you wouldn't believe me if I told you," she said.

"Ya, we've been attacked by half-breeds and seen a dokkaebi army formed from your blood. What won't we believe?" Kwan snapped.

Taejo was shaking his head. "But what about Jindo and Major Pak? They're waiting for us. We have to go back for them!"

"When they are completely recovered, they can return to us," Kira said. "But it is urgent that we help Kyoung."

"Sunim, you must return with Shaman Won to Kim Jaewon's village. The dokkaebi army will protect you. Once Jindo and Major Pak are recovered, head for the closest port. By sea will be the fastest way south," she said.

"But how will we find you?" he asked.

"The dokkaebis will lead you straight to her," the shaman replied. "After all, they are of her blood."

"You've had an exhausting night and climbing the mountain will be dangerous," Jaewon said. "Why don't you rest for now? The mountain will still be here in the morning."

"But first tell us what we'll find at the top," Kwan said.

Kira grinned with glee. "Chollimas!"

32

In the morning, all the remaining dokkaebis lined up before Kira. They were half their original number and many of them looked bruised and battered. To Kira, they were still a beautiful sight.

"Thank you for protecting us from the demons," Kira said. "You are all the bravest and strongest soldiers I've ever had the pleasure of fighting with."

The dokkaebis cheered loudly, banging their cudgels on the ground.

"I will leave you with two last tasks to perform for me," she continued. "Please take Brother Woojin and Shaman Won to North Wagay Village. Then once Major Pak and Jindo have healed and are ready to travel, I ask you to stay with them and protect them on the journey south again. You must find me. I will be waiting for all of you."

All the dokkaebis grunted in agreement, bowed, and dispersed.

While Taejo talked in private with Brother Woojin, Kira went to speak with Shaman Won, her faithful shadow Gom following close behind.

Shaman Won cocked an eyebrow at Kira when he saw Gom by her feet.

"I do not believe that one will be leaving with us," he said.

Gom shook his head and held tightly on to Kira's leg as if worried someone would pry him off her.

She smiled and scratched him behind his ear. "I feel safer having him with me."

Jaewon and Kwan both laughed.

"We don't go hungry with him around!" Jaewon said.

"But too bad he can't cook, also," Kwan said. "I do miss Seung a lot."

"What are you trying to say about my cooking?" Jaewon asked.

Kwan pulled a face. "You might want to stick to baduk."

As the monk and the shaman prepared to leave, Kira's worries resurfaced.

"Will you be all right?" she asked. "Will you be able to travel safely? Maybe we should build some litters so you can be carried home."

As soon as she spoke, several dokkaebis appeared brandishing their cudgels. They pounded them on the ground, and several blankets appeared.

Bang, bang, went the cudgels again, and four long bamboo poles and some twine appeared. The dokkaebis quickly used the materials to form two litters.

Everyone was surprised but the shaman.

Shaman Won gave the dokkaebis a rueful look. "Dokkaebi magic is a conjurer's magic. These blankets and poles were taken from somewhere else. Given that the closest settlement is ours, I have a feeling someone from our clan is wondering where their blankets are."

Kira suppressed a laugh. "I will have to be careful what I ask of them."

She bowed in gratitude to the dokkaebis, who all bowed in unison, pleased by her reaction.

It was a tearful parting for Taejo and Brother Woojin. In the nearly ten years that Kira had known the old monk, she'd never seen him cry before. She saw the worry and concern on his face as he covered her hands with his.

"Your job is not done. You must move on to the third treasure," he said. "Remember, it is at Jindo Island in the Tiger's Nest Temple. But please be very careful."

"I will, I promise," she said.

"But there's something I didn't tell you before that is important to know."

"What is it?"

"About the monks there—"

"Yes, I know: they are savages."

Brother Woojin shook his head and pulled her closer, whispering in her ear. "They are cannibals. They eat the flesh of their enemy. And you are their greatest enemy."

"Why me?" Kira asked.

"Because you are the Dragon Musado and they have sworn never to let the jade dragon's belt fall into your hands. For they believe that it will bring about the destruction of the world."

Her eyes widened, but she stayed silent. Now she understood the monk's secrecy. Her brother and Jaewon would never agree to let her near the temple if they knew of this. She had no intention of telling them. All it would do is worry them even more. They would redouble their efforts to stop her and that she just didn't want to deal with. For there was no choice. She had to go to Jindo Island. But she would go alone.

The dokkaebis lifted their litters and carried the two elderly men to North Wagay Village. She watched the procession until they were gone.

Jaewon and Kwan had packed up their gear and stood ready to leave camp.

Only Taejo loitered, sitting before the embers, warming his hands.

"What is it?" Kira asked, sitting down by his side.

He shrugged, avoiding her gaze.

"Are you scared?"

"No!"

"Are you worried about Jindo?"

He didn't answer.

"You'll see him again, I promise," Kira said.

"It's not that."

Kira waited patiently for him to continue.

"Everything has happened so fast. I feel like my life is out of control and there's nothing I can do about it. Nothing I can do to feel better," he said. "I don't even know if I want to be king."

Kira nodded. This she understood. But what could she say?

"Maybe you will be king, maybe you won't. I will not tell you what to do. These are choices that you must make. It isn't too late to join Sunim and return to the village. I can ask the dokkaebis to come get you and take you to North Wagay. You can stay in the village and be safe. Between the dokkaebis and the shaman, nothing will harm you there. I will not fault you if that is your decision. As much as I would miss you, part of me would prefer that you stayed safe in the village. But I must go on," she said.

"Why can't you stay with me?" he asked tearfully. "You are supposed to always protect me!"

"There will be no reason to protect you if the Demon Lord wins," she said. "My choice was made the minute I accepted that I was the Dragon Musado, and I will do everything in my power to fulfill the prophecy. But it seems to me that you are not so sure of yourself. I have no answer for you. I know only this—I could not have made it this far without you. So the choice is now yours. You can choose to be safe, or you can choose to seek your destiny."

She stood up and joined Kwan and Jaewon.

"Let's give him a few minutes. He's only twelve," she said. "Sometimes I think we are asking too much of him."

Kwan gave her a pointed look. "Strange, I feel the same way about you."

She raised an eyebrow at him and shook her head. "I feel I've already lived a lifetime in less than a year."

Her brother sighed. "I'm sorry for that, little sister." He went to check their bags one last time.

Jaewon gave Kira a friendly nudge. "So now do we also call you Dragon Slayer?"

"I doubt that I killed him," she responded.

"Even if your shot didn't kill him, if he's trapped in his cave, then you've given him a death sentence," he said.

The thought depressed her. Would it have been better to kill the dragon rather than have him die a slow, painful death?

Over and over she threw herself against the wall, reveling in the cracks. Laughing as the wall began to break free.

Disquieted by another glimpse into her vision, Kira shook her head. It was impossible. Fulang could not escape without the jeweled dagger.

Taejo approached, a determined look on his young face.

"Let's go," he said.

Kira smiled in approval. "I knew you would come."

Before they started, Jaewon handed Taejo a small wooden carving.

Taejo looked at it with wonder. "It looks like Jindo," he said.

"That way he's always with you," Jaewon said.

Taejo caressed the little figure lovingly. "Thank you."

As Jaewon hoisted up his bag, Kira mouthed a silent thank-you. He shrugged in response and continued to prepare for their climb. Soon they were all ready to tackle Mount Baedu.

Gom found the quickest and safest route up the mountain. They hiked around to the northern pass, where hot springs and geysers filled the frigid air with thick clouds of mist. They walked parallel to a rushing stream before soon hearing the roar of a waterfall that came from a lake at the top of Mount Baekdu. Gom pointed them past the waterfall to a steep path. They climbed for an hour through snow and ice, taking it slow and steady.

Finally, as they reached the summit, Kira swore she could smell the freshness of spring. The closer they got to the top of Mount Baekdu, the less snow they saw. Kira was surprised to find soft green grass below her feet, and the strong tingle of magic in the air.

The top of the mountain looked as if had been broken off, leaving jagged peaks that looked like old temple ruins surrounding an unearthly paradise. Standing above the cloud line, it was as if they'd climbed their way to heaven.

She walked down onto the soft black sand shore of a lake with waters that were a pure sparkling emerald green.

"Amazing. I've never seen water so beautiful," Kira said. Taejo nodded in awe.

The other two spun around at her words.

"What are you seeing?" Kwan asked. "All I see is a frozen lake."

Jaewon huffed. "Is this like the last time? When you got to see the Heavenly Maidens and we didn't? So unfair!"

"Perhaps only Taejo and I can see the enchantment," she said. "So you probably can't see an island in the middle of the lake either."

The two men glared at the lake, similar looks of bewilderment on their faces.

"Are those chollimas, the flying horses?" Taejo asked, a note of wonder in his voice.

Kira nodded and smiled in sympathy when Jaewon made a garbled noise of frustration.

In the middle of the lake there was an island, where a large herd of chollimas was grazing in the grass. Some flew in playful circles. Their wingspans were as long as their body lengths. Their coats and manes were a variety of colors—white, yellow, brown, black, spotted. There was even a brilliant red horse that soared high in the air, its wings blocking the sun.

They were beautiful, and Kira could have stood there all day watching them. A young white chollima flew over to them, whinnying and nosing them with curiosity.

"Great heavens! Where'd it come from?" Kwan shouted in shock.

Jaewon crowed in delight, but both of them stayed behind at Kira's signal.

Kira greeted the horse and then retrieved the tidal stone and jeweled dagger from her bag. The horse neighed loudly and flew back to the island. Minutes later several chollimas landed on the shore before them. A large black chollima stepped forward and tossed its head at Kira.

Inside her mind, she could hear the chollima's thoughts.

I am called Raiden. No human has ever come to our home. Are you friend or foe?

She bowed low and held out the tidal stone and jeweled dagger.

"I am Kang Kira, the Dragon Musado, and I have found two of the Dragon King's treasures," she said.

The chollima whinnied loudly. The rest of the herd echoed him, fanning their wings.

We were once the steeds of the great Dragon King. Although we no longer serve man, we are indebted to the Dragon King and his heirs. What is it that you want from us, Bearer of the Dragon King's treasures?

"Until this moment I thought you were a myth. To see you now is a dream come true. But it is urgent that we go as quickly as possible to the shores of Jinhan, where my oldest brother is fighting the demon invasion. It is said that you can travel one thousand li in a day. Can you take us there?"

Raiden conferred with the others in the herd before returning with three chollimas.

We will help you, he said. *It will take a few hours, so it would be best if we leave right now, while the sun is still high.*

The chollima knelt before her with his wings folded, allowing her to mount him. Gom climbed on behind her. His cudgel was tucked between them while his hands gripped firmly on to Kira's belt.

"Is flying like being on a boat?" Jaewon asked in a panic-stricken voice.

Tell your friend that he will not suffer from sickness, Raiden said.

"You'll be fine, I promise," she said to Jaewon. "Just trust your chollima."

With a nervous expression, Jaewon mounted a brown flying horse, who stood perfectly still.

Kwan and Taejo had no such hesitation, each eagerly bonding with the beautiful creatures before them. Happy and excited, Taejo climbed on top of the pure white chollima, giving him many admiring pats, which the chollima enjoyed. With a great burst of energy, the chollimas soared into the skies and away from Mount Baekdu.

It was as cold in the air as it was climbing the mountain. Raiden took the lead as they flew faster than any horse could ever gallop. Through the breaks in the clouds below them, she viewed the rapidly changing landscape.

She wondered how far they had traveled.

We have passed beyond the Guru boundaries, Raiden answered.

Below, Kira admired a sprawling city that she didn't recognize. It reminded her of home. She missed the walls of Hansong and streets of the city. She missed her parents and her aunt. So many memories. So much lost. Kira worried about everyone she was leaving behind. She wondered if she'd ever see them again. And then Shin Bo Hyun's face flashed before her eyes.

I told you I would do anything for you.

Kira rested her face against Raiden's mane and cried.

33

The sun was completely overhead when Kira smelled sea air. They'd reached Jinhan and were heading to its port city of Dongnae. On the bluffs above the beach, Kira viewed the Iron Army and her brother Kyoung with a group of generals in the front lines. Farther away, she saw General Kim leading his men.

Like in the vision Kira had seen, the seas were filled with hundreds of ships flying the banner of Daimyo Tomodoshi. Yamato soldiers possessed by demons poured off the ships and onto the sand by the thousands. Soon, the beach was filled with the roar of the enemy army. Kira flew straight for her brother, the others right behind her.

The Iron Army erupted with joyous cries. As people recognized Kira and Taejo, they began shouting, "Musado." Kira circled over the line of soldiers, flying first in front of her brother's men and then General Kim's. She kept her eyes steady on the general's as she flew by, enjoying his rage.

She headed to her brother, where the soldiers moved to allow the chollimas to land. The cheers were deafening as the sight of the chollimas reinvigorated the army.

Kyoung approached and helped Kira down, hugging her hard in the process.

When Taejo dismounted, everyone bowed before him.

"Here is the rightful heir to the Guru throne!" Kyoung shouted.

The army roared in approval. Even General Kim's men cheered.

"Thank you," Kira said to the black chollima.

Raiden inclined his head, and with a loud neigh vaulted into the sky, followed closely by the others. Everyone watched as the flying horses disappeared into the clouds. They began to chant Taejo's name, until the cheers reached a deafening level.

Kira stood at the edge of the bluff right above the beach. She barely paid attention to the drama behind her. She watched the numbers of the Yamato army grow. The stench of demon was overwhelming. Although the majority of the Yamato soldiers were demon-possessed humans, Kira was dismayed to realize that the daimyo had been very busy creating his half-breed army. There were at least a thousand of them.

The enemy didn't approach. They seemed to be waiting for something. It wasn't long to see what it was. Ten large cages were carried onto shore, each containing an animal never seen by human eyes.

"What in the world is that?" Jaewon asked. He'd come with both her brothers to observe the enemy lines.

"Another crossbreed," Kira said. "This time with some kind of animal."

Gom whimpered at Kira's feet. She couldn't blame him. The animal was terrifying. It had the face of a vicious wolf, the big bulky body, and the claws of a bear. But where there should have been fur, the creature had jet-black scaly skin.

"How can we kill it?"

Kira grabbed her bow and nocked her arrow. Taking quick aim, she shot the creature through the bars of its cage. Her arrow bounced off its skin, clattering to the floor. The creature went wild with rage, but the half-breeds let out a howling laugh that was ghastly to hear.

A strident order rang across the beach as a figure appeared before the Yamato army. Kira strained to see who it was, hoping it was the daimyo.

"Is that Daimyo Tomodoshi?" Kira asked Kyoung.

"No, it is Lord Kaneda. The daimyo has not left Yamato," Kyoung said.

"Coward," Kira sneered.

Lord Kaneda was speaking to his army of demon soldiers. They could not hear what he said until the soldiers
chanted his order.

"Kill the prince! Capture the Musado!"

Taejo had come to stand beside Kira. She pushed him
out of the enemy line of sight.

"Do you hear them? You're their main target," she
said. "You must stay back."

"They're after you too, Noona."

"But they don't want to kill me," she said.

The chants of "kill the prince" grew louder and faster
as the Yamato prepared to open the cages. Kira placed a
hand over her chest, feeling the outline of the tidal stone.
It pulsed with heat and filled her mind with a suggestion.

Use the jeweled dagger. Bring forth an earthquake.

Quickly, Kira leaped from the bluff, a straight drop
two horse lengths long. She half rolled and half ran onto
the sand below.

She raced forward as the cages were opened and the
creatures targeted her. Pulling out the jeweled dagger,
Kira slammed it hard into the sand. Nothing happened.
She hit it over and over, but the dagger had no effect.

The sand, it's too loose, she thought. Spotting an outcropping of rocks below the bluffs, she began running.

The beasts were howling. Glancing over her shoulder,
she saw the creatures lumbering toward her, their bulky
bodies slowed by the sand.

Her lungs were tight, breathing was painful, but she

pushed herself harder, trying to run faster in the sand.

She could hear the arrows thudding off their hides. They were getting close.

The smell was overwhelming and she could feel the heat of their foul breath.

Desperate, Kira called for her tiger spirit. Immediately, she was filled with a burst of pure energy. She leaped for the rocks and stabbed the jeweled dagger into the outcropping. It sank into the stone as if it were made of paper. The creatures were so close.

With a roar, the first of the demon animals leaped for Kira's throat. Rolling onto her back, Kira kicked the creature in its chest and heaved it over her body. Before another could reach her, she twisted the dagger handle hard.

The earth began trembling and the sand around Kira swallowed all the demon animals.

She pointed the dagger handle toward the water and sliced it through the same outcropping. A large chasm formed from the point of Kira's dagger all the way across the beach, parallel to the water. The Yamato soldiers tried to run to their ships but the sand disappeared under their feet and pulled them into the abyss. At the same time, a tidal wave swept away the ships from land and sucked then down into the ocean. The shaking continued until no one but Kira remained on the beach. She pulled the dagger from the rock. The chasm closed and the ocean returned. There was no hint of the vast demon army that had just been there.

Cheers from the soldiers above her broke the sudden quiet. Exhausted, she smiled as Taejo, Jaewon, and Kwan raced down the bluff and over the sands. Gom was running around in excitement, leaping over the sand with Taejo.

The earth rumbled again. Everyone stopped. Kira looked at the dagger in her hand and then where the sand was breaking apart.

A vision of her nightmare raced through her mind. *Her massive body felt slow and lethargic, but she could feel anger giving her strength. Over and over she threw herself against the wall, reveling in the cracks. Laughing as the wall began to break free.*

The trembling stopped and then an explosion of sand erupted from the ground as a massive blue body flew out of the chasm.

"Fulang." And then her vision made sense. She had been dreaming as the dragon. It had been a warning that she had not recognized.

The dragon turned his head in Kira's direction and shot a stream of fire at her, but he missed her completely. His eye was maimed from where she had shot him with the arrow.

Kira aimed for his other eye, narrowly missing it and nicking his nostril.

He screamed and twisted his massive body. A barrage of arrows soared through the air at him. Most bounced off his scales, but two of them made impact. Roaring in pain, he shot a stream of fire at the archers. The soldiers scattered or held up their shields and quickly prepared for another attack.

The dragon caught sight of Taejo and sped toward him. Kira was running, but she was too far away to save her cousin. All she could do was shoot her worthless arrows. She watched helplessly as Jaewon tried to stop the dragon and was sent flying by a hard strike of Fulang's head. Kwan stood before Taejo, his sword raised before him when the dragon struck out with its claws, piercing Kwan through the abdomen. He fell to his knees but still tried to fight when the dragon struck him again.

"No!" Kira screamed.

The dragon scooped up the screaming prince by his claws and shot straight into the air. Quick as a wink, Gom grabbed hold of Taejo's legs and they were both lifted high into the sky.

She could hear Kyoung ordering the archers to hold their fire.

"Musado, if you want to see the princeling alive, then bring what you have stolen from me to Tiger's Nest Temple on Jindo Island. You have ten days," he said.

His great wings swirled up the sands as he lifted his prisoners into the clouds and disappeared from view. She could hear Taejo's shouts and Gom's distressed cries.

Kira ran after the dragon, yelling Taejo's name. Screaming for the chollimas. Screaming for help until finally she fell to the ground weeping.

Strong but gentle arms embraced her, murmuring that all would be fine. Kira clutched at Jaewon's sleeves as she tried to contain her tears. Suddenly remembering her brother, she scrambled up onto her feet and raced to Kwan's side.

An army doctor had removed Kwan's armor, and was tending to his wounds.

"Oppa!" Kira sobbed.

Kwan looked at her with pain-filled eyes. "Don't worry, it's not as bad as it looks," he said.

The doctor agreed. "He was very fortunate that his armor took the worst of it." He began to bind Kwan's wounds tightly.

Relief made her collapse, her body folding over as she covered her face and wept.

"Kira." Kwan raised her chin with his fingers, forcing her to look at him. He was now bound in numerous bandages and sitting up with Jaewon's help.

"It's all my fault," she sobbed. "He should have taken me, not Taejo!"

"No, it is still all part of the prophecy," Kwan said. "Remember what Sunim said. To find the third treasure you have to go to Jindo Island."

Kira heaved a shaky breath and nodded. "Jindo Island. But Sunim is not here! I need him to tell me what to do!"

"What are you talking about? He's never told you what to do—you've always figured it out yourself! It's all right, you'll be fine. Taejo will be fine. Your little protector is with him. He won't let anything happen to the prince," Kwan said.

"Gom." Kira sighed. "Poor Gom."

"That fierce dokkaebi will guard Prince Taejo with his life," Jaewon said. "We'll go after them and get them both back."

"You'll have to take a boat," Kwan warned.

Jaewon closed his eyes and then sighed. "The things I do for your sister."

Kyoung, who had just arrived, had been listening to them, but when Kwan and Jaewon started arguing about how to get to Jindo Island, he pushed them aside.

"Why don't you go help prepare Kira for her trip," he said.

Once they both left, Kyoung knelt in the sand before Kira.

"Little sister, this is not your fault. Nothing could have stopped that dragon. And he won't harm Taejo as long as he thinks you will bring him what he wants."

"I wish Father were here," Kira cried. "I miss him and Mother so much."

"I do, too," Kyoung said. "But they are both looking over us from heaven and I know that they are so proud of you, just as I am. You are my baby sister and yet I believe that you are the greatest hero of our world."

Kyoung pulled her into his embrace and hugged her hard.

"Dry your tears. You've got more work to do. But I know that you will save our prince," he said.

Kira let out a shaky breath and wiped away her tears.

"I'll get him back, no matter what," she said.

"I know," Kyoung said. "Now let me go get you a boat."

With one last hug, he left her alone.

She sat on the sand, staring off into the waves. She watched as the skies began to turn indigo blue and the sun's rays diminished in a reddish haze.

Her fingers clenched around the jeweled dagger as she thought of the trip she must take. Danger awaited her on the island. Half-breed demons that wanted to destroy her, cannibalistic monks who would hunt her as their prey, and a sea filled with enemy ships. On top of it all, an oath to the ghost of King Eojin to break his curse or damn herself to eternal hell if she failed.

The stakes were high and very dangerous. Yet Kira focused on one thing. There was only one thing she now cared about, for which she would risk everything.

"Fulang," she said, "this time, I will kill you!"

Glossary

Baduk—Korean term for the ancient Chinese board game Weiqi and the Japanese game Go

Chollima—winged horses that can fly

Daegam—Your Eminence or Your Excellency; term of respect used for high-ranking officials

Daimyo—powerful Japanese feudal lord

Dokkaebi—goblinlike creatures made from inanimate objects; always carry cudgels, which is where their magic comes from

Dongji—winter solstice; usually falls on December 22 of the solar calendar

Gisaeng—female entertainers

Haetae—mythical fire-eating dog

Hanbok—traditional Korean dress

Hanja—Korean name for Chinese characters used to write the Korean language

Imoogi—half-dragon, half-snake mythical creature

Jangseung—totem poles made of wood or stone traditionally used to ward off evil spirits; also used as village boundary markers

Jesa—memorial service

Ki—life-force energy

Kumiho—nine-tailed fox demon

Li—Korean measurement unit; 1 li is equivalent to 500 meters, 0.5 kilometers, or 0.31 miles.

Makkoli—milky rice wine drink

Musado—warrior

Nambawi—traditional winter hat

Noona—boy's honorific term for an older sister

Ondol—a floor heating system unique to Korea

Oppa—girl's honorific term for an older brother

Sang gum hyung—double-sword form

Saulabi—soldier

Suchae—untouchables, the lowest members of the caste system, including actors, butchers, hunters, and prostitutes

Sunim—honorific term used for monks

Taekkyon—the original martial art form of ancient Korea that has evolved into what is referred to as tae kwon do

Ungnyeo—name of woman who used to be a bear and was turned into a woman by the Hwanung, a son of the Heavenly Father

Ya—hey; can also mean "you"

Acknowledgments

Writing book two was an incredible challenge and completely different from my experience writing my first book. Luckily for me, I have an amazing network of support systems.

The HarperCollins team, led by my brilliant editors Phoebe Yeh and Alyson Day and the remarkable Jessica MacLeish, who all worked with me to make *Warrior* the best book it could be. (Phoebe, you taught me so much and I am forever grateful!) Alana Whitman, my marketing guru whom I adore and who could always be counted on to give me excellent advice, which I was smart enough to listen to. My fabulous marketing team made up of the following amazing people: Emilie Polster, Olivia deLeon, Jenna Lisanti, and the amazing Epic Reads gals Margot Wood and Aubry Parks-Fried. My brilliant art directors Amy Ryan and Joel Tippie, who surpassed themselves by creating the most beautiful cover in the world. (No, I'm not biased. It really is the most beautiful cover!) And of course the remarkable Kate Jackson, editor-in-chief, and Susan Katz, publisher extraordinaire.

I'm also incredibly lucky to have Awesome Agent who is Awesome—Joe Monti, who has perfected the very important art of keeping me sane (and on task), along with the genius-man Barry Goldblatt and the wonderfully bright and fantastic Tricia Ready.

Thanks to my wonderful beta readers Caroline Richmond, Mike Jung, and Martha White, who are always there for me, even when I make irrational and unreasonable demands. You guys rock! (How do you put up with me?) My writer friends Cindy Pon, Juliet Grames, Marie Lu, Robin LaFevers, Shannon Messenger, and Elsie Chapman, who could always be counted on to raise my spirits and help me through even the most difficult of times. And the incredibly talented Virginia Allyn for being the brilliant illustrator that she is and a true friend.

My network of family support includes my best friends Sylvia (my soul sister) and Stewart Lara, Anna Hong Kim, Jennifer Choi Um, and John and Virginia Rah. I really love you guys and I'm blessed to have you all in my life! My sister, Janet, and my brother-in-law Laurent Poirot—what would I do without you both? My mom and dad for always being supportive. My three brilliant, beautiful, and wonderful daughters, Summer, Skye, and Gracie—you girls are my everything! And of course, my husband, Sonny, who really is my better half.

One last, heartfelt thank-you to all my readers and supporters, wherever you may be—you keep my faith alive. Thank you.

Read an excerpt from Book Three
of the Prophecy Trilogy!

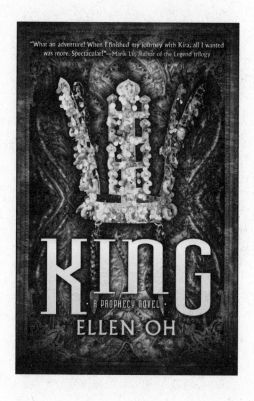

"What an adventure! When I finished my journey with Kira, all I wanted
was more. Spectacular!"—Marie Lu, author of the Legend trilogy

KING
· A PROPHECY NOVEL ·
ELLEN OH

1

Kira sat staring at the waves lapping on the sandy shore. She hadn't moved since Taejo had been snatched by Fulang over two hours ago.

Behind her, her brothers and friends were busy trying to prepare for her new journey. They'd left her alone, knowing she needed time to think. She'd gone from anger to despair to anger again. She burned with it, a fiery volcano.

In her mind's eye, she could still see the blue dragon's great wings beating up a sandstorm as he lifted Taejo and Gom into the clouds and disappeared from view. She could still hear Taejo's screams and Gom's distressed cries.

It was all her fault. She should have killed the dragon in the shadow world when she'd had the chance. Why had compassion stayed her hand? If anything were to happen to Taejo, she would have broken her oath to her uncle and father. Kira closed her eyes in pain. She couldn't bear the thought.

This is not your fault. This is fate.

Kira's eyes flew open in surprise. It sounded like Brother Woojin's voice. But he was three thousand *li* away. It would take him weeks of traveling to reach them.

"Sunim, I'm so sorry." She spoke into the wind, as if it would carry her words north to him. "It was my job to protect the prince and I failed."

You must have faith, my child.

Kira didn't know if it was really him somehow communicating with her or if it was just her mind telling her what she wanted to hear.

She sighed. "Faith is nice, but not much help right now. What I need is a plan. But I don't know what to do."

Brother Woojin's voice was silent. Instead, she heard the dragon again.

"Musado, if you want to see the princeling alive, then bring what you have stolen from me to Tiger's Nest Temple on Jindo Island. You have ten days."

Gritting her teeth, Kira had to fight the rage that rushed through her once again. So much of the anger was directed at herself for failing to recognize the meaning of her weird visions. It was all so clear now that it was too late. Now that she had to chase a blue dragon to an island that had already been invaded by the Yamato and seek a temple filled with cannibalistic monks who considered her their greatest enemy.

Her head hurt.

Someone came and knelt in the sand next to her. "Your brother sent me to tell you they are ready for you," Jaewon said.

Kira rose to her feet, feeling stiff and tired. The afternoon sun had shone down brightly on her head and she was feeling the effects. Silently, Jaewon passed her a water bag. With a grateful look, she drank, feeling the slight headache start to give way.

They climbed up the dunes and over to the command center. Inside the large open tent, Kyoung, Kwan, and several military leaders were conferring. Her brother Kwan should not have even been there. Badly clawed by Fulang, Kwan was in no state to be standing for very long. She was about to tell him to rest when he spotted her.

"Kira, this is madness!" Kwan exclaimed. "You of all people are the one Daimyo Tomodoshi wants. He will use everything in his power to capture or kill you. And Jindo Island is swarming with Yamato!"

Her eldest brother seemed to notice her immediate aggravation. He grabbed Kwan by the shoulders and pushed him onto a short stool.

"Actually, Admiral Yi has figured out an ingenious way to get her to the island," Kyoung said.

The admiral bowed and stared at Kira with piercing eyes under shaggy, graying eyebrows that even his helmet couldn't cover up.

"Kang Kira, we may be in luck. For this is approximately the right time of year for the miraculous land bridge to appear between the islands of Modo and Jindo," he said.

"Miraculous bridge? What is it?" Kira asked.

"It's a well-kept secret that only the islanders know about. It occurs two to three times a year in the spring and summer. A land bridge that lasts for about an hour forms between the islands of Modo and Jindo."

"Only an hour? What time of day does it occur?"

"That's one of the problems. In the last five years, the first of the pathways has formed progressively later in the day," he said. "Our navigator predicts that it will open in the next four days and will be at around sunset. But it is also the most dangerous time. When the tide returns, it comes in hard and fast and will sweep you deep into the ocean."

"If it's not dark enough, we also risk being seen on the road," Kira said.

"That's the other issue."

"How is this helpful, then?" Kira asked sharply. "There's a bridge that may or may not form, and if it does, it might be while it's still bright out, in which case we'll be visible to the Yamato patrols. And even if we cross it, we risk being drowned by the tide!"

"I know it sounds like madness," the admiral said.

"There may be no choice," Kyoung said. "The entire Jindo coastline is heavily patrolled by the Yamato."

"This is not going to work!" Kwan said.

In the ensuing quiet, the admiral stared at Kira, appraising her.

"To be honest, I'd rather you not go at all. Our intelligence informs us that you are the number one priority for the Yamato. They want you captured alive."

"This is nothing new," she responded.

"The daimyo needs you for some reason. He is more interested in you than the prince. Falling into his hands will mean disaster for all of us."

"I understand, but I have no choice. I must go after the prince," Kira said.

The admiral seemed to be carefully pondering his next words.

"I must ask you if this is the right thing to do," he said slowly. "If they get their hands on you, it might be more dangerous than losing the prince."

"Never say that!" Kira responded fiercely. "He is our future king!"

Kyoung pulled Kira aside and placed a comforting arm around her shoulders. She could see the blackened fingers of his left hand, the remnants of his encounter with the Demon Lord's cursed blade that killed their uncle. She was reminded again of how much they had lost and suffered since the start of the war.

Lowering his head, he spoke to her in a soft undertone. "Kira, he speaks the truth," Kyoung said. "There can be other kings but there is only one Musado."

Shaken by his words, Kira pulled away. She was reminded of Shaman Won from Jaewon's village. The shaman had claimed that Brother Woojin was using Kira only to protect the prince. He'd accused the monk of not respecting Kira and seeking to minimize her role in the prophecy.

"Even recognizing that the girl is the Dragon Musado, your mind seeks a more acceptable interpretation. That she is only part of the prophecy instead of the only one. She is only relevant to you as the prince's protector. But what you fail to recognize is that everything is irrelevant without her."

The shaman was right. This was something that she was as much at fault for doing as everyone else. It had been difficult for her to accept that she was the Dragon Musado, and when she did, she still downplayed her own importance. To Kira, Taejo was the prophecy. He was the one she had to protect. When she'd gone to the Diamond Mountains and found the first of the Dragon King's treasures, the tidal stone, the Heavenly Maidens had told her that Taejo was the future king. It was her job to ensure that he saw his future through. She swore to take care of Taejo. It was a promise she would never break.

"I understand why it is you feel this way," she said carefully. "I appreciate your feelings. But please respect mine. I made a vow to his father and ours to protect

Prince Taejo. I must go after him. I must save him."

"Then we will honor your oath and speak no more of this. We will do whatever is needed to help you," Kyoung assured her.

They returned to the group. "The matter is decided," he said. "She must go."

With a decisive nod, the admiral began the discussion again.

"I understand that my plan sounds crazy, but here is what I propose. We set sail for Modo tonight, on the evening tide. It usually takes a full day of travel, although the seas have been unpredictable of late. We will arrive from the east, which will keep us out of sight of Jindo. You'll be dropped off in a small craft as close as we can get to shore. We cannot drop anchor, as we would risk being seen if a Yamato ship should pass by. It will be late in the evening and low tide, so it should be relatively safe," he said. "Once you get to the island, you have two options. The first is to keep an eye out for the bridge and make a run for it. The second option is to row over to Jindo. But it would take too long by yourself."

"I'm going with her," Jaewon cut in.

The admiral eyed Jaewon with approval. "Well, with two of you, it should take only an hour, provided the seas are calm. But that leaves you sitting ducks for the Yamato if they spot you."

Kwan cursed. "That's an even worse option!"

Kira rubbed a finger along the scar that ran from her

eyebrow to her cheek. "We must pray to the Heavenly Father for a moonless night."

The admiral's expression turned crafty. "Well, here's the exciting part of my plan. We will create our own diversion." He pointed to the map of the southern tip of the peninsula. "Our navy has had great victories against the Yamato in the East Sea. We have pushed them west. But I have an idea that will send their naval forces a punishing blow."

He pointed to Jindo Island on the southwestern tip of the peninsula. "Modo Island is this tiny point right here to the east of Jindo Island. The channel between Jindo and the mainland is called the Roaring Channel because of the fierceness of its tides. It is the fastest of all our waters. This strait is treacherous, for it shifts directions from north to west and then back every three hours. We will draw the Yamato fleet into the Roaring Channel as the tides are changing. My sailors know how to navigate the channel, but the Yamato don't. If we time it right, they should incur tremendous damage without us even firing a shot at them."

"But how does that help my sister get to Jindo?" Kwan asked.

On a piece of parchment, the admiral used a fine paintbrush to highlight the area. "Here is the pathway. It leads to this shore point. The patrols cover several areas along the coastline. Four nights from now, you will wait on Modo for my signal." He then drew their attention to a small covelike area on the eastern side of Jindo. "We will engage all the Yamato on the north side of the island. At the same time we will attack this entire northeast coastline, drawing all the patrols away. When you see the night sky light up in flames that will be your signal. Only then should you run across the pathway, if it is there, or row your boat over to Jindo. Hopefully that will buy you enough time to cross over without being seen."

"We really need to know how long that path will stay open," Jaewon said, "and whether there will be time enough to cross it."

The admiral's craggy face was creased in concern. "While we think it is approximately an hour, we've noticed that the later in the month that the pathway forms, the shorter the time it stays open."

"Exactly how far is it?" Kira asked.

"Almost seven li," he said.

Kira smiled in relief. "That would only take us half an hour to run," she said.

"I have to warn you that its appearance is gradual. That's why you must be vigilant about watching for it. The hour starts as soon as it shows. You must plan accordingly."

Jaewon and Kira looked at each other uneasily.

"Admiral, if it is open less than an hour, and we have to wait until it is dark enough, there's a chance that we won't make it," Kira said.

"Or we wait until it is completely dark and row over," Jaewon said.

Kwan shook his head in frustration. "Rowing takes a

lot longer. More time for a patrol to come back and spot you. Neither of these options will work."

It was dangerous, relying on the fallibility of the Yamato patrols and the aggressiveness of the admiral's naval attack.

"I know it's risky but it's the best option available to us," Kira said.

Kira thanked the admiral. "It's an audacious plan, but I worry for the safety of your ships and men."

The admiral smiled. "This old guy has quite a few surprises left in him, ready to be unleashed on the Yamato. Don't worry, young Musado. We will be fine. But be careful: along this stretch of coastline there is a village nearby, nestled right into the mountains. You must avoid it, as the Yamato have taken it over. Even though Tiger's Nest Temple is located in the heart of the mountain range, you will have to go the long way around."

"I think it's quite brilliant," Kyoung said. "And Admiral Yi is the best naval officer in all of the Seven Kingdoms. I have faith in him."

The admiral and his men left the tent, Kyoung walking out with them.

Kwan held Kira back. "I don't like this. Even if you get to Jindo safely, it's a trap. The dragon is leading you right to the temple monks who want to kill you!"

"I have no choice!" Kira snapped.

"Let me go in your stead," Kwan said.

Her eyes widened as she took in her heavily bandaged

brother. "You can hardly stand."

"But they aren't after me—"

Kira shook her head. "This I know in my heart. It must be me. If Sunim were here, he would say the same thing."

Her brother closed his eyes. "I'm scared," he said. "I feel like I might not see my little sister again."

"Don't worry," Jaewon cut in. "I'll be with her."

Kwan gave Jaewon a dirty look. "That's what I'm afraid of."

DEMON SLAYER.
GIRL WARRIOR.
THE ONLY HOPE FOR HER KINGDOM.

BOOK 1

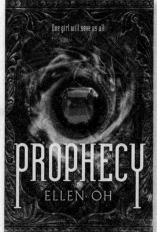

One girl will save us all.

PROPHECY
ELLEN OH

BOOK 2

"What an adventure! When I finished my journey with Kira, all I wanted was more. Spectacular!"—Marie Lu, author of the Legend trilogy

WARRIOR
A PROPHECY NOVEL
ELLEN OH

BOOK 3

"What an adventure! When I finished my journey with Kira, all I wanted was more. Spectacular!"—Marie Lu, author of the Legend trilogy

Don't miss a heart-stopping second of this swee